A LITTLE ONE-ON-ONE

"Swoosh!" Elation filled Rob as he hit a three-pointer. He couldn't remember the last time something so pure and simple as a basketball game had excited him. He grinned at Jane and strutted his stuff. "There it is."

She rolled her eyes, but when her gaze met his, happiness danced in their green depths. "Show-off."

They battled another two scoreless change of possessions. She ducked around him and hit another shot, taking the lead by one.

He shot. She jumped, caught a piece of the ball and knocked it off course. It hit the backboard with a thud. He jumped for the rebound, but landed his front to Jane's backside. Her firm buttocks pressed against him. Heat—her heat—radiated through the thin material separating their bodies, scorching his brain.

Rebounding plummeted to the bottom of his priority list.

JANE
MILLIONAIRE

JANICE LYNN

LOVE SPELL NEW YORK CITY

To the hero of my heart, my husband, David.
Love you whole big bunches.

LOVE SPELL®

December 2005

Published by

Dorchester Publishing Co., Inc.
200 Madison Avenue
New York, NY 10016

ISBN 0-505-52664-6

The name "Love Spell" and its logo are trademarks of Dorchester Publishing Co., Inc.

Printed in the United States of America.

Visit us on the web at www.dorchesterpub.com.

ACKNOWLEDGMENTS

I'd like to thank everyone who voted for *Jane Millionaire* in the American Title Contest. Thanks to Dorchester Publishing and *Romantic Times* magazine for sponsoring the contest and to Kate Seaver for seeing something special in my entry. Thanks for giving me a shot at my dream. Also, a big thanks to Leah Hultenschmidt for stepping in and making my first publishing experience a fabulous one.

Without the following groups you would not be reading this book, so I have to send out a special thank you to The Writer's Playground, who make awesome campaigners and are the best friends a girl can have; to www.wetnoodleposse.com for being my sisters in spirit; and to the Vote 4 *Jane Millionaire* Yahoo group who cheered me each step of the way. Thanks for believing in me from the beginning and for working so hard to make my dream come true.

No thank you would be complete without mentioning my family and God; through them I am the person I am. And last, but not least, my heartfelt thanks goes to my children, Jessie, Jacob, Abby, and James, for putting up with Mommy "always being on the 'puter." Thanks for filling my life with love and for giving my dreams meaning, because without y'all, I'm nothing. This one's for you!

JANE
MILLIONAIRE

CHAPTER ONE

Uh-oh, the tall, raven-haired god circling Jill Davidson already knew she was an imposter.

"You look different from your photos." The sexy executive producer scowled. His voice echoed off the stone walls of the fourteenth-century European castle the film crew had leased.

"Uhm." Jill stalled by glancing around the large, high-ceilinged room that had been converted into a studio. Her gaze landed on the cluttered far corner, where expensive computer equipment screamed that this was a first-rate operation.

And she was a first-rate fraud.

Her heart raced, pounding so loudly it wouldn't have surprised her if he could hear the thunderous beat. She'd known no one would take her for her drop-dead beautiful sister. Okay, so they looked a lot alike in some ways, but when it came down to it, they were as different as Madonna and Mother Teresa. She'd told Jessie. But would her sister listen? Did she ever listen?

"I darkened my hair." *Brilliant. That should convince him. Ugh.* She mentally cringed at her lack of finesse.

Rob Lancaster continued to stare, threatening her composure with his intense scrutiny. Scarier men had tried to intimidate her and failed. Jill did not squirm. At least, not under normal circumstances—not that this was in any way normal. Besides, she had a feeling the sweat beads popping out on the back of her neck had little to do with her supposed identity and everything to do with the velvety gaze sliding over her body.

"You, well, you appear to be a little heavier than in your pictures."

Great, just what every woman wanted to hear. This sexy man who stole her breath with his honey-colored eyes and Latino good looks *would* comment on the extra five pounds she carried in comparison to her size 2 sister. "Maybe a few pounds."

"The camera isn't kind to additional weight," he said.

"I can lose it." Could she? She hated dieting and usually ate like a—well, she wouldn't go there.

Gorgeous eyes studied her some more. "No, you'll do."

Was that skepticism she heard in his voice?

"Just see to it you don't gain any more."

Ouch. "Yes, sir." Jill resisted the urge to salute. It wouldn't do to get off on the wrong foot with the sexiest man she'd ever met. Especially since she'd be working closely with him. His spicy scent filled her nostrils. Close was good.

For the next six weeks she was in Rob's hands—too bad not literally. She bit back a grin, then remembered the cold, hard facts of why she was here. Six weeks. How had Jessie talked her into a reality show? How did her

2

sister ever talk her into anything? It was easy enough to figure out. Jessie asked and Jill did. Just like always.

With each second that passed, Jill questioned her motives for agreeing to her sister's pleas so readily. Part of it had been an excuse to avoid seeing Dan, which Jill couldn't do in San Padres. And why shouldn't she enjoy these next few weeks? For once, she'd be the center of male attention, treated as a desirable woman. She could look at this as a holiday. She wouldn't really fall for any of the bachelors. Past relationships, including the one with Dan, had taught her better, but she could enjoy herself. After all, it had been years since she'd had a holiday. Being Jane Millionaire could be the vacation of a lifetime—a vacation *away* from *reality*.

"Have you read the materials you were sent?"

She ran her gaze over his strong facial features and six-foot-tall, jeans-and-T-shirt–clad frame. When he wasn't scowling, he looked more like a movie star than a behind-the-scenes man.

"Yes, I read it on the plane." Now that she thought of it, he had done a few acting stints early in his career. A former actor. He ought to have this "reality" thing down pat.

"What! You waited until *when?*" He threw his hands up in apparent disbelief—or was it disgust? Several of the crew milling around the studio turned to look in their direction.

"Uhm . . ." How could she explain she hadn't known she was coming until the day before she'd gotten on the plane? She hadn't even known her sister was supposed to come. Jessie had failed to mention quite a few things in the past few months. Like having auditioned for the lead role on a reality television show.

"I'm a fast reader." Thank God it was true.

His dark brows drew together, creating an intense look on his handsome face. "This is a job, not a joke."

A joke? It was reality television, for goodness's sake. Could there be a bigger joke? "No, sir." She pressed her lips together, suppressing a smirk.

Whiskey-colored eyes narrowed. "Are you mocking me?"

Jill raised her hand to cover her twitching mouth. He was serious. "Well, it's just television."

"'Just television,' she says." He glanced around the room as if he were talking to an invisible audience. Turning back to her, he drew quotation marks in the air for emphasis. "'Just television' is going to make you famous, 'Princess.'"

She didn't want to be famous. Her flighty, attention-seeking sister did, or had right until the last minute when she had gotten engaged and just couldn't possibly go to Europe to fulfill her contract obligations by acting like a princess.

Acting. That's what reality TV was. A bunch of nuts acting like they weren't acting. Jill had better things to do. Like putting criminals behind bars at her job on the San Padres police force. She loved living and working in the small community, which was about an hour's drive outside L.A. But here she was in a tiny, never-before-heard-of European country, pretending to be her sister for the next six weeks as the star of Wolf Television's latest idea of entertainment, *Jane Millionaire*. What a joke.

She blinked at the annoyed man, who sort of reminded her of Benjamin Bratt from *Law & Order*. Rob was still scowling. "You're serious."

"To the tune of the hundred million dollars the network expects to bring in."

The room spun; her ears roared. If Jill hadn't known better, she'd have thought the castle was under attack or zinging through the air like Dorothy's house on its way to Oz.

"Are you okay?"

No, she wasn't. "Did you say a hundred million dollars?"

"Yes. And your pretty little face is how we're supposed to do it. Millions of viewers will tune in to see which one of the bachelors you spend your all-expenses-paid honeymoon with."

A honeymoon? She didn't remember seeing anything about a honeymoon in the packet of papers Jessie had stuffed into her hands at the airport. Jill prided herself on her legendary knack for details. She wouldn't have forgotten such a significant detail. And her sister sure hadn't mentioned any honeymoon.

"I have to marry one of these wackos?"

"Wackos? I assure you none of them are crazy. They're carefully selected bachelors from around the world." Lines on his forehead deepened into a V above the bridge of his nose.

"Whatever. If you ask me, anyone who'd agree to do a reality TV show has to be a bit strange."

His lips inched upwards and Jill's heart rate kicked up a notch at just how attractive he really was. "*You* agreed to do a reality show. Not only agreed, but competed for the privilege."

"Point taken."

His eyes twinkled with amusement. Her insides turned to mush. *Oh Jessie, what have you gotten me into this time?*

Put her in the line of fire up against hardened criminals, and she was as cool as a cucumber, but pretending to be a princess for a reality TV show? She almost broke out in hives at the thought.

She met Rob's eyes and wished she could tell him the truth, but he didn't look as if he'd understand. Jessie had signed a contract and spent the advance the network had given her. Jill had no choice but to see this charade through if she wanted her sister to remain happy. The memory of just how happy Jessie looked when she'd waved her bejeweled left hand kept Jill's mouth closed. She'd just have to think of the show as an undercover job. But as the center of twelve men's attention?

Her gaze dropped to her bare arms to be sure big red welts weren't popping out on her skin. "What if they all hate me?"

He scanned her from head to toe. A slow perusal that made her feel as if he could see right through her no-nonsense khaki slacks and short-sleeved navy blouse. She resisted the urge to shift her weight as he lingered at her chest. So she wasn't a D-cup like Jessie, but she'd never had any complaints about her generous B's. Okay, so she hadn't had a lot of compliments either. Still, more than a handful went to waste, right?

Jill looked up at the dark-haired hunk eyeing her.

Tiny hairs on her neck stood at attention, a reaction she usually experienced only when confronting danger. His gaze unnerved her in ways even the toughest thug couldn't. Her heart pounded. Yep, he was more dangerous than any criminal she could imagine. He was too damn attractive. Her breath caught.

"They won't hate you." His tone left no doubt. Lethal. Rob Lancaster was positively lethal. Maybe she should handcuff him to herself just for safekeeping—not that he'd be safe from her if handcuffs and his body were involved.

"How can you be sure?" she asked, fighting the mental image of the man handcuffed and at her mercy.

"Just take my word for it."

Jill's eyes widened. This wonderfully scrumptious man saw her as a woman, a desirable woman. But having practically asked for his assessment, she felt foolish. She was a fool. Just being here proved that. Intellectual, tough-as-nails Jill Davidson—practical till the end.

But not for the next few weeks.

For a short while she had to be Jessie Davidson, her younger sister by ten months. Her irresponsible sister who was everything Jill wasn't. Feminine. Flamboyant. Sexy. Jessie, who had always been popular with the men and who was the center of attention no matter where she went. Jessie, who would run her tongue invitingly over her lips and offer to let Rob handcuff *her* to the bed. Jill gulped at the mental image.

She was tired of being one of the boys.

Rob's gaze made her feel deliciously female, and she liked the unfamiliar sensation.

"Thank you." She smiled. If he was an example of what the bachelors would be like, the next few weeks might not be so bad, after all. Too bad he wasn't one of the bachelors. She could make her pick right now and save the film crew a lot of hassle. "I look forward to working with you." That had to qualify as the understatement of the year.

Her hand automatically extended, and he shook it.

"That's some grip you've got there." His eyes danced.

Heat infused her face. She wasn't sure if it originated from his comment or from the lightning that streaked through her from where they touched. She jerked her hand away.

"I work out." Competing in a man's world, she had to.

"Obviously, *Jane.*" His gaze raked over her with renewed appreciation. His lips curved.

Her heart flip-flopped.

The man had a killer smile and a tall, muscular body that probably made women drop at his feet. She took a deep breath and shoved aside the wicked thoughts his smile inspired. She had enough to worry about without complicating matters by lusting after the producer. She would lose her job, her reputation and possibly her freedom if she got caught and the network pressed charges. Fraud. That's what she was, and she needed to keep as much distance between herself and Rob as she could. "You know, Jane isn't really my name."

"Only J.P. and I know your true identity, and we both think of you as Jane. You have no other name. And to answer your question, no, you don't have to

8

marry one of the bachelors." He plowed a hand through his hair, then added with a thigh-melting wink, "Although it might help the ratings if you did."

"That's a relief. I have no desire to get married." Not to some guy she met while pretending to be her sister.

He looked taken aback. "That's not what you said during your interviews. I may not have physically been there, but I did read over the transcripts."

Transcripts? Her stomach plummeted. Had she just made a major slip?

They had recorded Jessie's interviews.

She needed to get her hands on those so she'd know what "she" had said.

Rob's eyes narrowed at her continued silence. Darn, she usually thought fast on her feet. In her line of work she had to. What was it about this guy that had her acting like some knock-kneed teenager in heat?

"You want someone to sweep you off your feet, marry you and make lots of babies," he continued in an almost mocking tone, as if he found the prospect repulsive.

Jessie had said that? Nausea rose in Jill's throat. Her sister better not rush into motherhood. Visions of changing diapers and walking the floor at all hours during the night caused Jill to shudder. She had enough responsibilities just looking after her sister without adding a little munchkin to the clan. Jessie better stay on her birth control or else.

"Don't you remember what you said during your interviews?"

"Of course, I do." *She* hadn't said a thing. Jessie, however, had given an embellished mixture of both

Jill's life and her own. Mostly Jill's, from what her sister had admitted during her teary good-bye at the airport. "Isn't a girl allowed to change her mind? Maybe I could read over those transcripts?"

"A woman's prerogative and all that jazz, huh?" He stared a few moments longer with a cocky grin on his face, shook his head and walked across the large room with confident strides. Several people scurried after him.

She sighed in relief. He'd bought it. He'd believed she was Jessie. He hadn't offered to let her read the transcripts, but oh my God, she'd pulled it off.

"Jane?" A thin, well-dressed man with a young friendly face, paisley silk shirt, and too-tight pants walked up the moment Rob disappeared through one of the high-arched doorways of the castle-turned-set.

She blinked. Twice. Jane. Oh yeah, that was her.

"I'm Gregory Bell. I'll be doing your hair and makeup," he explained as he stunned her by kissing both of her cheeks. "How are your accommodations?"

Her accommodations? They were staying in a castle. "Like something straight from a fairy tale."

The dashing man winked, bowed his head and gave a wave of his beringed hand. "Well, you are royalty."

"So I've read."

He clicked his tongue. "You don't sound as if you understand the coup you've landed. You were chosen out of thousands of hopeful women to play Her Royal Highness Princess Isabella Jane Strovanik."

"Coup," she muttered as she followed him to a catchall-room-slash-beauty-salon. He pointed to a stylist's chair.

"You're not cutting my hair." She grabbed her long tresses, which were free from their usual clips. She hadn't cut it for the police force. She sure wasn't cutting it for these TV jokers.

His mouth fell in exaggerated horror. "Absolutely not. Just a little snip here and there to give you some verve." He stepped around her. "And a few highlights."

She didn't release her protective hold.

"Don't worry," he assured. "I'm just going to take you from beautiful to absolutely breathtaking."

"I hope you've got the fairy godmother and her magic wand stashed back here somewhere." She looked around in vain.

He laughed and patted the chair. "In you go."

She sighed. What could a trim and a few highlights hurt?

Jill stared at her reflection in the antique full-length mirror set up in her suite. Gregory had taken her drab brown hair and added subtle streaks that shone in the light, making her resemblance to Jessie even stronger. He'd plucked her brows to almost nothing and performed magic with his makeup brushes. That stunning woman couldn't be her. She was a tomboy, not a homecoming queen—or princess, as the case was supposed to be. Not even with a few practice poses could she believe herself to be a princess.

With one last look of disbelief, she left her spacious room and descended the curved staircase. Masterpiece paintings of "her" ancestors lined the walls. An intricate crystal candelabra hung from the ornate ceiling.

Three men stood in the large marble-floored foyer:

11

Gregory, an older man she'd yet to meet and God's gift to women. Rob Lancaster. Her heart fluttered. Man, he was gorgeous.

Her steamy reaction to his magnetism surprised her. She'd rarely dated since her breakup with Dan two months earlier. She'd thought Dan was the one—that special someone just for her. They'd gotten along so well, perfect partners on the force, with complete trust in each other. Too bad there'd been no passion. She'd accepted mediocre sex as a small price to pay for the affections of a man like Dan. Obviously he hadn't been willing to make the same concessions.

She returned her attention to Rob, who did a double take. His throat worked. His gaze darkened as it slid over her bare shoulders and the generous amount of cleavage revealed by the gown Gregory had insisted she wear. Wicked slivers of desire sizzled through her at the way he dragged his gaze back to her face—as if he had to force himself to look away from her body.

When had a guy made her pulse race with just a glance? But race it did. Indy 500, look out. Rob didn't see her as one of the guys. Not by a long shot.

Delicious heat pooled inside her. Moist, burning heat. She'd never felt more like a woman than at this moment, wrapped in Rob's masculine approval.

Gregory glanced up and grinned. He made a grand gesture and bowed. "May I present Her Royal Highness Princess Isabella Jane Strovanik?"

She nodded at the other two men before facing Rob again. Something in the way he stared reached inside and made her ache for the fulfillment his eyes promised. Instinctively she knew nothing he did would rank as mediocre. Could you fall head over heels for a man simply because he looked at you as if you were the most desirable woman he'd ever seen?

"You're stunning," exclaimed a silver-haired man, in his late fifties or early sixties, when his bushy-browed gaze landed on her. "Much more so than in your photos and interview tape."

She did feel beautiful, but for him to say she was lovelier than her sister—no one was lovelier than Jessie.

She tipped her head in the manner she'd practiced with Gregory and held her hand out to the distinguished older man who had to be J.P. Scott. "Thank you. You are too kind."

He took her hand, lifted it and pressed his cool lips to her warm skin. "Just look at her, Rob. She's absolutely perfect."

Rob *was* looking. He hadn't been able to quit looking from the moment he'd spotted her. Like something from a fairy tale, she'd practically floated down the ornate staircase.

His body took notice of every minute detail. From the delicate curve of her exposed throat, to the creamy skin of her shoulders, to her firm arms. He skimmed her gown's tight bodice and swallowed to wet his dry mouth. Full breasts narrowed into a tiny waist. Hips flared to legs his imagination worked overtime envisioning as long and shapely. He'd have liked to push the layers of her gauzy skirt aside to know for sure.

Red-hot lust threatened to knock his normally steady feet out from under him. He couldn't remember the last time he'd had such an intense response to a woman. He wanted her. In a bad way.

But of all the women in the world, Jane was one he had to deny himself. Which was a shame, as he could see recognition of his longings in her shimmering green gaze. Recognition, curiosity and a desire of her own. Damn. A sexual attraction between them would screw up everything.

Jane was here to fall for one of the twelve bachelors chosen to compete for her affections. J.P.'s career teetered on whether or not Rob could make this show a success. A success that wouldn't happen unless Jane fell for one of the men and convinced millions of viewers she had found her Prince Charming.

"Yes. Stunning. Very well, then—" Rob paused, feeling like an awkward schoolboy. He squelched his rising libido. He was a grown man and could restrain his physical needs. He *would* control them. However, Jane's sweet, flowery scent was quickly demolishing his resolve. He needed distance. Now. Without another word, he strode away, ignoring J.P.'s frown, Gregory's wide eyes and Jane's confused expression.

Rob slammed into the room he'd be staying in for the next month and carefully avoided glancing at a connecting door he didn't want to acknowledge. He headed straight for the shower. A cold shower. An icy shower.

He wasn't supposed to want to rip Jane's clothes off and ravage her shapely body. The twelve clowns that would show up next week were for that. Still, Jane naked and beneath him was exactly what he craved. He groaned and hooked his fingers under the hem of his T-shirt to tug the material upwards.

A knock rapped at his door.

He froze. Excited anticipation filled him. "Who's there?"

"J.P."

Rob let out a breath he hadn't realized he'd been holding. Did he really think she'd followed him to his suite? And if so, he'd only have to send her away. Frustrated, he opened the door and stepped aside, letting J.P. enter.

J.P. glanced around the room and let out a whistle. "Nice."

"It ought to be for what we're paying." He sounded gruff. Too bad. He didn't feel like socializing.

"Castles don't come cheap." J.P. sank into a high-backed eighteenth-century chair with deep, blue velvet cushions. "So what did you think of Jane?"

She's sexy as hell, and I want to know if she's as toned under those clothes as I think she is.

Aw, hell. He had to quit thinking like that. Right now.

"She's not what I expected," he finally admitted, his mood easing some.

"How so?"

"I figured you'd go for some blond Pamela Anderson wannabe to play Jane." That much was true. He'd wanted to make the final decision, but had been tied up with another production.

"Casting narrowed it down to the top five choices. I picked her based on her interviews, looks and background. You've seen her portfolio. She plays every sport and excels. She rides, shoots and can probably kick my sorry hind end into the next country. A modern-day Belle Starr. She's amazing."

"I'll say," he muttered. God, he hated reality TV. Even when it had first hit the airwaves he hadn't bought into the crazy phenomenon. The thought of contributing to such a phony production repulsed him. He'd worked damn hard to build a quality reputation after his one career blunder. His involvement with *Jane Millionaire* could revive old media clips of his one and only failure. He might not recover a second time.

But J.P. had believed in him when he'd been a greenhorn from East L.A. itching to make a name for himself, had believed in him even after his show flopped thanks to the antics of his ex-wife. Without J.P., the doorway leading down Hollywood's golden path might never have opened a first, or second, time.

Only J.P. could have talked him into this reality sham.

"She'll get the works over the next couple of days. Then we'll go over the agenda for the show, what our expectations are, and brainstorm on how she'd like the men to prove themselves." Oblivious to Rob's inner turmoil, J.P.'s voice grew louder with each word. "She's fully trained in martial arts, holds a black belt. It might be interesting to let her duke it out with the guys."

"Should work." Suspicion snaked through Rob as J.P. shifted in his chair for the third time. "What aren't you telling me?"

"You always could read me like a book." J.P.'s laugh bordered on nervous.

Rob didn't smile as he waited. Whatever J.P. had to say, experience said Rob wasn't going to like it.

"Last night when I met with the Wolf rep, I mentioned the series you were writing. Your name alone had him salivating. I gave him a copy of the script."

Rob cursed. He'd been playing around, toying with an idea for a new prime-time series. He planned to write, direct and produce the show—what he'd wanted to do from the beginning, but a pricey mistake with the help of his ex-wife had kept him on a narrower path. On a whim, he'd asked J.P. to look over the script. *Gambler* wasn't ready to pitch to a major network. J.P. shouldn't have taken the liberty.

"He called. If we pull off *Jane Millionaire*, they'll give *Gambler* a prime-time slot."

"You're kidding." He had to be. *A prime-time slot.* Rob's heart threatened to explode.

"No. They loved the idea. All we have to do is make *Jane* a success."

"Just what kind of success are they looking for?"

"At least twenty mil in the eighteen-to-forty-nine adult viewer range."

Rob whistled. "Not asking for much, are they?"

"If we hit over twenty, you get complete creative control over *Gambler*, and they've promised me a Tuesday night sitcom, and a sizable bonus for both of us." J.P. mentioned a figure that had Rob whistling a second time as he shook his head.

"Twenty million-plus viewers?"

"You've seen Jane. Viewers are going to love her. She's tough, yet has an innate vulnerability in her eyes. She's classy, yet not afraid to get dirty." J.P. stood and walked to French doors that led to a private balcony. "She's the ticket to my staying out of the retirement home for has-been producers and your shot for

Gambler. How many of our colleagues would kill for this chance?"

"Every single one," Rob conceded.

"We have to hit twenty mil."

"How do you propose we do that?" Rob muttered, knowing the answer, yet unable to contain that very male part of him that didn't like what J.P.'s response was going to be.

"We have to make sure Jane falls in love with one of the bachelors, all of America falls in love with both of them, and we give our viewers the fairy-tale romance of a lifetime."

CHAPTER TWO

Jill cringed at every creak of the floor. How was she supposed to sneak around an eerily quiet castle in the middle of the night when the floors moaned and groaned with each step she took? Jeez, it was a wonder she'd made it to the studio without waking up the entire crew.

She'd picked the studio's lock, and although she saw a spare cell phone tucked away in a cabinet, Jessie's transcripts were nowhere to be found. Ugh. She had to find a copy of those interviews. It would make life so much easier if she knew what her sister actually said while auditioning for this part.

Another step. Another creak. Another cringe.

Had she made that last creak? Tiny hairs prickled along her neck. Man, if she didn't know better, she'd think this place was haunted. Where was her Glock when she needed it? Not that her gun would do much damage to a ghost.

She was almost to her room. Only a few more steps, creaks and cringes and she'd— A hand covered her mouth.

Oh my God! Adrenaline coursed through her. She cocked her elbow to nail her ghostly assailant at the same time as Rob whispered in her ear.

"What are you doing out here?" He let his hand fall away from her mouth.

"About to crack a few of your ribs. Don't grab me like that. I might hurt you." She pulled free of his loose hold, her arm brushing against naked flesh, and with a sharp jolt of electricity she realized he was wearing only a pair of unbuttoned jeans. Wow. Where were her handcuffs? Covering abs like his definitely constituted criminal activity.

Rob chuckled at her warning, obviously not taking her seriously, although he should have. She could easily bring down a man twice his size, and trained other women to do the same in the safety courses she routinely taught.

He opened the door behind him and motioned for her to step inside. Light from the room illuminated his golden skin. Her gaze raked over his bare chest and the wispy smattering of hair that disappeared into his faded, snug but not too tight jeans. Maybe someone should handcuff her before she discovered firsthand where that fine tracing of hair led. Uh-oh. She was in trouble. In more ways than one.

"Where were you coming back from?"

Did he know she'd broken into the studio? She stalled by looking around the suite—similar to her own from its lush historic décor to the pleasant citrus scent. The suite next to her own. So that's where that locked door in her room went. "Why is there a connecting door between our rooms?"

20

"Because it was me, J.P., one of the crew, or one of the bachelors. Guess I'm just lucky that way." He sounded as if he didn't consider the privilege an honor. Had he been assigned to baby-sit? Or spy, maybe?

"And you were wandering around the castle because?" he prompted, sliding one hand into his jeans pocket. Had that unbuttoned gap just widened? She wasn't going to look. She was *not* going to look.

She looked.

Was the sweat on her neck from fear of getting caught or thoughts of peeling Rob's jeans right off his pin-up-poster body? Gulping down the lump in her throat, she tore her gaze from his exposed flesh and met his amused expression.

"I couldn't sleep?" Now, why had her words come out sounding like a question? She'd been making a comment, damn it. And she hadn't been staring at his hard abs. Uh-uh. No way.

"And needed a drink of water?" Mischief danced in his golden eyes.

"Water?" She blinked. "Oh! Water. Yes. I was thirsty."

He grinned, and she had no doubt he was on to her. Ugh. She was a trained police officer. Posing as Mafia Max's girlfriend hadn't made her this nervous. Why was she coming across as a total moron?

He nodded at a high-backed settee and a chair with finely stitched velvet padding. "Have a seat."

Unable to answer her own questions about why he affected her so intensely, Jill sat in the chair.

"Did you quench your thirst?" His deep timbre pulled her gaze back to his six-foot-plus frame.

"I, uh, never made it to the kitchen." But looking at him did make her thirsty. Desperately so. His smooth golden chest and abs were cut like the proverbial washboard—and she had a sudden longing to do laundry. Heat flushed her face—as well as other, more hidden parts of her body.

He walked over to a small refrigerator cleverly disguised to blend with the room's antiques. He took out a bottle of water and tossed it to her. She twisted off the lid and swallowed a long sip of the cold liquid, hoping to cool down her body and thoughts.

Sinking onto the settee, Rob drank some of his water. After a long moment, he spoke. "Want to tell me what you were really doing in the hallway at two in the morning?"

"What were *you* doing out in the hallway?" she challenged, having regained some of her usual aplomb. She had learned long ago that the best defense was to go on the offensive.

"I heard a noise and came to investigate." The corner of his mouth lifted, and she was pretty sure her stomach had taken up skydiving because it rose and plummeted with his sexy grin. "Have to admit, I wasn't expecting to find you."

"Really? What *were* you expecting? Ghosts?" she asked, hoping to distract both him and her sex drive. Those dark hallways had been a bit spooky, but she'd rather be beaten than admit that out loud.

"Not hardly." He shook his head. "Actually, you're not what I was expecting, period."

Now he'd distracted her. She leaned forward. "What do you mean?"

"You seem more real than the type of woman I'd have thought would audition to play Jane." His gaze bored into her.

"More real," she laughed, relaxing a little. "I'll take that as a compliment."

"I meant it as one."

She swallowed. If she poured the rest of her water over her head, she doubted it would douse the fire he'd started. An attraction to the producer could only lead to trouble, but how did one explain this to a body that, for the first time ever, seemed to be on sexual hyperdrive?

Without looking away, he took another drink. "Why are you here?"

" 'Here' as in your room? You dragged me in." So she was still stalling. Maybe it would work.

"I mean in Europe as part of this show."

She shrugged. "To be Jane Millionaire, of course."

His lips quirked at her flippant tone. "Why?"

Every instinct told her to be honest, to give him the truth or at least as close as she could manage. Damn. She really didn't want to admit to the boring shambles of her personal life, but he'd see right through her if she tried to lie, and she preferred honesty anyway. The more she could stick to the truth, the less likely she was to trip up.

"Because my boyfriend decided to resign from his position in my life. My overrun-with-one-problem-after-another sister is currently engaged, and she seems blissfully happy for the first time in ages. I feel like a party pooper." She looked away from his penetrating gaze. "Leaving California for six weeks right now is a godsend."

"You were in love with this man?"

"What's love?" She laughed to hide her pain. She had fancied herself in love with Dan once upon a time. She'd wanted to love him as she'd believed he loved her, and he had—as a best friend. Ugh. She hadn't wanted another friend—she'd wanted a lover. Her gaze collided with Rob's darkened one.

His expression remained unreadable for several seconds. She got the impression he wanted to ask more, but had decided to change the subject instead. "I read you played college ball. You were predicted to go pro. Why'd you drop out?"

Just how much of her life had Jessie listed as her own? She'd said she'd fibbed a little, borrowing a few aspects of Jill's life—not the whole thing. From what she'd encountered up to this point, Jessie had listed more of Jill's history than her own. Why wasn't she surprised?

"At the beginning of my sophomore year, my parents died and I had to take care of my sister. I found a day job, took night courses to finish my degree, and eventually, got a job on the police force, and the rest, as they say, is history."

"Is this the engaged sister you mentioned earlier?"

"Yep." Jessie had danced around like a child with a prized toy when she'd shown Jill the diamond her latest beau had given her. That had been right before she'd begged Jill to pretend to be her. Although she was beginning to question whether she was pretending to be herself. Why had Jessie listed so much of Jill's history?

"How much younger is she?"

Jill sighed. "Ten months."

"Ten months?" His forehead creased. "And you had to drop out of school to take care of her? She would have been what? Eighteen? Nineteen?"

"She was eighteen, but she didn't deal well with our parents' death. She needed me, and I was there." Jill shrugged and didn't explain the legal fiascos Jessie had landed in following their parents' fatal car crash. Why bother? Things had worked out for the best. If not for Jessie's minor transgressions with the law, Jill wouldn't have seen the job posting on the police department's bulletin board, wouldn't have personally known the chief. Now she couldn't imagine any other career. Law enforcement was in her blood.

"I hope she appreciates the lengths you go to for her."

If he only knew.

"Yeah, me too." She finished her water in one swig. "Why did you leave so quickly earlier tonight? You seemed upset. Did I do something wrong?"

Oops. She hadn't meant to ask that. But she did want to hear his answer. Her head still spun from his abrupt departure. One minute she'd been staring at the man, moved with desire, the next she'd been re-tracing every minute detail, wondering what she'd done to scare him off.

He took a swallow of water and regarded her. "Your entrance was perfect. I left because"—he paused and quasi-shrugged—"I needed a drink."

"Oh. A drink. Right." Jill smiled at the way his eyes twinkled mischievously. Her gaze dropped to his bare, muscular chest and her stomach flip-flopped. Before she stuck her foot in her mouth by asking why he'd needed a drink, she stood. "Guess I should let you go back to sleep."

"I wasn't asleep." Which explained why he'd heard her creeping around outside his doorway.

"It's two-thirty in the morning. Why aren't you in bed?" *With me.* Oh! Where had that last thought come from? If she wasn't careful she was going to get herself into megatrouble.

"I was reviewing your portfolio, making notes on ideas for the show." He nodded to a desk littered with papers, several bound notebooks and a laptop that had a photo of Jessie on the screen. "The pictures you submitted really don't do you justice, nor does the interview video."

Do her justice? Jessie was the beauty queen, not Jill.

"I never photograph well." Which was true enough. Her gaze lingered on the notebooks. Was one of them the transcript?

She walked over to the desk, hoped she appeared casual, and picked up a photo of Jessie. Jessie's beauty never failed to move Jill. She'd never seen this shot before, but then she hadn't had a lot to do with Jessie's pursuit of acting.

For once her sister had attempted something on her own, and Jill had been relieved. She should have known better. Look where leaving things to Jessie had landed Jill. In Europe in a sexy man's suite in the wee hours of the morning. Hmm. Maybe she needed to rethink this and send Jessie a thank-you note. If only Rob weren't forbidden territory. As things were, she couldn't risk him finding out he had the wrong

26

woman. Just how far could she push things before he'd realize the truth?

"Personally, I like this one." She stared into Jessie's eyes, almost identical to her own. How could two sisters be so different, yet so similar? "Of course, my hair was lighter then."

"I like your hair darker. It suits you."

Startled, she turned to face him.

"Thank you." She touched her hair. "Gregory lightened it quite a bit when he highlighted it. Do you think it's too much?"

"No. It's just right." He shook his head, eyeing her from head to toe. "I've also decided I like how the extra few pounds fill out your face. You looked a bit gaunt in a few of those pictures. You were too thin."

What was with the compliments? Didn't he realize she already liked him too much? Add a great personality, intelligence and compliments to his hot bod, and she was in for some major problems.

"You know, I find it odd. Thanks to airbrush technology, people rarely look better than the photos they submit, but none of your pictures even come close to portraying your beauty. Casting couldn't have chosen a more suitable woman. You're sexy as hell, intelligent, and have a genuineness about you that can't be faked."

Right then and there she fell just a little bit in love with Rob Lancaster. *Sexy as hell.* Had a better compliment ever been paid?

Her gaze met his, and she shivered. How could she shiver when her insides were in total meltdown? This man made her hot.

"I plan to supervise your publicity shots. I want to make sure our photographers capture the real you, unlike whoever did your portfolio," he continued.

His words were a sharp reminder that Rob wasn't a man vying for her affections. He was her producer. She'd do well to remember that rather than fantasizing about what could never be.

Disoriented by the confusing emotions running through her, she dropped the photo back onto the desk. It landed on a stack of books. There it was. The transcript. Boldly labeled as such on its blue cover. She ran her finger over the smooth cover and wished she could magically absorb the contents, could magically be the woman Rob Lancaster thought she was.

"Looking for some late night reading material?" He stepped up behind her. She could smell his wonderfully male scent. Was that spicy mixture a cologne or pure Rob? And could she possibly purchase a few gallons of the stuff to pour on her pillow so she could breath in his intoxicating aroma all night?

"I'm not really sleepy. Would you mind? The thought of reading my interview converted into a transcript fascinates me." Not realizing how close he stood, she swiveled. Less than a foot separated her from his magnificent bare chest. Why had she been wasting her time running her fingertip over paper when something much better stood before her? And why buy bottles of a fragrance when the real thing was within sniffing range?

Acting on instinct alone, she reached up to touch his tempting pecs. She yearned to smooth her palms over his wide chest, his sinewy arms, but he captured her fingers before she made contact. His larger hand clasped hers longer than necessary before he gave a gentle squeeze. Electric zings zapped their way to her brain, singeing her nervous system in the process. Holy smoke. How had he done that?

"Take the transcript if you want to read it. I'll see you at breakfast." He released her hand and stepped away.

"But I—" Had she been about to beg for more zings? She wasn't sure what she'd intended to say.

Rob shook his head and opened the door to his suite. "Goodnight, Jane."

Two days later, Jill could feel Rob watching her. All morning he'd been in and out of the studio where she was working with Gregory on everything from memorizing her royal heritage to perfecting her princess etiquette. Who would have thought there was so much to learn to star in a reality show?

Jessie couldn't have realized how much effort this would be. Her sister was highly allergic to anything that remotely resembled work. Jessie. Jill inhaled deeply. After reading the entire transcript two nights ago, she'd concluded her sister had stolen her life. Jessie had listed Jill's accomplishments—both during her competitive sports days and while on the police force. She'd listed her job with the San Padres Police Department, her hobbies, her likes, her dislikes. Everything. Her sister had pretended to be her in all but name—and she'd even gone so far as to state that her friends called her Jill in order to explain all the references to "Jill Davidson."

The question was *why*? Why would her fun-loving,

sexy sister want to use Jill's dull background when interviewing for an acting job? Jill couldn't fathom her sister's train of thought—but she would ask the moment she returned to California.

Refocusing her attention on the scheduled meeting, Jill glanced around the studio. She sat at a long, heavy wooden table with yellow legal pads all around. J.P., Rob, the director of photography, a couple of assistants and several others she couldn't remember occupied the table, too. She was the only woman present. Come to think of it, she hadn't seen another female since arriving earlier this week. She leaned back in the gray metal fold-up chair.

"Why aren't any women working on this crew?"

All eyes turned to her.

"We decided it would create a higher level of sexual tension if you were the only woman at the castle. We didn't want to take any chances on one of the bachelors being distracted by one of the crew members or castle staff," J.P. answered. Jill liked the older man. He had a fatherly air about him, although she'd heard rumors that he'd been a babe magnet in his day—still was, according to some sources.

"You eliminated the possibility of me having competition. Nice thinking." Lucky her, she'd truly be the center of the bachelors' attention. Why wasn't she more pleased at the prospect? Her gaze shifted to Rob sitting at the head of the long, crowded table.

What precautions had they taken to keep her from falling for him? A paper sack over his head might help for starters. And gloves. He'd definitely need gloves to prevent conduction of those lightning bolts his finger-tips had zapped to her nerve endings.

She wasn't sure any of those things would diminish her crush on Rob. From the moment she'd met the sexy producer, she'd wanted to be the center of his attention. And in many ways she was—until the filming ended. His quick wit and looks of pure male appreciation over the past two days had only heightened her already keen awareness of everything about him.

He looked up and caught her ogling him. Where had he gotten those honey-in-sunshine eyes and dark good looks? She'd expected a Spanish flavor to his words, but his accent was pure southern California. Regardless, she could listen to his sexy baritone for hours on end.

She smiled before she could check herself. He immediately averted his gaze to his notepad without acknowledging her gesture. Her smile sagged. Since their late-night encounter, he seemed determined to keep their relationship as producer/actress—which was just as well since the more time she spent with him, the more she liked and respected Rob in ways that had nothing to do with anything physical—and the physical soared right off the Richter scale.

Rob Lancaster was dangerous to her sanity and to her bogus identity. She needed to be careful or he'd distract her right into one big mess-up and presto! Everyone would know what a fake she was.

She was making a mockery of everything she held dear, worked hard to uphold, simply by being here. She was usually the one seeking out the truth, not perpetrating a crime. Guiltily, she admitted to herself that she was no better than some of the criminals she helped lock up. If she made a slip of the tongue, her honor, her freedom and her job as a police officer would all be on the line.

Slip of the tongue. She'd like to slip her tongue into Rob's mouth. She swallowed, ran her gaze over his strong features one last time, then forced her attention to J.P. who had talked nonstop during her fantasizing about Rob.

J.P. continued the brainstorming session. "Okay, the first week the guys are here, they get the opportunity to wine and dine Jane. While they're still at the hotel, they'll write a letter of introduction. At this point, Jane won't have met any of them. She can choose which ones she likes best based on their notes, and her choice will be made without the bias of outer appearances coming into play."

"This portion is interactive as well. The audience will vote on which letter they like best, and that bachelor receives a night out with Jane and a cash prize of ten grand. A special kickoff vote of sorts," a creative assistant said with excitement in his scratchy voice.

"We've also added a viewers' choice to air at the end of each episode," Rob informed. "Viewers will have twenty-four hours after the show airs to vote. Audiences are much more likely to tune into the next show if they've participated in the decision process. They'll want to know how their choices compared to the rest of the viewers'."

"The audience is going to pick the guy I have to go

on the pretend honeymoon with?" Jill didn't like that thought one bit. What if they chose someone she couldn't stand?

"No," Rob said. "Ultimately, the choice between the last four bachelors is yours. Just like you'll have information about the men that will be cut from the actual footage shown, we'll give the audience different inside information." He clicked the tip of his pen back and forth as he continued, "We'll show clips of the men discussing you, etc. They'll form their own opinions about which men are sincere and which ones are after the prize money that comes from being chosen."

"Prize money? The guy I choose gets prize money?" This was news to her. Why hadn't the packet they'd sent Jessie included this information? Or had it, and Jessie just hadn't seen fit to pass those pages along? Jill bit her lip to remain silent.

"The bachelors win a prize for each episode they advance. The chosen bachelor gets the choice of going on the honeymoon with you or taking a hundred thousand dollars cash." J.P.'s dismissive tone made it seem like this point was no big deal. A minor detail. Wrong.

"Holy smoke," she exclaimed. The plot thickened. "So even though all these guys are going to be kissing my fanny for the next month, ultimately I'm going to be made a fool of when he walks away with the dough and I'm left alone on national television?"

"If one of the men falls in love with you, he'll choose you, not the money," Rob assured her from the opposite end of the table. He sounded confident, but she knew better. Men fell in love with Jessie, not her.

And that was when nothing was at stake but her heart. Add in the bonus of a hundred grand for walking away, and Jill Davidson didn't stand a chance.

"In a month's time, some guy is supposed to fall so in love with me that he'd choose me over that amount of money?" she scoffed. "It'll never happen."

Not that she wanted it to. She was here to save Jessie's butt. If she happened to have a little fun along the way, well, that would be an added windfall. It was beginning to look more as if her usual luck remained true to form. What man would choose a tomboyish woman over that much cash?

"Ah, but you're forgetting the guys don't know you're not really Jane." Rob leaned back in his chair, regarding her thoughtfully. "They believe you're a princess, and someday they'll be crowned king if they marry you."

"So if the guy does choose me over the money, I still won't know if he's choosing me or hoping for a bigger payout," she mused out loud. This just got better and better. She should have known there was a catch. There was always a catch.

"After he's chosen you, you'll tell him the truth. That you aren't a princess, but in truth, work at a low-paying job," Rob said.

Her police salary wasn't that bad—well, maybe it was to a big-time Hollywood producer like Rob Lancaster. But at least there she knew where she stood and didn't have to take any crap from anyone— except the commissioner, and the mayor, and the . . . Okay, so she had to take some crap there, too, but at least it was acceptable crap. Most of the time.

"Either way, I'll be humiliated when he takes off. Humiliated in front of millions." Just great. She rolled her eyes to the ceiling, staring at the exposed wooden beams that glistened with richness and age.

"If you've found true love, he'll stand by your side." The words were spoken low but evenly. She glared at him, but he refused to make eye contact.

"Yeah, right." She snorted with disbelief. Surely he didn't buy the garbage he'd just fed her? Regardless, she knew better. Dan had proved how much she knew about love. And about picking men.

"Whether or not any of the bachelors truly fall in love with you depends a great deal upon you." Still the irritating man didn't meet her eyes. He seemed to look anywhere but at her. "Choose how you spend your time with the bachelors wisely. Think about the worst dates you've had and what made them that way."

"My worst dates?"

Rob nodded. "We'll recreate them and see how these guys react in similar situations."

"You want to recreate my *worst* dates?" Jill scowled. Was he out to torture her? She'd thought having to be constantly exposed to him when he represented prohibited goods was punishment enough. Apparently not. "I thought I was going to be romanced for the next month."

She wanted a little romance—even contrived romance had to be better than constantly being considered just a good friend.

"People convince themselves every day they're in love when things are bright and sunny. It's when the rain comes that the truth is exposed. What they thought was love turns out to simply be lust." Rob's gaze bored into hers. "I want you to put these guys in situations to bring out their true nature. Make them work to show their charm."

She rolled her eyes. Oh, she knew quite a few ways to kill the look of romance in a guy's eyes. She had a lifetime's experience. "Jeez, just put me in a game of one-on-one with them."

Rob's dark brow rose.

"I'll win," she clarified. She took a deep breath, trying to stifle her frustration at this whole setup, and failed. She glared at the overabundance of testosterone at the table. "Men don't like to lose to a woman. At anything, but especially not at sports."

Several snickers sounded around the table.

"Okay, we'll let you play them in a game of basketball." He turned to an assistant. "There's a gym here, isn't there?"

"Yeah, some NBA star leased this place for a month of R and R after a media fiasco. He had one put in."

"Make sure cameras are installed." Rob scribbled on his notepad.

"Cameras are everywhere except the bathrooms and the west wing," one of the crew assured.

"Why not in the west wing?" Jill asked. Heck, she'd been here for several days and had yet to make it through the place. But she hadn't known she wasn't supposed to go in certain areas of the castle.

"The west wing is off limits to everyone, including the crew. The castle owner's private quarters are located there," J.P. answered.

"How are we going to liven up this contest to make

it more interesting to the viewers?" Rob's gaze touched each crew member.

The sound of J.P.'s pen tapping against the tabletop grated on Jill's nerves. Several people tossed out ideas. Rob rejected each one. *Tap. Tap. Tap.*

Jill forced herself to ignore the tapping. Unfortunately, this left her mind free to ponder Rob. She snuck a look. His lips pursed as the wheels visibly turned in his head. What would those lips feel like against hers? Would Rob's kiss steal her breath? She closed her eyes, daydreaming of Rob jerking her to her feet and lowering his mouth to hers.

"What are you thinking, Jane?" Rob's voice murmured in her fantasy.

"Kissing." Jill blinked. Had she said that out loud? Shoot. Her wistful voice had been all too real.

"Kissing?" Rob and J.P. asked simultaneously. "What does kissing have to do with you playing the bachelors in a game of basketball?"

Thinking quickly, she grabbed J.P.'s pen, wrote "kiss" across the top of her notepad and slid it across the table.

"Instead of playing regular basketball, play a version of H-O-R-S-E, only we'll call it K-I-S-S. If my opponent beats me, I'll kiss him."

Rob's throat worked, his eyes narrowed and then he nodded. "Okay, each bachelor will be given the opportunity to 'score.' "

A harassed crew member rushed into the studio and headed straight for Rob. He looked like the bearer of bad news who feared for his life. Jill watched curiously as the man leaned over and whispered something in Rob's ear.

"What?" Rob's pen landed on the table with a thunk. "You're kidding."

The man grimaced and shook his head.

"Aw, hell." Rob looked directly at J.P. "William's agent called and says he's canceling. Personal reasons."

Every male mouth at the table dropped open.

"So some guy canceled. We'll just have eleven bachelors instead of the twelve. No big deal." Jill shrugged. Eleven, twelve, it made no difference. She was afraid an entire army of men wouldn't be able to distract her from Rob.

"William wasn't one of the bachelors." Rob corrected her mistaken assumption. "He was the host."

"There isn't time to line up someone else," J.P. announced, not looking one bit worried. "We'll just have to use someone here who's already available." The older man shot a glance in Rob's direction. "Rob's got showbiz experience. He'll just have to fill in."

"Hell no." Rob was on his feet.

Several of the crew and Jill flinched at his exclamation.

"You know I'm not into publicity. Putting me in front of the cameras is out of the question. I don't want every gossip columnist in Hollywood poking around in my private life." Rob's jaw set in a determined clench. "I won't do it."

J.P.'s bushy brow quirked upward. He and Rob stared at each other, silent messages flying back and forth between the two tense men. Just as Jill wondered if they would come to blows, Rob flopped down in his chair in apparent defeat.

Her mouth fell open as the crew visibly sighed with

relief and more than a little disbelief that Rob had conceded to J.P.

The older man flashed a triumphant grin and slapped Rob's shoulder. "Say hello to our new host with the most."

CHAPTER THREE

"I don't appreciate how you put me on the spot a few minutes ago." Rob leaned back in his worn leather chair, toyed with a pen and tried to remember that his friend had meant well.

J.P. had escorted Jane to the door after Rob had called a quick end to the meeting, then hung around until they were alone in the makeshift studio.

"Had to." J.P. didn't look one bit repentant as he took the chair next to Rob's.

"Explain."

"I know you."

Rob frowned and waited for J.P. to continue. He didn't have to wait long.

"You'd have found a way to wheedle out of going on-screen if I hadn't made my suggestion in front of the crew. Now they're all excited at the prospect of you hosting, and it'll be more difficult for you to squirm your way out."

He ran a hand through his hair. What was J.P.

talking about? Why would he even want him to be on-screen?

"Exactly why is it that you think I shouldn't refuse? You of all people know that being in front of the camera holds no appeal to me."

"But you were damn good, boy."

Rob snorted. "Circumstances and you put me in the limelight. My goal was never to continue acting. I can't say I'd change the past if I could, but the thought of being center stage again gives me heartburn."

"Don't you think it's about time you got over that?"

"Uhm." Rob thought about his answer for all of two seconds. "No."

J.P. shook his head. Disappointment similar to what Rob imagined a father felt toward a son who'd fallen short shone on the older man's face. J.P. had been more of a father to him than the bastard who'd run off when Rob had been barely out of diapers.

"Aw, hell, J.P.," Rob relented, unable to stand the look in J.P.'s eyes. "I'm a behind-the-scenes man. Not some pretty-boy host."

J.P.'s lips twitched as he stood and clapped his hand against Rob's shoulder. "Now, that's not how I hear it. According to *Tattler*, you're a pretty boy, indeed. Although your hospitality is only known when it comes to charming the ladies."

Tattler. He hated that rag. He'd been raked over the coals one time too many, but not in the past few years. He'd intentionally skirted situations that would call media attention to him for other than professional reasons. Until this crazy reality TV stuff.

"Yeah, well, thanks to you, I'll probably make the cover. 'Reality TV Host Has Millionaire Alien Baby Who Looks Like Oprah' or some other such nonsense."

J.P. laughed. "Just think of the free advertising that would give Jane."

Rob shook his head, but grinned, grateful the disappointed expression on J.P.'s face had vanished. "Always planning ahead, heh?"

Practically rubbing his hands together in glee as he agreed, J.P. grinned in a way that left Rob's stomach unsettled. "Always."

"Rob, wait," Jill called as she jogged to catch up with him. He'd not said much after calling an end to the meeting. She'd wanted to linger, but J.P. had practically pushed her out of the room, and it would have been too obvious if she'd gone back.

Obvious and stupid, much as she was right now. But she didn't seem to be able to stay away from the man.

Spotting him running in the gardens while she'd been staring out her suite window had been a godsend. Or the devil's most seductive temptation. Either way, she intended to take full advantage of the opportunity to spend time with him. She'd jerked her hair into a ponytail, thrown on some jogging clothes in record time and bolted through the castle and the garden to catch up with him.

Which explained why her chest heaved and her lungs burned.

At least that's what she was blaming her breathless

state on. Rob's damp hair, glistening skin and bulging muscles ran a close second.

His pace slowed, but he didn't turn to look at her. The high, tense set of his shoulders made her question whether or not he welcomed her intrusion. Had he and J.P. argued after the meeting broke up?

"Hey, you." She intentionally kept her tone light as she fell into stride beside him.

His gaze cut to her briefly. "Hey."

That quick look was enough to set Jill's heart to pounding. Of course, the fact that he'd managed to scan her from head to toe might have played into her racing pulse.

"What did you think of my K-I-S-S plan?" she asked just to have something to say.

He shrugged and kept running. "Brilliant."

She grinned. "Brilliant" worked for her. "You really think so?"

"Sure. It's competitive, fun, and yet sexy. Viewers should love it."

Viewers schmeewers. She just wanted Rob to love it.

"Maybe I should practice a little before the bachelors arrive." Okay, so she was trying to flirt without technically flirting. She certainly wouldn't say no if he offered to help her practice. Not that she needed to. For a few glorious years, she'd lived, eaten and breathed basketball. Then her parents had died and her life had crumbled around her.

"Maybe." She blinked her depressing thoughts away and focused on Rob. She wasn't going to live by Jill Davidson's rigid "have to be responsible" guidelines for life. She was free to enjoy every moment without having to be sensible and cautious. For once, it was okay for her to go with the flow. To take chances. Just so long as she didn't forget that Rob thought she was her sister. "You wanna play me sometime?"

"A game of K-I-S-S?" Rob stumbled and came to a halt. They were at the far end of the gardens, the castle a long way off in the distance. A soft breeze blew through the leaves, creating rustling background music.

"Well, I meant regular basketball, but"—she wiped moisture from her brow, wishing the breeze would whip this way to help cool her down—"I'm game if you are."

His lips twisted in a smirk. "Seems like everyone is trying to set me up today."

He stretched forward, touching the tips of his white sneakers. Jill almost sighed in appreciation of the play of muscles beneath his thin T-shirt and gray gym shorts. Yowzas, the man was built like an athlete.

"You two had me worried there for a bit," she admitted, trying to keep the drool in her mouth from running down her chin.

He motioned toward a path to the left and she nodded. They fell into a brisk walk.

"Who, J.P. and me?" Rob laughed. "There's no need. We go way back."

"Really?" The scenery around them was amazing, with tall trees full of vivid green leaves and flowers of every color and variety. Fresh, crisp air filled her oxygen-hungry lungs, and the breeze had finally descended enough to blow against her clammy skin. But by far the biggest attraction was the glistening man walking two feet from her.

"Let's just say he feels comfortable pushing my buttons and for some crazy reason I let him get away with it." The good-natured way he spoke hinted at a deep bond between the two men.

"Sounds like you're good friends."

"The best."

Odd that his best friend would be a man twice his age.

"What about you?" he asked, causing Jill to steal another look in his direction.

A tiny drop of sweat trickled down her breasts as she stared at his tanned features. "What do you mean?"

"Tell me about your friends." He flashed a grin. "I doubt your best friend is as ornery as J.P."

"No. My partner on the force is my best friend." Although things had been rough after Dan had given the "let's just be friends" spiel, he was still her dearest friend and she his. Too bad his latest girlfriend wasn't thrilled by their continued closeness. Dan's overly jealous girlfriend—just another reason she'd wanted to leave California for a while.

"How many female officers are there in San Padres?"

"Just one. It's a small community. Very quiet and family-oriented. A great place for raising a family." Jeez, she sounded like a walking ad for the San Padres Chamber of Commerce. What was she trying to do, convince him to move there?

"Just one?" He turned toward her, his brows drawn together. "Your best friend is a man?"

"He likes to think he is," she teased, wondering why

they'd stopped walking and why he didn't look pleased.

"Is he your lover?"

She inhaled deeply and faced him. Her breath caught. He regarded her intently, clearly wanting to know. Fool that she was, she wanted to tell him.

"Not anymore. I'm not involved with anyone." She laughed, although even to her it sounded fake. Her insides churned in what she guessed had to be called feminine coyness. Rob's blatant sexual interest reduced her to a sniveling idiot. "I wouldn't be here if I had someone waiting on me at home."

"Good point." He glanced around almost nervously, which didn't fit with his usual confident air. Maybe she wasn't the only one sniveling? His stance tightened. "We should head back. Gregory will be looking for you."

Had she just heard a loud thump as he'd slammed those walls up between them? She sighed. Free to take chances and enjoy life or not, she didn't need to forget that there were some chances she couldn't take. One slipup and she and Jessie would be in a whole heap of trouble.

"Yeah, you're probably right." But she'd really rather have kept walking with Rob and ignoring the little voice warning her that spending time with Rob was riskier than facing an armed robber. "Tell me, how is it that a famous big-screen producer is working on a reality television show?"

"I'm not that famous."

She snickered. "Yeah right. Since when?"

Rob chuckled. "Had you ever heard of me before you auditioned for *Jane Millionaire?*"

"I remember hearing the girls talk about you when I was in college. You starred in some romantic comedy that was all the rage. I never saw it. Actually, I don't think I've ever seen any of your movies or shows. I'm not a big movie or TV person." Sports had been her life. Watching a movie would have required sitting still too long.

"Really?" He sent her a look of mock horror.

"I rarely watch anything more than the late-night news. Too busy working and volunteering."

"Good thing there aren't more people like you in the world, or I'd be out of a job." He grinned and the tension from moments before eased. "What kind of volunteer work?"

"I teach self-defense classes to women and work with San Padres High School's after-school drug-prevention program, among other things. But somehow I think you already know all these things about me. They would have been listed in my bio information, right?"

"Yes, I read about your extracurricular activities." He grinned. "Still, I find your volunteer work interesting. Noble, even."

"Necessary."

"In quiet, family-oriented San Padres?" His tone teased. She reached out and punched his shoulder lightly.

"Even in the most serene settings, you just never know when someone's going to knock you off your feet." She tossed him a challenging look, as though he'd better watch out or he might find himself on the ground. Of course, that being the case, she'd be right there with him. "I'll race you back. First one to touch the castle wins. Loser has to buy the first round at the tavern tonight."

"You're on."

They bolted toward the castle.

After slapping her hands against the cold stone wall of the castle, Jill doubled over with laughter and the need to catch her breath. "Who won?"

"I did." Laughter and breathlessness inflected his words.

"No, you didn't."

"Yes, I did." He laughed. "But I'll be a gentleman and spring for the first round tonight anyway. I'm a gracious winner."

She rolled her eyes. "I can tell. Apparently, you're a gracious loser, too."

His rich chuckle warmed her insides in a way the heat from her brisk run couldn't touch.

"You better get inside. Gregory's not going to like the damp-hair look."

Her hands lifted. Oh, she bet she made a pretty picture all hot and sweaty. She looked at Rob and realized he was staring at her clingy T-shirt, not that he could see much through the material and her sports bra. But it didn't matter. Her nipples budded under his scrutiny. Heat of a different kind spread through her.

Maybe she didn't look as bad as she'd imagined. Or maybe it was because she was the only female he'd seen in over a week.

"Uhm, I'll catch you later." His gaze lingered a moment longer before he waved and took off.

Jill watched as Rob disappeared. If he'd moved that fast during their race, he would have won.

* * *

Jill glanced around the tavern, eyeing a pay phone at the far end of the room. Apparently, all phones had been removed from the castle, except the cell phone in the filing cabinet. It was unlikely she'd get another opportunity to make a call home.

What was Jessie doing?

She slid off of her barstool and smiled at the seven men sitting at the two pushed-together tables. She grinned. Jane Millionaire and the seven studs.

"Be right back."

Rob's hand shot out and grasped around her wrist, stopping her departure. *Zing. Zing. Zing.* Electricity shot through her. "Where are you going?"

"The ladies' room." And she'd make a detour by the phone on her way out.

"Just give a shout if you have any problems." J.P. raised his mug in salute.

Jill smiled. She doubted J.P. would be able to do a thing if she had problems she couldn't handle, but it was sweet of him to offer.

"I'll do that." She winked at him, eliciting a lot of good-natured ribbing from the crew. Rob watched without commenting and Jill scooted away before he suspected her duplicitous motives.

Three minutes later, she hid behind a burly man as she charged a call to Jessie's cell number. *Ring. Ring. Ring. Come on, answer.*

Jessie's voice mail picked up.

"Jessie, where are you?" she mumbled into the phone. "I'm not sure when I'll get another chance to call, but if you need anything, call Dan."

She hung up the phone and snuck a glance at where the crew sat. No one had noticed her. Her gaze lingered on Rob as she took a moment to study him undetected. Dressed in his usual garb tonight, he wore snug blue jeans and a T-shirt depicting a superhero character from a film she'd read that he directed a couple of years before. J.P. had kindly provided her with an entertainment magazine that had done an unauthorized spread on Rob.

As if sensing he was being watched, Rob scanned the room. Jill ducked back out of view.

She needed to quit dallying and check on Jessie. She grabbed the phone again and punched in Dan's cell number and her PIN to charge it to her calling card.

"'Lo," Dan answered on the third ring. His voice sounded muffled. Still, the familiarity of his voice felt good. She hadn't realized she was homesick. Maybe she was, just a little.

"Catch you at a bad time?"

"I was sleeping." Sounded like he still half was.

Jill did a quick calculation of the time difference. "Oops. Sorry about that. Wasn't sure when I'd get another chance to call."

"It's okay. What's up, Your Royal Pain in the Butt?" he teased, sounding more awake. She could picture him scooting up to a sitting position in his bed, blond hair tousled and a sleepy look on his face.

"I wanted to check on Jess, but I couldn't reach her when I tried calling."

"She's twenty-five," he reminded.

"So?" Jill twisted the curly phone cord around her finger.

"So, if she doesn't answer her phone, maybe it's because she's busy. Probably with that new fiancé of hers."

Jill sighed. "You're right. I just wanted to check on her. You know how she is."

"You're her sister, not her mother, Jill. For once, why don't you worry about yourself and the mess she's gotten you into this time? You should have made her go."

"Actually, it hasn't been too bad so far. I'm staying at a castle surrounded by lots of men all catering to me. What more could a girl ask for?"

"Trying to make me jealous?" he joked.

"Could I?" she asked, not sure why. She'd already worked out that Dan had done the right thing breaking off their romantic ties. She valued their friendship, but she wouldn't take him back as a lover, would she?

"No. Nor do you want me to be."

She sighed. He was right. "Yeah, I know that and you know that, but does the perfect girlfriend from hell know that? I take it she's there with you?"

"Yep."

"Tell her I said hi."

"Now's probably not the best time to do that."

Jill snickered. "Okay, you're right." From the corner of her eye, she noticed one of the crewmembers standing up from the table. Uh-oh. "Look, I'm going to have to go in just a sec. Have you checked on Jessie lately?"

"Saw her yesterday, and she's fine. Quit playing mother hen."

Was that what she was doing? And, of all people, he should know why she had to look out for Jessie. He'd worked on the force during all those legal fiascos.

For that matter, without Dan she might not have ever made it through Jessie's rebellion after their parents' death. He'd been at her side from the beginning.

"You know what kind of trouble she gets into. I just don't want to come home to a mess."

"If she makes a mess, let her clean it up. She might amaze you by acting like a grown-up."

Jill scowled. "You make it sound like I'm smothering her and her irresponsibility is my fault."

The line crackled with silence.

"Dan," she started, and glanced up to look directly into Rob's tawny eyes not two feet from her. Uh-oh. "Speak up a bit, please. You're calling for a Dan Jones? Just a minute and let me see if there's someone by that name here." She placed her hand over the mouthpiece and called out, "Is there a Dan Jones here? There's a call for Dan Jones." She met Rob's narrowed gaze and shrugged as she spoke into the phone.

"I'm sorry, but no one's answering to that name."

"What in the hell are you talking about?" Dan demanded. "Is someone listening? Jill, are you okay?"

"Yes, that's quite all right. Maybe you'll catch up with your friend soon."

"Someone's there, but you're 'quite all right,'" Dan correctly guessed. "If I didn't think it was good for you and Jess for you to be out of her pocket for six weeks, I'd strangle her for getting you into this mess."

"Oh, he's not your friend?" Jill waved her hand at Rob, acting as if she were just being polite. She needed to know Dan was going to look out for Jess. "A brother? Wow, I always wanted to have a big brother to watch out for me. Little sisters need watching out for, you know."

"Hint taken, Your Royal Pain in the Butt. Take care of you, and I'll keep an eye on Jess. No worries."

"Well, good luck. 'Bye now." Her heart squeezed from missing Jess and Dan, but she carefully kept her emotions checked as she replaced the handset and smiled at Rob. "Sorry about that."

"Just what was that about?" He looked suspicious.

"The pay phone rang as I was walking by, so I answered it." She shrugged, reminding herself that he couldn't tell her heart was racing. "I think the poor guy had the wrong number."

"Wrong number, huh?"

"Yep."

"Kind of odd for someone to be looking for a Dan Jones in this country, don't you think?"

"Now that you mention it, you're right. Still, that's who he asked for." She reached out and ran her finger down the front of his shirt, knowing she had to distract him before he pried the truth from her. "Wanna dance?"

Not that she knew how to dance to the wild music playing in the background, but she'd figure it out if he said yes. The prospect of being in Rob's arms threw her heart into a wild rhythm of its own.

An odd look passed over his face, as if he wasn't sure what to make of her. "No, we don't need to draw any more attention than two tables full of Americans in the middle of a European bar already do."

She laughed, hooked her arm with his, and enjoyed the zings as they walked back to their tables.

"You think everyone in this tavern doesn't know an American film crew rented that monstrosity where we're staying?" Jill asked. "I promise you, they all do."

"You think?"

"I know." She winked at him. "Now, tell me about the bachelors and how they were chosen."

"Eenie, meenie, miny, moe, catch a bachelor by his toe." Rob started with a gleam in his eyes.

She slapped his arm playfully.

"I bet you've chosen some real winners with that foolproof scientific method."

"Just wait. One of them will sweep you off your feet and romance you to the tune of twenty-million-plus viewers."

Yeah, that's what she was worried about, because she'd already met the man she wanted to romance her. Too bad he was plotting for another man, actually a dozen men, to do the job instead.

CHAPTER FOUR

"The bachelors will be here tomorrow night. I'm so nervous. Will they like me? Will I be attracted to any of them?"

Rob watched the video clip of Jane contemplating the bachelors' arrival. She sat next to him in the cluttered studio, leaning in as she pointed at her image on the screen. She wore jeans, a T-shirt and one of the headsets so that she could listen to the recordings. Her hair was swept up in a ponytail. She'd apparently scrubbed her face clean, because she no longer wore any of the makeup Gregory had painstakingly applied prior to a photo shoot and the filming of the scene they watched. Most of the women he knew would rather take a bullet than be seen without their armor of paint.

Mandy sure hadn't let him see her sans makeup. Apparently, Jane couldn't rid herself of Gregory's artwork soon enough.

"I feel ridiculous watching myself think out loud,"

she mumbled as she stared at the monitor in obvious distaste.

"Just don't do it in front of the bachelors." Rob grinned. J.P. was right. America was going to love Jane. And when they did, *Gambler* would really happen—if he could keep his hands off of his current star. Which he would. Somehow. No woman was worth losing this shot at success.

"You don't have to worry about that," she assured. Something in her tone made Rob wonder what he'd learn if he could hear her thoughts out loud at this moment.

"Are you excited about tomorrow night?" he asked. This evening most of the crew had traveled an hour away to the hotel where the bachelors roomed. The men were being filmed in the hotel's bar discussing the princess.

She shrugged. "I'm meeting twelve guys who are competing for my affections so they can dump me for a hundred grand. What's not to be excited about?"

"You're too young to be so cynical." Not that he necessarily believed his own words, but the phrase seemed like an appropriate response.

"What about you? Do you think one of these guys is really going to fall in love with me while all of America watches?" Her emerald eyes challenged him to be honest.

Rob adjusted the earpiece he wore. What could he say? He wasn't an advocate for love or reality TV. Most of what he'd seen when researching this project was about as bogus as television got.

Love. Reality television. Ha, what was the difference?

He knew just how *real* love was. It lasted just as long as you could help a woman one more notch up the proverbial ladder of success. Once she'd clawed her way up your back, love lost all its allure.

"It could happen," he said; after all, stranger things had.

"But it won't."

Why did she make comments downing her appeal when she exuded confidence in so many other ways? Hell, he was pretty sure he'd never met a more together woman than the one sitting next to him. Too bad she wanted Hollywood's glitter. Lust for stardom would ruin her.

Not that his high opinion of her mattered. Jane was hands-off in so many ways, somebody should post warning signs. Certainly, the prospect of her finding love on a reality show warranted a "Danger Ahead" notice.

Distracted, he said the first thing that popped into his head. "The question is whether or not you will fall in love with one of them."

"I've already told you, I don't believe in love." Her eyes glowed a hypnotic green, like kryptonite. Fortunately for him, he was no superhero. His heart rate picked up anyway, throbbing so loudly the booming beat probably echoed throughout the castle. Actually, his entire body throbbed, making him wonder if he should run while he could—before she sapped his ordinary male strength that was quickly succumbing to her supernatural feminine appeal.

"One bad experience and you're shelving happilyever-after for life?" It bothered him that he wanted to know as Rob the man, not Rob the producer. Maybe he should invest in a red cape and a bright S for his chest. If it would help him resist her allure, he might be tempted to wear blue spandex.

"How do you know it only happened once?" A quick shimmer of pain flashed in her eyes.

His grip on the computer mouse tightened. Just how many men had hurt her? And why the hell should he want to track down complete strangers just so he could pound their sorry faces?

Maybe her green gaze had robbed his sanity right along with his strength. No spandex tights were going to protect him.

"What about you? Any gaping chest wounds in your past?"

He blinked at her question. "We aren't discussing me."

And he certainly didn't want to rehash any of his old flames. Not now, not ever. He looked at the computer screen, hoping she'd take the hint and let the subject drop.

"We are now."

Damn, she was quick on the comeback. He laughed in spite of himself, admitting, "A few."

"And do you still believe in together forever and all that jazz?"

He considered her question before answering. "I believe a man and a woman can have fun for as long as the attraction lasts. But once it's gone, forever is a hell of a long time."

"You say that like you've had a few long relationships."

He didn't turn from the computer monitor, but knew her gaze remained on him. "Only my marriage, and I doubt that classifies as long."

"You're married?" She sounded distressed, and he looked at her. She stared at his bare left hand, her face pale.

"Not in the past ten years. Mandy and I divorced when I was twenty-one." He hadn't regretted that decision a single time. Any bitterness he held came from how he'd given her his heart and all she'd really wanted was a free ride on his determined path to Hollywood success.

"Twenty-one? How old were you when you got married?" She leaned closer, her chair squeaking with her movement. He got a whiff of flowers, not strong, just a subtle scent that made him want to inhale deeply.

"Eighteen and old enough to know better." Just like he was old enough to know better than to inhale. *Don't inhale. Don't inhale.*

He inhaled.

The scent of roses seduced him.

"What happened?" Genuine concern and curiosity shone on her face, and Rob shifted in his chair as much from his intoxicating lungful of Jane's scent as from the conversation.

How had they gotten into a discussion about Mandy? And why was he telling Jane about her? He never talked about his disastrous marriage. Why bother when everyone else had already read about his biggest failure thanks to media rags such as the *Tattler*. His marriage had ended because his wife stayed busy sleeping with anyone she thought capable of advancing her career. He bit back an ironic snort. Not that she'd been doing any actual sleeping in her bed-hopping adventures. Over the past ten years, she'd periodically begged Rob to take her back—usually when she was between husbands or her career was going a bit slowly. Not once had he been tempted.

As during their run in the gardens, it surprised him that he'd revealed so much about himself to Jane. He generally guarded his privacy with a tenacity that would frighten off the most determined.

"I'm sorry. I have no right to pry. Being a cop, I'm used to asking questions, and expecting people to answer." She smiled apologetically, tucking a stray strand of highlighted chestnut hair behind her petite ear. "Sometimes I forget I'm not wearing my badge."

Glad for the change of subject, he ran his gaze over her, trying to picture her in her everyday life. "It's hard for me to imagine you in a uniform chasing down bad guys."

"Why?"

Their chairs were side-by-side. Less than two feet separated his body from hers. It wasn't nearly enough space. Two miles might not be, not when her expression was warm and inviting—and completely stole his breath.

"I see you as Jane and not a police officer," he answered honestly. Why had he just leaned closer to her when he'd meant to shift as far away as his chair would allow?

Her eyes danced with humor. Apparently oblivious to his inner stirrings, she broke into the theme song from *Cops*.

Bad boys was right. Rob could think of a few things he'd do if she *came* for him. Like explode deep inside her. Aw hell. Where had that come from? He grimaced at his own usage of the word. He needed to pull his mind from the gutter. His other wayward body parts, too.

"Seriously, I've been awarded Officer of the Year two years in a row." Her chest puffed with pride and the hair she'd just tucked aside fell back across her face.

Still battling his lustful demons, he longed to push that strand back into place. His gaze traveled over her beautiful face, lower to the rise and fall of her chest with each breath. He glanced up and didn't bother to hide the lust slamming through him. What would be the point when he'd been as obvious as daylight? "I can see why."

Her bright smile faded. "Just what are you saying?"

Her chin jutted forward, her shoulders squared and her glare slashed into him, which should have dampened the heat surging through him. So why hadn't it? He should have run when he'd realized her gaze packed kryptonite. Even the man of steel would have gotten out of Metropolis. He had to douse this flame between them. Fast. Too bad he didn't have a red cape. Leaping tall buildings would be a breeze compared to ignoring his attraction to Jane or intentionally hurting her. Damn, he hated this, but he'd do what needed doing.

"It's unlikely you outperformed the men you work with. I imagine a female officer is cut a lot of slack."

Her indrawn breath cut him to the core, but he didn't take back his intentional slur.

"I got those two awards because I earned them. Both times." Her chin tilted at a proud slant.

"I'm sure you did."

She eyed him as if he were a snake that had crawled out from under the lowest rock. And even though he'd accomplished what he'd set out to do, the sinking feeling in his gut told him he'd messed up. Big time. That's what he got for allowing his crotch to distract him. The only thing he should be worried about where Jane was concerned was ensuring this show's success. Not anything personal. They had to avoid personal at all costs.

"I'm a damn good police officer, and not because of anything I've done while lying on my back." She quietly stood, pushed her chair back and walked out of the studio with her head high. Regal as a queen—er, princess.

Remorse gnawed his insides. How had he instinctively known how to hurt her? Even worse, a part of him had believed his chauvinistic comment. He really was a low-down, belly-crawling snake. But the women he normally dealt with used their bodies to get ahead, to accomplish what they wanted. Why should he expect Jane to be different?

Because she was different. Different from anyone he'd ever met. He liked her. Too much.

The thought of having sex with her had sent him into testosterone overload, and he'd purposely offended her. Now she'd think him a jerk, and maybe the undercurrents between them would fizzle.

He grimaced and rose from his chair, not liking where he was headed. After Jane. Bad. Bad. Bad. He should let things stand as is, but he couldn't. He owed her an apology.

Not to mention her thinking him a heel had him feeling like one in the worst kind of way. Bad boy indeed.

Jill pushed the castle door open and strolled to the garden with an outer calm she didn't feel. Her insides bubbled with frustration and the need to escape Rob's arrogance.

Men! She'd thought he was different. Not that it mattered. He was totally unavailable. But, darn it, she'd wanted to believe in him.

He might see her as a woman—a desirable woman, even—but he suffered from the same affliction as every other man in her life. She'd had to work twice as hard to get respect. So she had, and did. She'd finally earned her fellow officers' respect. They'd voted for her because she'd deserved the honor and not because of any favors she'd given them—at least not the sexual kind. No one could accuse her of using sex.

Not even Dan. If anything, he'd done *her* a favor by their having sex. He'd probably had to clear away cobwebs, she'd been out of commission so long. It had been years since her previous lover. Her one and only previous lover, and those few disappointing fumblings during college shouldn't even count.

A bluebird flew over her head and landed on a flowering bush to her left. The bird tweeted a short melody. Jill sighed at her peaceful surroundings, so in contrast to her inner turmoil.

None of her fellow officers would accuse her of using her gender to advance on the force. She'd put in long hours, performed flawless investigations. Outwitted, outmaneuvered, and usually captured her quarry. How dare Rob question her integrity?

She kicked a foot-high stone container of sweet-scented flowers. Along with a tiny puff of pollen, a bee buzzed from the bright yellow blooms.

"Ouch." Jill jerked to dodge the insect she'd disturbed. She sneezed and grabbed her throbbing toe.

"I'd probably make a softer target—unless you aimed at my head," a deep baritone said from behind her.

Almost toppling over, she spun at Rob's voice. "Oh, you don't want to hear what target I'd like to aim at."

Both hands covered his groin in mock fear, and he grimaced. "You wouldn't."

"Don't count on it." She turned away. She didn't want to see him. Just looking at him made her eyes water. *Water*. She did not cry. Not when her parents died. Not when Jessie had gotten involved with the wrong crowd and experimented with drugs. Not when she'd given up her athletic aspirations to take care of Jessie. Not when Dan had said he just wanted to be friends. Now certainly wasn't the time to start.

"Jane?"

She blinked, hoping to clear the moisture. She must have stirred up more than just a little puff of pollen when she'd kicked that container, because she was *not* crying. Damn allergies.

"Look at me."

She didn't budge. His hand closed around her upper arm. *Zing. Zing. Zing*. There went those sparks again. She ought to toss him on his electrifying butt. It would serve him right.

"I'm sorry."

Maybe she wouldn't throw him to the ground after all. And the zings from his touch were . . . not supposed to happen. "For?"

A soft chuckle escaped his throat. "You're not going to make this easy, are you?"

"No."

"I'm sorry I insulted you. I was a jerk."

"Yes, you were."

"Forgive me?"

If you kiss me and make it all better. Okay, so she couldn't say that. But the intensity of his gaze made her want to, did that count? She had to get her emotions regarding Rob under control. She couldn't afford any slipups that might reveal her as an imposter.

Annoyed with herself and consumed with guilt, she swiped at her eyes and faced him. "If you meant what you said."

"About being a jerk?" His lips twitched.

She stifled the grin wanting to replace her glower. "Oh, I *know* you meant that. I was talking about the sorry for insulting me part."

He threw back his head in laughter. Her insides fuzzed over—all nice and warm. Uh-oh. Rob Lancaster was wheedling his way beneath her protective armor. She already wanted his bod. What red-blooded woman wouldn't? But she didn't want to like the man quite so much. Maybe he should go back to being a jerk. For both of their sakes. Because she had a pretty good idea he wouldn't be too happy to have his show ruined by discovering he had the wrong "princess."

He wrapped his arm around her shoulders and

walked her back toward the castle as if everything was just hunky-dory. Didn't he feel those zings?

"You're priceless," he said, grinning.

She snorted. Priceless? "Yeah, well, let's hope one of the bachelors thinks so."

The night of the bachelors' arrival, Jill read over their letters in her private suite. A cameraman recorded her as she read the notes out loud and pondered over her decision. Of course, she'd have to spend an evening with whichever one received the most viewer votes.

She tried to ignore the cameras recording her every movement and let thoughts of Rob fill her mind.

A shiver ran down her spine.

She couldn't stop thinking about him. For the past week, she'd spent most of her waking time with him, J.P. or Gregory. And yesterday when Rob had wrapped his arm around her . . .

She reached up and touched one of the tendrils hanging from the elaborate hairstyle Gregory had concocted, and sighed. What would Rob think about the magic Gregory had once again created?

"Oh, that was perfect," the cameraman said.

Ugh. She'd forgotten he was filming. And she shouldn't give a flying flip what Rob thought about the way she looked. She had twelve men to choose from. Surely, one of them would float her boat and make her quit pining after the producer.

She turned and smiled at the camera like a good little pretend princess should. "Wish me luck."

* * *

Rob and J.P. mingled with the newly arrived bachelors in the magnificent foyer at the bottom of the curved staircase. For centuries the room had been used to host grand parties and introduce debutantes. Tonight was no exception. The air sizzled with excitement.

Along with lots of hidden video equipment, cameramen were everywhere, although most remained discreetly in the background. The entire evening would be recorded from every angle. All to catch the bachelors' first sighting of Jane. How would they react to meeting her?

Tonight was the night all the lunacy began. Rob let out a still-not-too-crazy-over-the-idea sigh.

He scanned the room. Which lucky man would Jane choose to spend a week with on a secluded island paradise? Unease festered as he inspected each of the twelve tuxedo-clad men. All healthy, good-looking specimens, he supposed. She had a variety to choose from. Average height to tall. Blond to coal black. Super-intelligent to super-jock.

None of them deserved her. Sure, they seemed like nice enough guys on the surface, but the thought of a single one touching her, kissing her sickened him. Which was all wrong.

A bachelor would claim her heart and woo her to the tune of twenty million viewers. At least until he and J.P. played the cards they held up their sleeves for the show's finale.

He'd make sure Jane and one of these men hooked up. J.P.'s career, Rob's reputation and *Gambler*'s future rode on doing so.

The music changed to an eighteenth-century waltz, the melody chosen for Jane's cue. The men stopped their conversations and drinking to line up at the bottom of the splendid staircase and stare at the landing where Jane would appear.

Rob's breath caught as she stepped into sight. He fought the urge to push through the line and claim her as his own.

What was the matter with him? Was it because she was forbidden that he couldn't think of anything but her? Or maybe her beauty was what held him captive?

Gregory had certainly outdone himself. Of course, he'd had a lot to work with. Jane was a stunning woman. Her long chestnut hair had been piled on her head into a mass of curls. Stray wisps begging to curl around a man's fingers framed her face. Her lips had been glossed and shined full and ripe, like the plumpest strawberries. Her skin glowed, and her high cheekbones had been powdered in a way that gave her an almost exotic look. Like Aphrodite or Venus.

The strapless blue designer gown straight from a Paris runway outlined her body to perfection. Her shoulders and upper body glistened. Had Gregory sprayed her with something? A sapphire and diamond necklace and matching earrings on insured loan from Tiffany's adorned her neck.

By far, Jane was the most breathtaking vision he'd ever seen. And that was saying a lot, as he'd been around more than his share of beautiful women. But then, he'd found Jane gorgeous the day before when she'd been wearing jeans and a T-shirt. He'd even found her beautiful during their run, when she was hot and sweaty. All he'd been able to think was that he wished he'd been the reason for her breathlessness, her sweat.

He should look at the bachelors to gauge their reactions, but he couldn't. His gaze remained glued to the goddess gracing the staircase with her beauty. With each step she took, his heartbeat drummed louder in his ears, like a seductive jungle beat calling to his primal instincts.

Large green eyes made up to dramatic perfection touched each man with an individual acknowledgement. Pure kryptonite. A soft smile played on her full lips, yet she didn't completely hide her nervousness. After she'd nodded at bachelor number twelve, her gaze searched the foyer until she spotted him. Her eyes flashed, and his heart stopped. It had been a hell of a long time since a woman had looked at him without ulterior motives. Jane's eyes shined with excitement and desire. Desire for him as a man. Not as a ticket to fame.

But he was her ticket to fame. Just as she was his ticket to fulfill the dream his ex-wife had stolen from him. He'd never again risk letting another woman jeopardize his career. Not even one that attracted him as much as Jane did.

With all his heart he wished he'd met her under different circumstances, wished he had the right to act on the chemistry burning between them. But he hadn't, didn't, and too much rode on *Jane Millionaire*'s success for him to give any encouragement.

With regret, he motioned toward the bachelors.

Indecision, then sorrow flared in her brilliant eyes, but she only paused on the bottom step long enough to allow the first bachelor to take her hand and bring it to his lips. Rob couldn't hear what the man said, but Jane's laughter rang out like music on a soft sultry night. Enchanting. Seductive.

Damn. He walked over to a waiter holding a tray full of champagne and picked up a glass to down the contents.

It was going to be a long night.

Jill's face hurt from smiling, but she kept her lips turned up as she shielded her nose from Bachelor #9. Bachelor #7 had wandering hands. Bachelor #8 had stomped her toes at least twenty times, and Bachelor #9, well, his morning breath had decided to stick around for the evening's excitement and smelled like something straight from San Padres's sewers.

Relieved that the song had finally ended, she excused herself as Bachelor #10 made his presence known. She bit back a sigh and forced her smile to stay put as yet another hunky man took her in his arms.

"You look tired," he commented as he gracefully led her through a waltz.

At least he wasn't stomping her already sore toes.

"Uh-oh. That's not supposed to show. I've still got two more dances." She was tired. Tired of dancing with all these men when what she really wanted was to find Rob.

No, she didn't want to find him. What she wanted

was to not even care that he was in the same room. Either way, it didn't look as though she was going to get what she wanted this evening. She kept smiling anyway.

"Maybe no one else noticed."

"Maybe." But she doubted it.

"And maybe the next two won't use your feet as target practice."

She laughed. A real laugh compared to the feigned ones at Bachelor #4's incessant jokes. Ugh. "That would be nice. Was I grimacing that badly?"

"No, you were very gracious and kept your smile in place even after most women would have politely—or not so politely—excused themselves."

"Most women aren't having their every movement, and word," she added, remembering the mike she wore, "taped."

"True." He smiled, and Jill relaxed. She took a closer look. Bachelor #10 was a ruggedly handsome blue-eyed blond who looked as if he should model Stetson cologne for a living.

"I can't remember your name. I'm sorry. I know it's terribly rude of me, as each of you introduced your-selves after I came downstairs, but the names ran to-gether," she said in her most practiced princess voice.

"Bachelor #10, Jeff Kensington." He grinned, not seeming to care that she'd had to ask.

"You're the safari doctor?"

He nodded, his smile reaching his eyes, letting her know he truly loved what he did.

"Tell me about your work."

As they swayed to the music, he did. The song ended quicker than she would have liked. Jeff was a wonderful dancer, and the medical missions he was involved with in Central America fascinated her. But Bachelor #11 patiently waited for his turn.

The next two dances passed pain-free, and she managed to keep a smile plastered on her face for the cameras.

The bachelors milled around sipping champagne and chatting. She joined the closest group—Jeff Kensington's group. She'd fulfill her obligations by mingling with the men and with any luck she'd see Rob before the night ended.

No, she didn't want to see Rob. She needed to forget Rob. She'd keep her eyes on the bachelors. However, if Rob just happened to wander into her field of vision, well, a girl couldn't be blamed for looking. She mentally rolled her eyes, but kept her smile bright.

The next two hours flew. Jill allowed the men to convince her to join them in a few more dances—just not #4, #7, #8, or #9.

Someone tapped on her shoulder, and she turned to see which bachelor wanted another dance, praying it wasn't one of the dreaded four. She'd only had two glasses of champagne, but her insides bubbled with giddiness when she saw the tall, obscenely handsome man standing next to her.

"Rob!" He was the last person she'd expected, but the one she'd longed to dance with all night, if she was honest with herself. She raked her gaze over him. His tux fit to perfection, emphasizing his broad shoulders and narrow hips. The crisp white of his shirt gave an added glow to his golden skin, and his whiskey eyes sparkled.

God, he was magnificent. *Benjamin Bratt, eat your heart out.*

"May I?" He extended his hand to her. Quivers of anticipation shot through her.

"Of course." She turned to the bachelors she'd been talking to and excused herself in what she hoped was a princessly manner and not an I-shouldn't-be-doing-this-but-I'm-going-to-anyway nervous bumbling as it really was.

"You are absolutely breathtaking," Rob whispered in her ear the moment she slipped into his arms. His warm breath tickled the inside of her ear, making the tiniest of hairs on her neck prickle to attention.

"Thank you. I was thinking the same thing about you." Her face flamed. She wasn't supposed to have said that out loud. And she'd forgotten to whisper, which meant the good old mike had captured every word.

"What is it about a man in a tux?" she laughed, another of those forced, fake ones. She'd spent the whole week with him, talking for hours on end; what was wrong with her that she suddenly couldn't think? Oh yeah, now she remembered. She hadn't been enveloped in his arms, hadn't been snuggled against his hard frame, hadn't been so close she breathed the same air as he did. That's why she could barely string two words together, much less obtain coherency.

"Actually, we look like a bunch of penguins, and you look like a beautiful fairy princess."

Her insides melted. Oh, why, oh, why couldn't *he* be one of the bachelors?

"I didn't realize I was allowed to dance with you." If she had, she'd have found him earlier, bachelor or not.

"You aren't." His voice was filled with frustration, rebellion and a hint of humor.

"Oh." She wrinkled her forehead in confusion.

"Now that all the bachelors have held you in their arms, I decided one dance between the 'host with the most' and the 'star of the show' wouldn't hurt."

She liked his reasoning. She liked him. Although "liked" seemed such a mild word for the sensations churning inside her at his closeness. "I'm glad you did."

His spicy masculine scent tickled her senses, dulling the reasons why she should resist this man. "You smell so good. Not overpowering or so strong it chokes a woman." Not like Bachelor #9. Ugh.

He chuckled and brushed his face against her hair. "You smell like flowers."

"I should. Gregory sprayed enough products on me to keep Sephora in business for a year. I've never been so powdered and perfumed in my life."

"Gregory's the best."

"Apparently. I couldn't believe it was me when I looked in the mirror."

"Why not?" His feet slowed, his hand gently pressed into the small of her back, his gaze searched hers.

"Because I looked . . ." She paused, searching for the right word and trying not to read anything into the way his eyes seemed to delve right into her soul or the fact that his body was noticeably hard.

"Beautiful?"

"Do you think so?" Her breath caught.

The sane, methodical cop in her poked her conscience with a reminder that she was a phony. Becoming emotionally involved with Rob Lancaster could only lead to trouble. Nevertheless, the woman in her craved what shimmered in his eyes.

He swallowed, his eyes glittering with the truth. He wanted her. "You know I do, but it would be better if I didn't."

She could barely hear his low words, but they touched her more than if someone else had screamed her praises over the intercom system at a Lakers game.

"Rob." She didn't say more. She couldn't. Not when all the cameras were focused on her. Not when everything said was recorded by the tiny microphone hidden between her breasts. They both knew it was there, although she wondered what Rob would say if technology wasn't capturing every word, every look, every touch. Would he kiss her? She wanted his mouth on hers.

Knowing she couldn't act on the lust coursing through her, she rested her head against his chest for the remainder of the dance, enjoying the beat of his heart against her cheek. Its steady, rapid rhythm told her he wasn't immune to her body pressed against his, not by a long shot.

The world faded, and she lost herself in his embrace, his scent, his warmth. Her own heart raced, as did her mind. She wanted Rob Lancaster. She'd never comprehended how a person could risk his or her freedom for a temporary pleasure—Rob's arms provided a crash course in understanding.

Forbidden, lethal and something she had to resist, Rob embodied the most potent ingredients of any addiction.

When the song ended, she reluctantly lifted her head. "Thank you for the dance."

"It was my pleasure, Princess." He stared into her eyes, longings of his own evident. But just as visible was the determination to ignore his attraction to her. She wouldn't ever know how strong their passion was for one another. He'd never give either of them the opportunity to find out. Which was a good thing, since she longed to throw caution to the wind and experience all this man could share.

She turned away before moisture gathered. Must be something about Europe making her all glossy-eyed. Regardless, she couldn't ruin her makeup. Gregory would kill her.

"May I have the honor of another dance?" a grinning hunk asked. She smiled at Bachelor #6, hoping her disappointment at leaving Rob's arms wasn't too apparent. At least her new dance partner wasn't #4, #7, #8 or #9.

"I'd be honored." Which was much better than saying, "Forgive me, Your Honor. It was a case of temporary insanity," as she'd be doing if she got caught.

Which was exactly what was going to happen if she didn't stay away from Rob Lancaster.

CHAPTER FIVE

Resigned to his fate of craving a woman he couldn't have, Rob watched as Jane slipped into the other man's arms and swayed to the music.

"What the hell do you think you're doing?" J.P. growled, joining him under the pretense of handing him a drink. A drink Rob didn't want as, minutes after Jane's descent down the stairs, he'd downed his self-imposed limit of two.

"Dancing."

"Uh, yeah. I noticed. As did all the cameras filming this blessed event." J.P. smiled as a camera panned their way. "What gives?"

"Nothing."

J.P. stared at him with wide ice-blue eyes. "Nothing?"

"I'm the host." Rob shrugged one of his shoulders. "I danced with the princess. No big deal." And if that were true, everything would be just fine. However, his insides still shook from how her body had fit perfectly against his, how her scent had wrapped itself around him and dragged him further under her spell, how—

Jane's laughter rang out across the room. Lyrical, beckoning him to return to her. What had the man said? He racked his brain for Bachelor #6's information. Ex-military. Athletic. His gaze assessed the other man's appearance. Looks most men would give their eyeteeth to resemble. Didn't he work as a private investigator now? He and Jane had a lot in common.

Damn it. He'd liked #6, too. The guy had reminded him of his die-hard military brother. An annoying tic twitched along Rob's jaw. Was #6 the bachelor she'd choose?

It didn't matter which one, just so long as she chose.

He couldn't have her regardless.

"You like her, don't you?"

Rob cut his gaze to a thoughtful J.P. "Jane?"

"No, the other 'her.' "

"Smart mouth." He turned to where she and the man danced. Damn. She looked as if she was enjoying herself with the come-to-life G.I. Joe. His tic worsened. Rob hoped J.P. didn't notice, but he imagined the twitch probably registered on the Richter scale and was impossible to miss.

This shouldn't bother him. She was supposed to enjoy herself—with any man but him.

Most likely, she was similar to all the other starlets he'd encountered over the years, willing to do anything to climb to the top of Hollywood's Most Wanted, including walking over him to do so. *Think about* Gambler. *Think about Mandy, how she used you to introduce her to bigger fish and then she'd* . . . He clamped his jaw tight in effort to stop the increased twitches.

Jane was staring up into Bachelor #6's eyes, looking totally captivated by whatever the man was saying. A lump formed in Rob's throat, threatening to cut off his air supply.

The evening was a success.

Too bad the knowledge held no pleasure.

Ignoring J.P.'s glare, he shoved his still-full glass back at him. Time for him to disappear to the studio to scan over tonight's footage to start edits for the show's premiere just two nights away.

"Just one more?" Bachelor #11 panted after Jane sunk her winning basket.

Rob watched on the monitor as she grinned and shook her head at the man who'd just allowed her to walk all over him.

"Not today."

"Can I have a kiss as a consolation prize?"

"Nice try, but no." She laughed as they walked to a wooden bench where they had left their towels and water bottles. Jane stretched her neck, then dried her face and throat with her towel.

"Just one?"

Rob snorted. The guy was pathetic, but he wasn't the only one. Why were the bachelors letting her win? Did they think they had to be chivalrous? Next week, more than twenty million viewers were going to watch them getting their butts stomped by a pretend princess. Didn't they care?

"Partaking in your favorite pastime?" J.P. questioned as he slid into the seat next to Rob.

"Huh?"

"Watching our very own WNBA star."

"Ha ha, very funny." Rob adjusted his headset and fiddled with the volume.

"I notice you aren't bothering to deny it."

"I'm being paid to host, produce and direct this show. Of course I'm watching Jane."

"Maybe keeping your tongue from lolling out the side of your mouth when you look at the star should have been listed in your contract."

Rob turned to his longtime friend. "That's enough. If you have something you want to say, spit it out."

"Don't worry. If you act out of line where Jane's concerned, I'll be doing more than spitting. I saw how she looked at you when she came downstairs last night. What's worse, I saw how you looked at her." J.P. sighed. "I know you have a way with the ladies, always have, and I've been damned proud of you for it, but this is one little gal you're going to have to leave alone. She's got twelve men to choose from. Thirteen is bad luck, and don't you forget it."

Rob watched as Jane blew a stray piece of hair from her eyes and faced her next opponent, Bachelor #6. The man who'd taken his place last night. A man who'd had a right to hold her in his arms and breathe in her sweet scent. A man who might be chosen to accompany her to a romantic paradise.

Jane's face lit up in delight as she joked with the guy.

"Promise to go easy on me." She swatted her towel at him. "You're my fourth game today."

G.I. Joe's gaze raked over her from head-to-toe and Rob squelched the urge to punch the guy's lights out.

"Oh, I promise. I'll be easy, and make sure you enjoy our game as much as I do."

Jane's eyes widened as she checked out the man's wide shoulders and bulging biceps, then her mouth lifted in challenge. "Why do I get the feeling you're no longer talking about basketball?"

"Because I'm not." He winked at a grinning Jane.

Rob scowled at the screen. He hated reality shows. He really, really did.

Jill practically tiptoed down the stairs. Maybe she could make it to the exercise room without any of the bachelors spotting her. She'd had her dates with the bachelors that morning. First she'd gone horseback riding with Bachelor #8, then she'd had a picnic lunch with Bachelor #12 and this evening she'd cooked dinner with Bachelor #3.

She discovered Bachelor #8 barely knew which end of a horse to avoid, Bachelor #12 had severe hay fever and Bachelor #3 should have the fire department on standby any time he stepped into the kitchen. The entire day had been a disaster. From start to end. But then, she had a feeling Rob and J.P. had meant for it to be.

She'd also played four more of the men, one at a time, in a game of K-I-S-S, two midmorning and two in the afternoon. Twelve games of K-I-S-S and none had beaten her, although Bachelor #6, Steve, had come close on that first afternoon. But she was pretty sure that was because he'd been fresh. She'd been playing ball for thirty minutes straight and had already played three games that day. Still, he had been good.

Of course, truth be told, none of them had really tried to beat her—not until she'd sunk the ball even when they hadn't meant for her to. Then pride had taken over and they'd tried, but to no avail. Except for Steve, who'd remained playful, not stressing when she'd score or outmaneuver him. Easy, he'd said. She smiled at the memory.

Regardless of the constant attention and flirting from the bachelors, she remained kissless.

It bugged her that she wanted to be kissed. Not by any of the dirty dozen, as she now thought of the bachelors. Not even Steve or Bachelor #10, Jeff, although both were great guys. She wanted Rob's kiss. Goose bumps pricked her flesh at the thought of his lips covering hers, demanding that she respond to him. And his kiss would be demanding. Of that she had no doubt. Rob wouldn't go easy on her. No way.

She sighed, shaking the image from her mind before she went into meltdown. Here she was in the middle of a castle full of gorgeous men wanting to woo her, and all she could think about was the one man she shouldn't want. The one man she needed to stay away from at all costs because she couldn't have him—and because if he discovered the truth, she'd have to face the legal repercussions of her actions.

A door opened. Her breath caught. She hoped. Could it be? J.P. stepped into the room. In disappointment, she let the air whoosh from her lungs.

"Jane." He looked around the grand foyer. "What are you doing here alone? I'm surprised one of the bachelors isn't with you."

Yeah, that made two of them. All day long, bachelors had shadowed her every move. At least one of the men had been with her from the time she'd left her room prior to breakfast.

"I snuck down after pretending to go to my suite for the evening. I'm headed to the exercise room to work out." She was pretty sure she'd find Rob there. During the time before the bachelors had arrived, she'd gone to the exercise room several times and found him pumping iron. They'd worked out together, laughed, talked, worked up a sweat. Her stomach flip-flopped at the memory of how he'd looked in his gym shorts. Oh man!

J.P.'s brows lifted, probably because her face had flushed from her heated thoughts. "I figured you'd be tired after the day you've had. What time are you meeting the bachelors for drinks?"

So she might be a bit sore in the morning. No biggie if it meant she got to see Rob without a crowd around them.

"At nine by the pool." She rolled her eyes at the thought of more time with the bachelors. Three full days in and she'd already wanted to eliminate half of them. "Maybe I'll drown a few."

"Why on earth would you want to do that?" J.P. scolded.

"I thought this would be more fun than it's turning out to be." And it would be, if she could spend her time with Rob the way she had before the bachelors showed up. She missed having her meals with him and the rest of the crew, having Rob devote hours of his time to educating her on her role, supervising her photo shoots, of having him smile and laugh with her. She missed Rob. Period.

Oh yeah, if she could have spent the entire month in Rob's company, she'd have been a happy camper. Instead, she'd barely seen him since the dirty dozen had taken up residence four days before. Not seeing him should have been a welcome reprieve, rather than sending her in search of his company. Rob embodied the biggest threat to her being found out, yet she yearned to be with him.

Jill sighed, not bothering to hide her frustration.

A worried look settled onto J.P.'s face. "You aren't thinking of breaching your contract, are you?"

She shook her head. She'd gone this far to ensure her sister didn't face legal repercussions. She wouldn't quit now. Who knew what would happen to Jessie if the truth ever came out? Or to her? The prospect of losing her job and possibly going to jail for fraud wasn't an appealing thought. Besides, ending this charade would ensure she'd never see Rob again.

"I'm seeing this to the end—whatever that may be."

She spoke with J.P. a few minutes longer, nervously glancing around the foyer in case one of the bachelors showed up. She didn't want anyone following her to the exercise room.

"Well, I'm going to get a quick workout in before having to meet with the bachelors." She smiled and gave a quick wave before heading down the long passageway that led to the exercise room.

Jill stood in the doorway and watched Rob lift weights in controlled repetitions. His dark hair was damp and his tan skin glistened. His sleeveless T-shirt outlined to-die-for abs and revealed biceps that bulged. She'd have liked nothing more than to cross the room and run her fingertips over his shoulders and arms.

She was used to working out around men. The police force gym was always full of half-dressed men, but none of them made her break out in a sweat before she'd started her work out. Watching Rob made her sweat. In a very naughty way.

He looked up and frowned when he saw her. "You need something?"

Yeah, she did. What would he say if she admitted she needed him to kiss her? Just so she'd know if his lips were as scorching as she imagined, if his lips zinged the way his fingertips did, if her knees would bend and her insides melt at the mere touch of his mouth to hers.

"I want to work out." Which was the truth. She did want to work up a sweat. Of course, the only special equipment she'd need was the man eyeing her with suspicion.

His brow rose, but he didn't point out the obvious—that she'd had a more than decent workout playing the men earlier. Instead, he glanced around the exercise room. "There's plenty of room. Help yourself."

Why had things had to change? Prior to the constant cameras, he'd smiled when she'd arrived in the gym. He'd teased her and even sat on the bench just talking when he'd finished his workout halfway into hers. Now, except for the dance, he'd barely acknowledged she existed. Of course, the only time she'd even seen him had been during filming. He'd remained in the background and she'd only been able to sneak quick peeks.

And she hated it.

Walking over to a bench, she dropped her fluffy navy-and-white striped towel. She pulled off her T-shirt, leaving only her black sports bra and matching shorts to cover her body. She stretched before hopping onto a ski machine. When she glanced up in the mirror lining the wall in front of her, her gaze collided with Rob's.

He looked away and continued his own workout.

Jill smiled. Rob's gaze had been full of sexual longing. Bachelors or not, Rob wanted her.

Maybe life wasn't perfect, but regardless of having to spend time with the bachelors, this was going to be the best month ever. A month without bailing Jessie out of one crisis after another. A month of not having to deal with crooks, con men, an ex-lover whom she'd always believed she'd eventually marry and said ex-lover's new girlfriend, who brought new meaning to the word "jealous."

Of course, maybe she'd had reason. Because Jill now admitted that until meeting Rob, she'd harbored hope that Dan and she would get back together. After all, they made a great couple and wanted the same things from life.

Dan was built, but he didn't begin to compare to the man pumping iron across the room as he pretended to ignore her, probably because of the camera in the corner recording every move they made. But it was more than Rob's outward appearance that attracted her to him. She'd watched him over the past week. He was a natural-born leader. Everyone on the crew, including J.P., looked to Rob for answers. He never hesitated to make a decision. He was a man who invoked trust in those who knew him.

She wanted to know more. Wanted to move beyond her twenty-six years of being a good girl, and just live for the moment—even if it was only for one month.

But what she wanted more than anything was for Rob Lancaster to make love to her over and over until she couldn't see straight. More caught up in her thoughts than her workout, she lurched and stumbled awkwardly on the machine.

"Ouch." She rubbed her hand over her calf as a muscle pinched into a spasm. She hadn't had a cramp in years, but lusting after Rob rather than paying attention to what she was doing had apparently triggered all sorts of aches.

"You okay?" Rob dropped his weights onto the mat and crossed the room.

"Charley horse." She groaned in total misery.

He knelt next to her and ran his hands over her calf. Her spasm eased as he massaged her tight muscles. Magic. That's what his fingers were. Pure zinging masculine magic. Jill stared at the top of his head, spotting a single strand of gray mixed in with his shiny dark hair. How old was he?

"Thirty-one. Not that it's any of your business."

Had she asked that out loud? Yikes. She needed to

be more careful, or she'd be begging him to kiss her—possibly more.

"Don't you want to know how old I am?" Now why had she asked that?

"You're twenty-five." He recited Jessie's age, reminding Jill she was living a farce in more ways than one.

"You know, it really isn't fair that you know everything about me, and I know next to nothing about you." His hands stopped massaging. "Don't quit. That felt great."

He frowned, eyeing her skeptically. "Did you have a charley horse?"

She flexed her toes upward. No pain. Had she had a real cramp, or had her body given her an excuse to get his attention? A reason knowledge of the camera wouldn't cancel out? Her leg had hurt, but her pain was gone now.

"Maybe you're so good my pain went away?" Okay, so she was feebleminded, and her excuse was even worse. His hands on her body had been worth it.

"Maybe," he conceded, his eyes briefly meeting hers. She wished she could read his thoughts, but those whiskey eyes revealed nothing. He stood and turned back to where he'd left his weights.

"Wait." She grabbed his arm, the one she'd been fantasizing about running her fingertips over. His biceps flexed, solid and hard, against her palm. The ever-present zings of their skin contact pulsated through her.

He slowly pivoted. "What?"

She leaned close and whispered the words in his ear to prevent their being picked up by the recording equipment. "I know I'm not supposed to be, but I'm attracted to you."

She held her breath as she waited for him to react to her foolish admission.

"Don't be." He pulled back, his body tense, his hot masculine scent tempting her nostrils.

"I'm not very good at the games men and women play. Maybe it's the cop in me, but I don't like to evade the issue." Her heart raced, and if not for the desire she saw in his gaze she would have chickened out, but her every instinct said he wanted her as much as she wanted him. She'd learned to trust her instincts long ago, and doing so had saved her life on more than one occasion. Of course, in Rob's case, her instincts sent out conflicting messages. *Stay away. Kiss him.*

She reached up, closer, almost close enough to press her lips to his ear. Heat, his heat, emanated, seduced her to go ahead, to taste his salty flesh. "I'd really like you to kiss me."

His muscles contracted beneath her grasp. "Don't say that."

"Why not?" She breathed in deeply, his musky scent adding to the longings building within her. The man oozed pheromones.

"I'm not one of the bachelors."

She could barely hear his strained words. Had that been a Spanish curse under his breath? Whatever it was, it sure hadn't sounded like an endearment.

"So? Can't I spend this evening with you? Somewhere away from the cameras? At least until it's time for me to show up at the pool? Or afterwards? No one has to know." Part of her was embarrassed by her boldness. Part of her warned that she was skirting with danger. Another reveled in her initiative. Jill Davidson was hitting on a man—and, for once, not with her fists. Cool.

"Not a good idea." He pulled his arm free but didn't step away.

"I've seen how you look at me." The same way he looked at her this very moment. His eyes told her that if a genie granted him one wish, he'd choose her as his prize without hesitation.

"That's why we can't spend any more time together than is absolutely necessary. I made a mistake by spending so much time with you before the bachelors arrived. I knew better, but—" He paused and ran his hand through his dark hair. Looking frustrated, he shot a glance at the camera, then leaned forward and whispered into her ear, "If we do, I won't be able to help myself; I'll have to have you."

And that was a bad thing?

"What if that's what I want?" She told him with her gaze that was exactly what she wanted.

"You *can't.*"

A bead of sweat trickled down his neck and she was pretty sure it had nothing to do with his workout. Her gaze followed its path until his sleeveless T-shirt absorbed the drop. Tension was visibly coiled through his body. He wanted her. She wanted him. Forget all the reasons why she shouldn't be with this man.

"But I do. So very much." Her lips parted in excited anticipation.

His head moved closer, his eyes locked on her

mouth. Abruptly, he jerked away. He stepped back, determination on his face.

"I won't ruin *Jane Millionaire* just to get laid."

He forgot to keep his voice down, or he simply didn't care if the camera picked up the sound. Jill was too shocked to remind him as he ripped her heart to shreds with his next words.

"And that's all a girl like you could ever be to a man like me. A fun roll in the sack."

A little before nine, Jill plastered a smile onto her face as she stepped outside the castle, clad only in a bikini. An itsy-bitsy, teeny-weeny green bikini. Ugh. She always wore a functional one-piece, but Gregory had insisted she wear the tiny scraps of shiny material. She had so much skin on display she may as well have been naked.

Oh, and don't forget the stiletto heels. Heels with a bathing suit. She rolled her eyes toward the star-strewn sky. The beauty of the cloudless sky with its expanse of twinkling diamonds failed to impress her. She was too busy concentrating on putting one foot in front of another. How ridiculous. She'd probably fall and break her neck, Jessie would have to fly overseas, and the truth would come out. Just peachy keen.

Wolf whistles greeted her.

Jill cringed on the inside, squelched the desire to fold her arms in front of her chest, and smiled as though she were auditioning for the role of Miss America as she click-clacked across the patio.

Just remember, you wanted all this male attention.

Even after she stumbled—*darn high heels*—she

forced herself to continue smiling. After all, two cameramen were sticking to her like glue.

"What'll you have, doll?" Bachelor #7 asked, placing his hand on her rear.

"Not you." She pulled away and suppressed the urge to toss him into the pool. Several bachelors laughed. Very conscious of her state of undress, she carefully swayed over to a poolside table, praying the entire way that she wouldn't fall smack-dab on her face. Who ever heard of wearing three-inch heels with a swimsuit?

Two of the bachelors grabbed her chair to pull it out.

"Thank you," she said as she winked at another. She would play the role J.P. had outlined for her—even if she felt ridiculous doing so. Her ego needed a boost after the beating Rob had given it in the exercise room. Not that he wasn't right, or that he'd told her anything she hadn't already known.

The best thing she could do was forget about the way he made her pulse race.

Too much was at stake. His hot, sweaty body had made her lose reason, but he'd doused her in cold reality. She needed to stay away from him before she forgot she was a fake in every sense of the word. Before she forgot that personal relationships with co-workers never worked anyway. She'd focus on the bachelors, hope she didn't get caught, and make it through these next few weeks. Then she'd go back to California and do as Rob suggested—forget he existed.

And maybe buy a little oceanfront property in Arizona while she was at it.

After two hours of smiling, laughing and, surprisingly, enjoying the bachelors' company, Jill excused herself. She walked through the house and toward the stairs minus the two cameramen who were still filming the bachelors—probably discussing her. She froze when Rob stepped into the foyer seconds after she did.

"You did a great job tonight." His eyes raked over her bikini-clad body even while he grimaced, as if he hated looking yet couldn't help himself.

Her nipples hardened to beaded pebbles beneath the scraps of green. How did he do that with just a look? She shivered.

"Cold?"

Damn him for calling attention to the fact her body responded to him even after he'd been a jerk to her.

"It *is* a bit nippy in here." She turned to walk away, determined to ignore how her body reacted to him, but his hand clasped around her upper arm.

"Surely you see the problems that would ensue if we act on the attraction between us?" he whispered into her ear, and she almost shuddered at the effect his closeness wreaked upon her senses.

"Whatever." She pursed her lips. How was she supposed to ignore how he affected her when he was touching her? "The only problem I see is your fingers on my arm. Unhand me, or I'll unhand myself."

His eyes glittered. "I'm not one of the bachelors who will let you make a fool of me."

"Oh really? You think they've been letting me kick their butts?" She poked her finger in his chest. "Maybe you'd like to see how you measure up, stud-muffin?"

"Don't push me." He clenched his jaw.

Jill was too far gone to care. She'd had enough of his

mixed messages. How dare he send her steamy looks, then give her the cold shoulder when she bared her heart to him and told him how much she wanted him?

"Oh-h, I'm so-o scared, dude." She tapped her finger against his solid pecs. "One-on-one. Basketball, hand-to-hand combat, boxing, the firing range. Name your game."

She tried to ignore the way her breasts brushed against him, the way his spicy, fresh-from-the-shower scent intoxicated her better judgment. A tiny tic along his jawline proved he wasn't as calm as he'd like her to think. Good. Calm was the last thing she wanted him to feel when she was so frustrated she could scream.

"Meet me in the gym in fifteen minutes." He pulled away and walked off, only pausing long enough to toss a parting shot over his shoulder. "You might want to change, as I don't intend to go *easy* on you."

The jerk. She ought to wear the bikini. It would serve him right. So what if she broke her neck while trying to run in her heels? Maybe she could use the spindly spikes to deflate that ego of his.

She watched until he disappeared up the stairs before making the climb herself.

He wanted her. She could see it in his eyes, in the way his breathing sped up when she got close.

Was it because of their enforced proximity? Or because of the forbidden nature of their attraction?

She didn't know. All she was sure of was that she wanted Rob more than she'd ever wanted any man and she couldn't have him. She really needed to stay away from him before she got in over her head.

But she knew she wouldn't stay away. How could she? He'd agreed to play her in a game of one-on-one.

She smiled in anticipation of what the night might bring.

Maybe she could convince him to play K-I-S-S.

CHAPTER SIX

"Hey, boss, you need to come see this," one of the crew working at the computer station called to J.P. as he stepped into the makeshift studio. "We just taped some interesting footage."

J.P. rubbed his neck, cursing the ache in his bones. Growing older was hell. And he needed a smoke something fierce.

"Yeah, catch something good on tape, huh?" he asked as he slid into Rob's leather seat. Crazy boy carted the worn chair everywhere he filmed. Said sitting in it got his juices flowing. Ask J.P., and he'd say that's what a willing woman was for.

Still, J.P. had been the one to give the chair to Rob. On the same day that he'd convinced the film production company he'd worked for to give a prodigy kid actor a chance to direct his own production. Of course, he'd had to agree to supervise the whole damn thing, but J.P. had never regretted the decision.

After a childhood illness, J.P. learned he'd never

have children of his own. But Rob Lancaster was like a son to him.

Settling back into the chair, J.P. glanced at the screen for the first time. He'd just come in from shooting the pool scene so he expected to see footage of the bachelors still at the pool, or Jane with one of the bachelors, maybe in an embrace. Probably #6, Steve Jernigan, or #10, Jeff Kensington, as she seemed to have taken a liking to those two.

"Holy mother," he cursed as his eyes took in the couple squaring off against each other in the foyer.

Jane's eyes flashed green fire that matched her bathing suit to perfection. Hands on hips, she glared at Rob. Rob didn't look too happy, either. Actually, he looked like a tortured man.

"When did this happen?"

"About thirty seconds after you walked through the foyer, Rob did. I think he was waiting for her. They've really been going at one another, but I can't pick up on most of what they're saying."

J.P. leaned back in his chair, regarding the screen. What was Rob up to? He'd seen how the boy looked at Jane, but Rob was a professional and was never led around by his trousers. At least, he never had been before.

"What did she just say?"

"I think she just threatened to kick his ass." Barely contained amusement laced the man's words.

Yeah, J.P. might have thought it funny, too, if one film company after another hadn't told him he was a has-been in the business and needed to retire. Until Wolf Television came through with this reality show gig, he'd been labeled as washed-up. He planned to prove every critic wrong.

Jane Millionaire's success decided too much of his future for him to risk letting things go awry because Rob got an itch in his shorts.

"They're going to play a game of one-on-one, sir."

J.P.'s brow shot up. Rob was going to play Jane in basketball? Didn't he know too much rode on this show for him to be dallying with her? He'd kick the boy's hind end himself if he went for a K-I-S-S.

Rob's angst-ridden gaze ran over Jane's barely covered body. J.P. grinned in spite of the seriousness of the situation. He could understand Rob's fascination. Jane was a great gal and a real looker.

For that matter, Jane seemed quite captivated by the man she was currently pitted off against. Much more so than any of the bachelors. Too bad she was the star of *Jane Millionaire*. She'd have made a great match for Rob and might have been the one to get him past the deep wounds dug by Mandy's repeated betrayals.

J.P. pulled a cigar from his pocket and chewed on the end, wishing he could light it and inhale its calming flavor.

He had no choice. He'd have to make sure whatever sparks were flying between them died a quick death by any means necessary.

Besides, as Jane Millionaire, Jane was the last woman Rob needed to be hooking up with. The boy avoided the media like the plague. When Jane returned to the U.S., she'd be a damn media magnet.

"Make sure all the cameras in the gym are on. Rob

will erase the main camera, as that's the one he'll expect to have been recording continuously. I want their game recorded on the other three as well. Save all the footage and bring it to me."

"Sir?"

"No one"—he stared at the curious man—"including Rob, is to know about this. Not a word. Understand?"

The man nodded. "Yes, sir, Mr. Scott. I'll bring the tape to you as soon as I'm finished recording."

J.P. steepled his hands, and regarded the man thoughtfully. "Excellent."

Idiot, Rob chided himself. What had he been thinking to take Jane up on her offer? That might be the problem—he hadn't been thinking. He'd been staring at her sassy lips, wanting to kiss the challenge from their fullness, wanting to run his hands over the toned flesh she had on display.

The woman was a walking advertisement for fitness equipment, and he'd challenged her to a game of basketball. Why? Because he'd dreamed of playing her? Of claiming the prize none of the bumbling bachelors had been man enough to take?

His midsection hardened. He didn't have time to take a cold shower and, blast it all, he'd already taken more cold showers in the past week than any grown man should. Two today. Not that the one following his encounter with her in the exercise room had helped. Her hot, whispered words haunted his libido like a ghost on Halloween night.

I want you to kiss me.

Aw, hell.

He was in trouble.

Rob managed to get his rebellious response under control without a cold shower—until he stepped into the gym and saw Jane in hip-hugging shorts and a tight T-shirt. He groaned and imagined being dunked into ice water, being back on the rough streets he'd grown up on, being married to Mandy again.

The last one worked.

His spine straightened and his resolve renewed.

"Practicing?" he called out.

"You know what they say." She turned, grinned, then tossed the ball into the air without looking at the basket. "Practice makes perfect."

The resounding swoosh of the ball passing through the net mocked him as he walked onto the gym floor.

"Are you sure you aren't too tired to play?" he asked, knowing she'd had a full day, and it was close to midnight.

"Afraid you might lose?" she taunted, looking way too bright and cheery as she rebounded the ball.

"Not in this lifetime. I didn't want you to claim that you lost because you were wiped out."

"I'm a big girl. You let me worry about whether or not I'm too tired."

She sure didn't look like she'd been on the go the entire day. She looked energetic and sexy in her shorts, shirt and ponytail. How had she gone from swimsuit model to sports jock in the fifteen minutes since he'd last seen her?

"My stamina would amaze you."

He almost tripped over his size twelves. She was blatantly flirting with him.

What had happened to the pissed-off woman he'd left in the foyer?

He averted his gaze, counted to ten and asked a question he wasn't sure he wanted to know the answer to. "What are we playing?"

Her lips curved. Wickedly.

God, he'd known he'd ticked her off in the exercise room. He'd meant to. *Had to.* Anything to put some needed distance between them. And in the foyer, what had that been all about? Why had he tried to explain why he hadn't taken her up on her enticing offer? She knew all the reasons why a relationship—even if just a physical one—was impossible between them.

Not to mention the ever-present cameras.

He'd rejected her, and now she planned to make him squirm.

Didn't she realize they were playing with fire and were going to go up in smoke if someone didn't extinguish the flames?

He swallowed and only managed to further fill his senses with her scent. He could practically taste her feminine sweetness. At least how he imagined she'd taste. Damn, he wanted to know.

"What would you like to play?" Her eyes danced as they traveled over his body. He refused to fidget—because that was definitely what she wanted. Too bad. Rob Lancaster didn't bow down to any woman. Not even one as feisty as her.

"H-O-R-S-E?" he suggested, knowing she'd refuse.

She did.

"Twenty points?"

She shook her head.

He *knew* what she wanted to play.

"I won't play for your kiss, Jane." But he did want to feel those plump lips against his.

"Fine." She shrugged as if it were no big deal, then shot him a sugary-sweet smile. "We'll play for *your* kiss."

"What?" His surprised yap echoed around the gym. Right then and there, he mentally bowed to her audacity. And her power to drive him beyond reason.

"If I reach twenty points first, you have to kiss me."

"You're crazy. No way in hell am I playing with those terms."

"Afraid you might lose?" she taunted with a sassy shake of her long dark ponytail.

Lose? With stakes like those, he wanted to lose.

Scratch that. He didn't want to give her any ideas. He had to convince her he was totally against an affair between the two of them. Of course, it would help if he could convince himself.

Besides, she couldn't beat him. Not at basketball. While growing up, he'd spent entire days at the neighborhood court. He and his brother sure hadn't had anything else to do during the long hours his mom slaved at one of her many jobs. Basketball was his game.

"Fine. What do I get *when* I win?"

"You don't want your kissing me to be the prize either way?" Her lower lip pouted almost imperceptibly, but he noticed.

Man, did he notice. Every single cell in his body stood to full attention.

He looked up, and his gaze landed on one of the

two cameras attached to opposite corners of the gym's ceiling.

"I'm sure." Sure kissing her was exactly what he wanted—but wouldn't do.

Her lips twisted in amusement as she considered him. "Name your prize, and it's yours."

"Anything?"

Her words had been heavy with innuendo. Hot desire flared, threatening to melt his tennis shoes to the gym floor.

"Anything," she whispered in a low voice, her lips parted. Her green eyes dripped with desire and fire.

Oh yeah, she planned to make him suffer for his rejection.

Every single drop of testosterone screamed for him to play for one night in her bed. For that one night he'd be the winner. But then he'd lose. Big-time. He had a feeling there was no way he could really win when it came to Jane.

"When I beat you, you have to kiss one of the bachelors tomorrow."

Had he said that? Idiot. What kind of incentive was that for him to win? For her to kiss another man?

Hell, he really did want to lose.

She looked taken aback, then shrugged with a saucy roll of her shoulders. "If that's what you want." She passed the ball. "Producers first."

Twenty points. Piece of cake.

Ten fast-paced minutes later, they were tied twelve to twelve. Maybe the bachelors hadn't let her win after all, he grudgingly admitted to himself as he dribbled down court.

"Do you give up?" She swatted the ball, but failed to steal it as he switched hands.

"You wish." He laughed in spite of his inner turmoil. What was it about her that made him feel good inside even when he was trying to hang on to all the reasons why he shouldn't be with her? Shouldn't let her close?

She slapped at the ball again, causing him to lose control. He snatched it before she stole it away.

"You really should go ahead and forfeit. You can't win this game." Yeah, he'd already worked that one out for himself. Was she still talking about basketball?

"I *will* win this game, and you *will* kiss one of the bachelors. Tomorrow." But damn if he wanted to think about another man tasting what he wanted.

"Which one would you like me to kiss? Jeff? Steve?" Her lips twitched.

None of them. "Whichever one turns you on."

"You turn me on."

He missed his shot.

What could he say? She turned him on, too, but not enough to ruin J.P.'s career. Or his. Or to get involved with a woman who craved the spotlight, for that matter.

She grinned, looked him over from head to toe and rebounded the ball. When he didn't respond, she dribbled out and cut through toward the goal for a layup.

He refused to allow her an easy score. He blocked her path, but she swapped hands, shot, and the ball bounced off the backboard and through the net. *Swish.*

"Nice shot," he admitted. "Enjoy it. You won't see another."

"You think?" She placed a hand on her hip, drawing his attention to how the cotton material stretched over her curves.

"I know." And he did. He knew he was in a hell of a lot of trouble if he didn't quit looking at how her breasts heaved with her rapid breathing. Or how her bottom looked as though it would fit perfectly in his hands as he pulled her to his hips.

"Come on," she urged, her eyes flashing as if she'd read his thoughts and teased him with her word choice. "What are you waiting on? For me to die from boredom? It's not going to happen, dude. Take your turn or pass me the ball."

He took the ball out, shot from three-point land, and, despite Jane's valiant blocking attempt, sank it through the net.

"Whoosh!" Elation filled him. He couldn't remember the last time something so pure and simple as a basketball game had excited him. Maybe not since he was a child and he'd beaten his brother for the first time. He grinned at her and strutted his stuff. "There it is."

She rolled her eyes, but when her gaze met his, happiness danced in her green depths. "Show-off."

They battled another two no-scoring changes of possession. She ducked around him and sank the ball for another two points, taking the lead by one.

He shot. She jumped, caught a piece of the ball and knocked it off course. It hit the backboard with a thud. He jumped for the rebound, but landed his front to Jane's backside. Her firm buttocks pressed against him. Heat—her heat—radiated through the thin material separating their bodies, scorching his brain.

Rebounding plummeted to the bottom of his priority list.

The ball hit the floor and rolled away. Neither of them moved. He honestly couldn't recall putting his hand around her waist, but it was there, so he must have. Her flat abdomen contracted beneath his palm. Every drop of blood in his body headed south.

She inhaled with a noisy catch as he grazed his thumb along the lower edge of her breast. Needing to see her face, he rotated her. She met his gaze with wide eyes full of passion. Every reason he shouldn't kiss her disappeared as desire for her filled him. He lowered his head—and almost stumbled backwards when she yanked free from his loose embrace to dart after the ball.

He frowned. What had happened? Why had she run off when she'd admitted she wanted him only minutes before?

Because she wanted him to pay for his callous comment in the exercise room. She wanted him to sweat. To squirm.

And he was.

Aw, hell.

The cameras.

He'd almost kissed her. He wanted to kiss her. And he was battling to ensure another man got what *he* wanted. *Idiot.*

He wiped moisture from his brow. He needed to win

this game and get away from the sight of Jane's sexy rear end. Pronto.

She pressed her way toward the basket, arm pushing, butt bumping as she held him back. He didn't want to touch her, but he wasn't going to let her score. She only needed two baskets to win.

And then he'd have to kiss her.

He blinked. She scored. Damn.

With a feisty grin she tossed him the ball. He inhaled, caught the ball and tried to refocus on the game.

He didn't score, but neither did she.

He fought to make two more baskets. She battled just as hard to make sure he didn't. She was good. He admired her spunk. Did she put her heart and soul into everything she did? Without a doubt, he'd never met anyone like this feisty woman.

"Give up?" He mimicked her earlier taunt, knowing she'd rather take a punch to the gut.

"Never!" she declared, swiping at the ball without luck.

He shot, missed, but caught his rebound and slammed it. One more and victory was his. No more squirming. Until he had to watch her kiss one of the bachelors. "Sure you don't want to call it quits before I humiliate you?"

She shot him an eat-crap-and-die look, and he burst out with laughter.

"Just make sure you don't blame it on your old age when I beat you," she warned.

"Okay, spring chicken. Bring it on."

She brought the ball in, and he blocked her shot. She got the rebound and shot again. He jumped and snagged the ball. She stayed on him, fighting gallantly, but he pulled back at the last second and sank another from three-point land.

Yes.

"Game over."

"Best two out of three?" She wiped her hand across her brow, then bent over to catch her breath.

"Not on your life." He tried not to look down the neckline of her T-shirt at the tantalizing glimpse of her sports bra–covered breasts. Tried, and failed.

She wasn't the only one trying to catch her breath. He was almost woozy from lack of air.

"Now who's chicken?" She looked up and grinned impudently when she caught his stare. Had she purposely provided him with the view?

"Nice try. Just see to it you keep your end of the deal."

Her lashes swept her cheeks. "You're sure you don't want to change your mind?"

"About?" he asked. Damn, but she was flirting with fire with her pouty lips and teasing eyes.

"Your prize."

Oh crap. He'd just won the game and lost her kiss to one of the bachelors. What had he done?

The right thing.

So why did it feel like the wrong move?

Still, he said what needed saying. "Make sure you wear kiss-proof lipstick on your outings with the bachelors tomorrow. You're going to need it."

CHAPTER SEVEN

The next morning, a frustrated Rob jogged around the corner of a tall hedge in one of the castle's many gardens. Until they'd rented the estate, it had been used as a private playground for the megawealthy. The setting was perfect for *Jane Millionaire*.

The sun was barely in the sky. Streaks of red and gold light broke through the haze. A bird chirped in the distance, singing its early morning song.

No matter that Rob should still be in bed. He hadn't been able to go back to sleep, and he'd needed to work off some steam. Out of the castle. Away from Jane.

Less than two weeks since he'd met the bewitching woman, and she occupied his every waking thought.

And a great many of his sleeping ones, based upon the dreams he'd had during the night. Dreams starring Jane. Hot dreams of them battling it out on the basketball court and his winning her kiss. Dreams of his stripping those tight shorts and T-shirt off her and making love to her right there on the basketball court. No cameras allowed.

Sweat trickled down his neck and he picked up his pace, hoping to exhaust his body to the point of forgetting her. If only for a few hours.

Jane. Had he ever wanted a woman more? Not even Mandy had wound him into such a blundering mass of hormones—and he'd been seventeen, hormonally overendowed and cocky with his film success.

Which explained a lot of things, but not his fascination with his current star.

J.P. had done an excellent job in choosing Jane. The bachelors were sure to be eating out of her hands before the end of the month. Only four days and they were already making fools of themselves left and right—not that he blamed them or could claim to be any better. He was doing a pretty bang-up job of foolhardy behavior himself.

When had staying away from a woman been so hard? Actually, staying away wasn't what was hard. He was. The mere thought of Jane had his body tightening into a contracted bundle of muscles.

The woman was driving him insane. The need to kiss her, taste her, plunge inside her. He groaned at the image of Jane arched beneath him. She would meet him kiss for kiss, touch for touch, thrust for thrust. She wouldn't lie there mentally rehearsing her film debut, planning her acceptance speech at the Oscars and her wardrobe for the Golden Globes—not like the last woman he'd accidentally let close a few years before.

"Oh!" A surprised feminine grunt sounded as a firm body slammed into his.

He stumbled back but managed to stay on his feet,

which was more than he could say for his early-morning attacker. "Are you okay?"

Jane stared up at him, dazed. She wore baggy jogging pants with a T-shirt that left little to his imagination—which had already been working overtime for hours on end.

"I wasn't expecting anyone to be out here this early," she said, making no attempt to get up.

Yeah, he hadn't expected to run into anyone either—especially not her. And not literally.

When she continued to sit on the hard ground, he reached to help her to her feet. Big mistake. He knew better than to touch her. Lightning flashed any time their skin made contact. He'd promised himself after their game last night that he wouldn't touch her. Not ever again. Yet here he stood waiting for her to grasp his hand.

Her eyes shifted to his outstretched hand, stared at it a moment, and then looked away. Without a word, she licked her lower lip and held her palms out to inspect them. A tiny drop of blood pooled on her scraped skin.

He'd hurt her.

His free hand clenched.

Unfamilar emotions rushed through him. Emotions he didn't understand and was pretty sure he didn't want. Emotions that demanded he protect this woman no matter what the personal cost.

He didn't like the feeling, didn't want to examine why he felt this way about her and why he didn't have the power to walk away when she needed him.

He bent down and lifted her to her feet.

"Are you okay?" he repeated.

She shook her head, not speaking. His arms still held her, and he became achingly aware of her body mere inches from his.

Her tongue darted out again. When he looked into her intense, desire-filled eyes, he knew he was a goner.

"Jane." He practically groaned her name. His heart pounded wildly, which seemed impossible as all his blood still loitered below his waist.

Not speaking, she lowered her hungry gaze to his mouth. She slipped her arms around his neck, her fingers tangling in his hair. Warning bells sounded loudly and clearly as her body melted into his, as she pressed her lips to his.

Her lips were gentle, her touch tentative, testing, tasting. Fire spread through him. Hot, raging fire that consumed everything in its path.

Pull away, his mind ordered. *Kiss her*, his body demanded.

A million reasons why he should stop her raced through his mind. None of them were strong enough to make him push her away. He stood frozen in time, unable to react one way or the other to the temptation she presented.

"Rob," she pleaded when he remained unyielding, barely able to control his physical response to her. "Please kiss me."

The vulnerability, the raw need in her voice, a need that matched his own, gave him no choice. He *had* to kiss her, taste her feminine pureness like spring's first dewdrop on the softest rose petal. Her beauty outshined every bloom in the well-tended garden. Her scent was sweeter than the most fragrant blossom.

He ran his hands over her rib cage and pushed against her lower back, pressing her fully to his aroused body. No longer caring if she knew how much he wanted her, he covered her mouth with his.

He'd been right. She was meeting him touch for touch, and her tight bottom fit perfectly in his hands.

A sheen of sweat that had nothing to do with the miles he'd jogged this morning covered his body.

Sweet heavens above.

She moved her hips, grinding her body against his hard midsection. Blinding heat flooded him. He wanted more. On cue her mouth opened. The need to plunge into her, to discover what she so generously offered, threatened to bring him to his knees.

But he couldn't. He shouldn't even be kissing her.

Where had they placed those cameras in the gardens? Damn, he couldn't remember. Anyone who happened to be in the studio early this morning could be watching them.

J.P. would kill him if he got wind of this.

"We've got to stop." He pulled back, but was trapped by her arms.

"Why?" Her eyes held confusion and a desire so hot he longed to say to hell with the cameras and take everything she'd give him, right here and now in the garden.

"This isn't right."

"It feels right." She touched her lips to his and proved her point.

His gaze fell on the soft green grass of the grounds

just a few feet away. He could lower her there and—
No, he couldn't. They had to stop.

"Well, it isn't." Even to his own ears, he sounded
lame. "You don't need to be out here alone before the
sun's up."

Her chin jutted forward. "I can take care of myself."

"Don't be out here alone. I won't chance something
happening to you and not being able to finish shooting *Jane Millionaire*." He tried to step back, but she pre-
vented him by tightening her hold.

She averted her gaze for a moment to stare off in the
distance before returning her attention to him. "Why
are you pretending you don't feel anything for me?"

She had every right to ask after the way he'd just
kissed her. He had to stop this now, before things got
any more out of control. Before he didn't care that he
would be ruining his friend's career, risking his own,
and losing out on his dream for *Gambler*. No woman
was worth those risks, he reminded himself. The sexy
one in front of him included.

He didn't want to hurt her, but it was the only way.
If she hated him, maybe she'd focus on one of the
bachelors. She had to, and he had to make it happen.

This time there would be no apologies.

He mentally cringed at what he was going to do.
His heart begged him to forget taking that next step
with his career and to explore his emotions for this
woman.

And maybe if that was all that was at stake, he'd
risk it.

Instead, he met her gaze without wavering and said
words he knew would kill any feelings she had for him.

"Pick one of the twelve to scratch your itch. Fall head over heels for him and forget I exist, because once this shoot is over, that's exactly what I'll do. Women mean nothing but a good time to me. If we slept together, it wouldn't mean a thing except sexual satisfaction. I doubt I'd even remember your name six months from now—or that I'd even care to remember."

Rob watched from the studio as Jane punched Bachelor #10, Jeff Kensington, much harder than she should have.

Thank God Dr. Dolittle wore protective gear.

The cameraman zoomed in on his face. Confusion shone in the man's eyes.

"Come on, hit me," Jane goaded, her gloved fists held high.

"My mom taught me not to hit girls," Kensington said, keeping his tone light.

She jabbed, making solid contact again. "Did she tell you to let a girl kick your butt?"

Should he tell the cameramen to cut? Probably, but he waited to see what Kensington would do. Would the guy give in to Jane's taunts?

He punched, pitifully, without any real effort.

"Is that the best you've got?" She rolled her eyes. "Knock me off my feet, and I'll invite you to my suite tonight for a private dinner."

He punched.

"Better," she jeered, parrying his shot. "But not good enough." She nailed him again, bouncing around a little. She held her gloves up. "Come on. I'll give you a clear shot to make it even."

He jabbed again, and she sidestepped.

Rob winced for the guy.

Yeah, he was going to have to stop this. They couldn't use it for the show anyway.

"Nice try." Jane tilted her chin in challenge and although her headgear hid most of her face, he knew she wore a stubborn expression.

"She's making an absolute mockery of him," J.P. commented as he stepped behind Rob to watch the live footage. "What's got that girl so ticked?"

Rob didn't look up, although he could tell J.P. was no longer watching Jane and stared at him instead. "Beats me."

"Is that what she'd like to do to you, and Kensington is taking your beating?"

Rob shrugged. "We'll edit this. She's acting out of character."

"Or maybe not. I think you've done something to piss her off."

J.P. eyed him, making Rob feel like he should open his mouth and spill everything that had happened between him and Jane. Not that he would.

"Want to tell me what's going on?"

"Nothing," Rob denied, hoping J.P. would drop the subject.

Instead, JP dropped into the empty chair next to him.

"I saw the kiss in the garden. You forgot to delete the footage from camera fourteen."

Damn. How could he have missed one of the cameras?

Maybe because he'd been in a rush to get them erased.

Or had been until he'd caught himself watching the man and woman on his computer screen with an ache in his chest—not to mention the one in his pants.

Kissing Jane in reality had made his dreams pale in comparison.

"I know you want her, but you've got to stay the hell away. Convince her she's not your type." J.P. wagged his finger at Rob. "Our show's star isn't available as another notch for your bedpost."

"Don't you think I know that?" he growled, frustration, regret and longing swirling within him like leaves caught in a whirlwind. "Besides, if you watched the footage from this morning, you know I took measures to put an end to whatever is between Jane and me."

"Just what is between you two?"

Rob didn't meet J.P.'s eyes as he muttered, "Nothing."

"Just look at what 'nothing' has done." J.P. gestured to the screen, where Kensington had called it quits, thrown down his boxing gloves and walked away before he lost his temper at Jane's taunts.

The guy had been holding back, letting Jane take her frustrations out on him, and J.P. was right. Rob was to blame.

He gritted his teeth, knowing he deserved the dressing-down J.P. was going to deliver, but bristling just the same.

"No more touching."

Rob didn't like taking orders. Not even from J.P. He didn't need to be told to leave Jane alone. Look at how much he'd already sacrificed to put distance between them. The most enchanting woman he'd ever met, and he'd pushed her away.

"I'll talk to her."

"Just so long as that's all you do."

Rob bit his tongue. "There won't be a repeat of what just happened with Kensington. I'll make sure of it."

"I'm more concerned about what happened in the garden between the two of you."

"There won't be any repeats of that, either," he bit out.

"You're sure?"

"Yes."

J.P. watched him a while before commenting. "You know, I told you I'd speak up when and if I felt I should." He paused until Rob glanced at him. "I'm worried she's gotten under your skin."

"She's just another woman." *Liar.*

"Maybe." J.P. shrugged, withdrew a cigar from his shirt pocket and lit it.

"Put that out."

Continuing to eye him with apparent thought, J.P. sank into the chair next to Rob and took a long drag on the Cuban.

"Ah, that's good."

Rob curled his nose at the pungent smell. Such a nasty habit, but J.P. often said he thought the cigars gave him an intimidating look. He sighed when J.P. blew a puff of smoke in his direction.

"Now, tell me about Jane." J.P. rocked back in the chair, blowing out another puff. "And I want the truth this time."

"She means nothing to me except as the star of my latest production. The rest is just physical." *Really big fat liar.*

"I hope you're right, because she's not going to be happy with either of us when she finds out she's being deceived along with the bachelors."

Isabella. Yet another of the many reasons he needed to stay away from Jane.

"Yeah, I know."

Jill plopped down on her bed, being careful not to muss her hair or the delicate, pale yellow, overtly feminine sundress. Gregory had dolled her up, insisted she wear the dress, and attached the microphone between her breasts before he'd left her suite.

Ugh. She'd behaved like a spoiled child during her boxing match with Bachelor #10, Jeff. Shame filled her at memories of how she'd taunted him in her need to relieve her frustration with Rob and the situation she found herself in.

J.P. had insisted she make amends, but she would have anyway. She'd invited Jeff to accompany her on a walk in the gardens. He'd responded like a gentleman to her temper tantrum.

Her, Jill Davidson, having a temper tantrum?

She was taking this pretending to be Jessie a bit too far.

A knock sounded on her door.

With reluctance she opened it, expecting one of the crew members had come to tell her it was time to meet her midmorning victim for the promised stroll.

Rob stood in the hallway, looking too good to be real in his worn jeans and navy T-shirt. Her heart lodged somewhere in her throat as she waved her hand.

"Come in."

He shifted his weight almost imperceptibly, but she'd been trained to read people's body language. At times her life depended on it. Whatever he had to say, she doubted she'd like it.

"I think it would be better if I stay out here."

"Coward."

"Smart," he corrected, but she'd seen the flash of guilt on his face and wanted to bang her hand against the door as a fresh wave of frustration filled her.

"I came to remind you to stay in character."

She nodded, feeling more than a little guilty at her earlier behavior. "It won't happen again. I've already told J.P. that."

"Good." He averted his gaze, looking ill at ease.

Warning bells dinged loudly in Jill's head. Here came the bad part.

"I also want to remind you that you lost last night's wager."

Her eyes widened. Was he saying what she thought he was saying? Surely he wasn't telling her to kiss another man? Not after this morning. Okay, so she meant nothing to him except as a woman he wanted to get hot and sweaty with. But he wanted her to kiss Bachelor #10?

"And?" she prompted, hoping she was wrong.

"You have to kiss someone. Today."

Crap, she'd been right. No matter. She wouldn't let him know he'd just added insult to injury. With a cocked brow, she smiled sweetly. "Maybe you've forgotten. I did kiss someone. First thing this morning."

"That doesn't count."

"Well, it should."

His forehead furrowed. "Why?"

"Oh, never mind. Wasn't much of a kiss, anyway." Head held high, she pushed past him to go find her garden date before she slugged the man whose kiss had been everything she'd ever dreamed a kiss could be.

CHAPTER EIGHT

"What's gotten into you?" J.P. asked when Rob barked at one of the assistants returning to the studio.

"Nothing."

"Lots of nothings going on around here."

Rob arched his brow at the older man watching the live feed from the garden.

"I saw Jane on her way out to the garden. She looked like she'd swallowed a lemon. When I asked what was up, she said, 'Nothing.' Seems like you're both reciting the same script."

Rob rolled his eyes. The last person he wanted to talk about was Jane. Especially after all the lectures J.P. had already given.

Especially after he'd practically demanded she kiss another man.

"Now that's interesting." J.P.'s gaze returned to one of the monitors.

He looked. He didn't want to, but he looked anyway.

Jane's arm was linked with Dr. Dolittle's. He led her through the well-tended shrubbery. She smiled. She batted her lashes. She flirted. Rob thought he might throw up.

He stared at the computer screen and could stand the silence no longer. He punched a button and Jane's voice came over his headset.

"You wouldn't happen to know the name of the bright orange blossoms on our right? They are so gorgeous. No? I'm going to have to remember to ask the gardener one morning," she cooed.

More benign conversation followed. Rob's ears perked up when she apologized for her behavior during their match.

"I was upset with someone else and shouldn't have taken it out on you. I think you were very gallant not to take advantage of me."

Take advantage of her? Ha, he'd never met a woman more capable of taking care of herself.

"Thank goodness you're so patient and gentlemanly. I feel so badly about earlier."

There went those long lashes sweeping across her cheek again. Lord, she was laying it on as thick as molasses.

"What I'd really like, Jeff, is to kiss and make up."

The guy loosened his collar. Rob tugged on his own, fanning air beneath the cotton of his T-shirt. When had it gotten so hot in here?

"You're serious? You want me to kiss you?" The poor sucker's eyes were wide. "You're not going to punch me in the nose afterwards, are you?"

Jane laughed softly and shook her head, a naughty expression on her pert face. "Kiss me."

The urge to yell, "Cut!" rushed through Rob as the grinning bachelor lowered his head to Jane's.

Cut. Cut. *Cut!*

He didn't want to see this.

He couldn't look away.

One of the cameramen zoomed closer.

Jane's fingers crept into the man's blond locks, and she twisted his hair.

Savage urges shook Rob. Her hands belonged on *him*. In his hair. If he went out there and choked the daylights out of Bachelor #10, reality TV would plummet into a whole new market. Murder and mayhem.

Of course, ratings would probably skyrocket. He could see the headlines now. HOLLYWOOD PRODUCER STRANGLES BACHELOR ON THE MAKE WITH CO-STAR. He slammed the button to kill the monitor instead of the unsuspecting bachelor who'd already had one undeserved beating today.

"You've got it bad." J.P. swore under his breath, leaning so far back in his chair Rob thought he might tilt right over. He pulled a cigar from his shirt pocket and chewed on the tip as he stared at Rob. "Maybe you should make a trip into the city, pick up some European hottie and work off your excess testosterone."

If Rob thought it would help, he'd do exactly that. But not just any woman would do. He stared at the blank screen. He wanted *her*.

"My testosterone levels are just fine."

J.P. snorted. "If you say so."

"I say so." Rob pushed back his chair and stood. "I'll be in the exercise room if you need me."

J.P. had the gall to laugh. "Tired of cold showers, eh?"

Rob called him a foul name and walked away, but not before hearing J.P.'s parting shot. "Just think, you're only stuck with her for another four weeks."

Aw, hell.

Murder and mayhem might be the theme of this reality show yet.

Princess Isabella Jane Strovanik paced across the floor of her private quarters in the west wing of Strovanik Castle. What had she done by allowing these crazy Americans into her home?

"Gregory, I think I have made a horrible mistake," she muttered to the dashing young man who had spent the past month learning everything he'd need to impart to the woman impersonating her.

"Your Highness?" he asked from where he sat in a wingback chair that had been her great-great-grandmother's.

"I should never have agreed to this."

"Why ever not?" He sipped vintage wine from her late father's wine cellar in a goblet that was three centuries old. Just the sight of it provided a reminder of what she had brought upon herself. All because of a man.

"I am making a mockery of my heritage, allowing another woman to pretend to be me. My father would be outraged if he knew."

"The film company is paying you good money for your role in this," he reminded her.

She threw up her hands in frustration. "I am not doing this for the money." Which wasn't entirely true. The royal coffers were not as full as they'd once been. Her father's refusal to modernize the workforce had stifled her country.

Gregory's shoulders lifted. "Then why are you doing this?"

Good question. She had sold herself a crock of lies, telling herself the media coverage would be good for her country's tourism industry, as the show would reveal the kingdom's beauty.

Yet, she knew it was much more complicated than that. Her cousin, Jiovanni Alarik, planned to lay claim to the throne if she didn't fulfill her father's last bequest and marry within the next three months.

Marriage. Shivers prickled her skin. And not to just anyone. Only a man of royal heritage would do.

Unfortunately, the spoiled playboy royalty she had grown up with left her insides cold.

Which is where the bachelor she'd insisted be sent a personal invitation came into the picture. He did not leave her insides cold. Quite the opposite.

She closed her eyes and inhaled deeply.

"When a representative from your television network approached me, I agreed for many reasons." Namely, she'd been searching for a way to see the man she'd met while doing mission work, the man she'd not been able to forget no matter how hard she tried.

"Although Jane is fabulous, I still think you should have done the show yourself. It certainly would have simplified things."

"No." She'd had to see him one last time, but being

forced to interact with him in front of the prying eyes of the film crew held no appeal. "I am not an actress."

"To play yourself, you wouldn't have needed acting skills."

"But the woman your show is portraying is not me." She'd watched the tapes of the woman's great athletic abilities. Her father would never have allowed her to develop such masculine talents. Performing charity work and looking beautiful were the expected activities of female royalty. Her country had much to learn about women's rights.

Which is why she couldn't just walk away and allow Jiovanni to control the throne. Her stoic cousin might set them back a hundred years on equality issues. She owed it to her people to marry soon.

And, once the filming had finished, she would accept one of the offers she had received. For now, she would continue her period of mourning for her father while hidden away at Strovanik castle.

"My heart is my own, but only for a short while. My methods may not make sense to one such as you, but I will take this time for myself, then I shall do what is right for my people."

"Yes, Your Highness." He saluted her with the goblet before taking another sip.

She walked to a window that faced one of the many gardens below. She gasped at the sight of the embracing couple.

"I have indeed made a grave mistake in allowing this invasion of my home."

And of her heart.

* * *

Crap. Would it look bad on national television if she spit to rid herself of Jeff's kiss? Kissing him just didn't evoke passion in her blood. It was nice enough, she supposed, but it felt kind of like kissing a brother—if Jill had a brother, which she didn't. One trouble-making sister was more than enough.

Jill suppressed her inclination to spit—just in case.

What a good little princess she was, she thought with ill humor. Her partner didn't notice. It seemed all was forgiven from her boxing match abuse. She glanced at him and smiled. He had been talking a mile a minute prior to their kiss. Uh-oh. What had he just said to her?

She hadn't a clue. No matter—his lips covered hers again. It was bad enough she'd had to pretend her heart weren't breaking because of one man, but she'd bitten the bullet and kissed another.

It felt so wrong. As if she was cheating.

She hadn't had a choice. Rob had won their game fair and square. Okay, so she hadn't thought he really meant for her to kiss one of the dirty dozen. Even after he'd told her to make good on their deal, she hadn't wanted to believe him. Some part of her had hoped he'd come charging into the garden and pull her away from Jeff. It would have saved her from kissing a man she genuinely liked, but who left her insides cold.

Was Rob in the studio watching? Of course he was. This show was all he cared about. She leaned closer to Jeff and tilted her head more, pumping up the enjoyment factor—fake though it was. So what else was new? Everything she did seemed fake these days—except for her kiss with Rob. That had been all too real.

"That was nice," Jeff said when he finally lifted his mouth.

"Nice doesn't begin to describe your kiss," she cooed. Knowing he would misunderstand her words and feeling guilty for misleading him.

"Guess I'll have to do it again, then."

Uh-oh. Jill ducked her head to avoid his oncoming lips. Once had been more than enough. She grabbed Jeff's hand and pulled him toward the castle. "We should probably head back." She smiled. "We'll have more time later."

She didn't want to think about that possibility.

Jill's stomach grumbled. Maybe no one would notice she'd snuck out of her room and into the elaborate, well-stocked kitchen, which was just like the rest of the castle—an appealing blend of old-world furnishings and modern conveniences. Oh yeah, and a camera monitoring her every movement.

Wondering if her late night snack would be allred, Jill rummaged through the industrial-sized refrigerator. Ham. Turkey. Chicken. Cheeses of more varieties than she could name. She placed her hand over her rumbling stomach and sighed in appreciation of the stash she'd uncovered. Heaven.

She pulled out packets of meat and cheese and a jar of mayonnaise, and popped a plump grape into her mouth, savoring the tart sweetness. Now, where would bread be hidden in this kitchen fit for a king?

She eyed the gleaming wooden cabinets lining the room.

"Try the third one to the right."

Jill almost choked on the grape as she spun at Rob's voice. What was it about him that shot her survival instincts to hell? She hadn't known he was there. How could she not have heard him entering the room? Something about him short-circuited her wiring.

"Thanks." She pulled fresh bread from the cabinet he indicated and tried to regain her equilibrium, which he always managed to knock off balance.

"Want one?" She nodded toward her pilfered deli supplies.

Laughter danced in his eyes. "Aren't we feeding you well enough?"

Heat infused her cheeks as she looked at how much food she'd dragged out. "I know you told me to watch my weight, but I've lost a few pounds since I've been here. One late-night snack shouldn't hurt."

His smile faded as he raked his gaze over her sweats and T-shirt with more than a little interest. His Adam's apple bobbed. "There's nothing wrong with your weight."

Hot flushes dampened her skin at the velvety darkness of his eyes. Her stomach grumbled again, and Jill wasn't sure whether it was from hunger or a growl of appreciation for the sexiness of the man lounging against the doorframe watching her. She dropped the bread onto the countertop. How dare he insist she kiss another man, then look at her like the chief of police salivating over a jelly doughnut?

Building irritation at the whole situation tangled with her ever-increasing sexual frustration. She found a knife and sliced two pieces of bread. Seething with annoyance, she piled her sandwich full, sliced it in half, and wrapped it inside a paper towel. She returned the meat and cheese to the fridge and grabbed a couple of sodas while she was in there. She tossed one of the plastic bottles to Rob.

"Come on. I don't like eating alone. Besides, we need to talk."

He opened his mouth, and she read the denial in his eyes.

"Oh, get over it. You've told me you're not interested and totally hammered the nail home by insisting I kiss Jeff." She picked up the oversized sandwich. "Fine. I can deal with that. It's not like you're the only fish in the sea. But we have to work together for the next few weeks. You can't avoid me."

"You know there are cameras." He glanced at the mounted video equipment in the far corner of the room. "We can't talk in here."

"Fine." She handed him half the sandwich. "Take me somewhere private."

Unable to ignore her stomach's demands, she took a bite. The meat had a smoky flavor to it and the cheese a sharp edge. Perfect. She closed her eyes and chewed, savoring the tasty combination.

"Oh, that's good," she said as she ran the back of her hand across her mouth. The cold drink she held brushed across her lower lip and sent a chill across her flesh.

When her gaze met Rob's, intuition told her she

stared at a tortured man. Or maybe his anguished look of lust and longing clued her in. Either way, she didn't have to be a detective to see his angst.

Darn him for making her kiss another man when she wanted him and he so obviously wanted her. Even if she understood and agreed with his reasons for pushing her away.

He opened his soda and took a long swig. "Maybe it would be safer if we stayed in here. I'll edit the tape later."

Safer? She hid her smile and set her drink and sandwich on the countertop a few feet from where he lounged. She hopped onto the counter to use it as a seat. "Okay."

He watched her but didn't comment on her very unprincesslike behavior. He took another drink, and Jill was racked with jealousy at the plastic touching his lips.

"So what did you think of your prize?" she asked.

A funny sound escaped Rob's mouth, and Jill got the impression he'd almost spewed soda. She smiled.

"My prize?"

"Sure, the one you claimed this afternoon. My kissing Jeff," she clarified. As if he didn't know what she was talking about.

"That prize." He shrugged. "I'm sure we'll be able to use some of the garden footage."

He'd answered without answering. Great. Not that she planned to let him get away with it. "Was it worth it?"

"What?"

"My kissing Jeff."

He swallowed. "It should help ratings."

Ratings? Jill took another bite of her sandwich to hide the burning pain caused by his words. Why? Why did she have to want *him* so much? Why had *his* kiss knocked her socks off?

Summoning her courage, she flicked him a glance. "If you say so. Just think, it could have been you, had you chosen your reward more wisely."

His gaze narrowed.

"Personally, I wasn't expecting to enjoy it quite so much." She moaned softly as if Jeff's kiss had been—well, like Rob's kiss. Out of this world.

"That good, huh?"

"Better." She lowered her gaze and pretended to be reliving a fabulous experience. "I can't recall when I've last been kissed like that. Must've been ages and ages ago."

"Must've been." His gaze bore into her for long seconds. A tiny tic twitched along his jaw like a live wire. He straightened from where he was leaning against the doorjamb and set his drink next to hers. His movements pulled his T-shirt across his chest, and a new wave of hunger panged Jill. Sexual hunger.

"Rob," she started, then paused as he stepped in front of her, leaned slightly forward and placed a hand on the counter to either side of her bottom. He didn't actually touch her, but his scent and warmth surrounded her. She wanted to wrap her arms around him, to feel his strong arms around her.

"Kensington floated your boat, did he?" Mere inches separated their faces.

She stared into his stormy eyes. Her gaze dropped to his all-too-kissable mouth. "Yes," she breathed.

Rob's mouth tightened at her lie. He bent in closer, and Jill held her breath. Was he going to kiss her? She licked her lip to make sure she didn't have bread-crumbs stuck in the corners of her mouth.

"Good." His word stuck like an arrow in her heart, and she lost her cool.

Good? What the hell did he mean, *good*? Oh yeah, ratings. Frustrated anger fumed within her as she glared at him. "Maybe we should play for my having sex with him just so those ratings will go up even more?"

Jill didn't so much as flinch beneath his unreadable stare. His warm breath caressed her skin. In the blink of an eye, his expression changed to one of amusement. "So you admit I'd win if we played again?"

Jill's mouth dropped open. "That's not what I said, and you know it." She poked her finger into his chest. "I'd win."

His gaze lowered to where her finger touched him, and her breath caught as she waited to see if he'd comment on the fire raging back and forth from that miniscule area where only the soft cotton of his shirt separated their flesh. He didn't. Only shook his head and half smiled. "That you might."

Without another word, he brushed her cheek with his knuckles and spun on his heels.

Jill's gaze dropped to the wedge of her sandwich she'd shared with him. Seemed Rob wasn't willing to let her satisfy any of his cravings. Just as well, since she needed to stay away from him.

She picked up the untouched half and took a bite.

How come she only remembered the reasons why she needed to avoid Rob when he was nowhere near?

CHAPTER NINE

A large-screen television had been set up for the bachelors to view the show's premiere when it aired in the U.S.—prime time there was early morning here. Most of the crew were in the media room with the bachelors. Jill wasn't allowed to watch the show, as it might influence how she reacted to the bachelors, and as far as anyone knew, she was fast asleep.

Instead, she snuck into the studio to call Jessie. She'd noticed the cell phone in the locked filing cabinet on the night she'd searched for the transcript of Jessie's interview, and had been waiting for the opportunity to use it.

With ease, she picked the lock again, opened the drawer and was relieved to see the phone still hidden there. She dialed her home number. *Please let Jessie pick up.*

Ring. Ring. Ring.

Where was she?

"Hello?" Jessie finally answered.

Jill sighed in relief at hearing her sister's voice.

She'd only been gone two and a half weeks, but she missed Jess. "Hello yourself. How's it going?"

"Oh my gosh! I'm watching you on television at this very moment. And if Larry wasn't right here with me to remind me why it's not me, I'd be pea green with jealousy that I gave you this part gift-wrapped."

"I'd much rather you had this part," Jill said, although she wasn't sure she meant her words. The thought of Jessie being here with Rob wasn't a pleasant one.

"You look like you're having a blast. If I didn't know better, I'd think you were a real princess, Jilly. You look fab!"

Jill smiled at her sister's use of the nickname their parents had given. "Thanks. Having a top-notch makeup artist at your disposal does that for a gal."

"Tell me," Jessie implored. "I want to hear everything. What's the castle like? And the bachelors? Man, they are so hot. They were showing clips of them at the hotel, and wow. Hey! Ouch!" Jill heard a scuffling sound, then giggles, and assumed Jessie's fiancé was punishing her verbal appreciation of the bachelors.

"Oops, sorry about that," Jessie said. "Now tell me about number six, that Steve guy. He's a certifiable hunk. And so is number ten. What was his name? I can't remember"

"Jeff."

"Yeah, that's right. And he's a doctor to boot. You go, girl."

Jill rolled her eyes. If only it were that simple.

"And that host guy is to die for. I'd about sell my

soul to sample a taste of him. Ow!" More scuffling and giggles came over the phone.

Jill was grateful for Jessie's distraction; otherwise she might have blurted out that Jessie wasn't the only one. She sighed, not meaning to, but unable to restrain her frustration at her situation any longer.

"I'm sensing negative vibes, and I'm on the opposite side of the world so I know, for once, that I wasn't the cause. What gives?"

"Nothing. I just wanted to check to make sure you're okay." Jill stalled, not willing to tell her sister about Rob. Besides, who knew if the phone was tapped? She could just see her conversation being aired for America's viewing pleasure. Would probably help Rob's precious ratings.

"I'm fine. Larry's taking very good care of me, if you know what I mean."

Yeah, she knew what Jessie meant.

Here she was the only woman in a house with almost thirty men, and Jessie was still getting more horizontal action.

"How's Dan?"

"Dan? He's fine. He's stopped by a few times to make sure I'm faring okay in your absence. Did you leave orders for him to babysit?"

"Yep." Knowing Dan was watching out for her sister offered Jill a great deal of peace of mind. At least as much as one could have with Jessie as a responsibility.

"Jilly, forget Dan. I mean, I love him dearly, but he isn't the guy for you."

They'd had this conversation before.

"Yes, I know," she said, and spoke the truth. If nothing else, this trip had convinced her that marrying Dan would have been a big mistake.

"You aren't surrounded by all those hunks and still moping about him, are you? 'Cause if you are, I'm gonna wring your neck," Jessie threatened.

"I love Dan, always will. After all, he's my best friend and partner, but he was right to dump me. I've realized that. I'm moving on. You'd be proud of me, because I've—" She paused. Cameras. Phone taps. She couldn't tell Jessie about kissing Rob. Who knew what would happen if the news leaked out that she was lusting for the producer?

"You're sure you're okay?" Jill asked, instead of mentioning Rob.

"I'm fine," Jessie insisted. "Now, finish what you were about to say."

"I've got to go. Love you. I'll call again if I can."

She clicked the phone off and slid it back into the file cabinet. In seconds, she had relocked the drawer. Phone conversations were not allowed. Period. If there truly were cameras in the studio, they were well hidden. Of course, if the phone was tapped, she was busted anyway.

She spun around to leave the studio and her gaze collided with Rob's narrowed one.

Uh-oh. How long had he been standing there watching her? Had he seen her on the phone? How much had he heard of her conversation with Jessie? And why hadn't she heard him sneak up behind her? Her face flamed.

She ran her gaze over him. His snug faded jeans and GOT MILK? T-shirt were molded to his body to perfection. For him, she'd get milk. Gallons and gallons of the stuff. Heck, she'd buy the whole cow.

"Rob!" she exclaimed, leaning back against the locked file cabinet, hoping she didn't look guilty as sin, knowing she did. "I thought you were at the viewing of the show."

"Obviously." His eyes flashed, and he stepped farther into the room. "Feel the need to reach out and touch someone this morning?"

"Huh?" Her gaze and attention lingered on the advertisement spread across his broad chest.

He gestured to the file cabinet behind her.

"Oh." Busted. She shrugged and plastered a sheepish grin on her face. "I needed to check on my sister. She's not got a great track record for staying out of trouble."

He nodded slowly, stopping about three feet from where she stood. "And?"

"She's fine."

He gestured toward his cabinet. "Did I leave my drawer unlocked?"

Crap. She should have left the darn thing open; then she could have fibbed and said yes. She had no defense, so she did what she always did under such circumstances. She went on the offense—distract and regroup. She tilted her chin, let her gaze wander up those washboard abs, broad chest and dynamite lips to meet his eyes.

"Wanna play basketball again tonight? New stakes?" She lowered her voice to a sultry invitation.

"Hell, no." His answer was swift and sure, but his weight shifted slightly and his Adam's apple bobbed.

Power washed over her. No matter what he said or did, or how forbidden their relationship was, Rob did want her as badly as she wanted him. "You aren't supposed to be on the phone. It's against the rules."

Guess her distraction didn't work. She'd try again.

"And do you always play by the rules?" she teased, enjoying needling him. After his callous remarks yesterday, he deserved it.

Okay, so he'd been warning her she could never be anything except a notch on his bedpost, but she'd never really thought otherwise. He was Rob Lancaster, movie producer. She was Jill Davidson, cop temporarily turned actress. She knew they had no future together. No doubt they wanted completely different things from life. But, truth be told, long-term wants didn't seem to matter so much when he stood right in front of her.

"Yes," he answered her question, but she knew he was lying.

"If you say so." She swept her gaze over him again in obvious appreciation, and then feigned a yawn. "Guess I'd better get back to my jail cell before the dirty dozen are released."

"San Padres's jail cells must be a lot cushier than the ones I've been in."

Hearing him use the name of her town churned up reminders that she wasn't who he thought she was. She kept forgetting he didn't know the truth about her. Her brow rose. "Just how many jails have you been in?"

"Six for various films. I've never been detained in one as you seem to be implying."

She grinned with mock innocence. "Not me."

They stared at each other for a long time, neither speaking, neither moving. Jill fought the urge to close the distance between them. Although she might yearn for him, she didn't intend to try to further their relationship. They wanted each other, but this situation was too complicated already. Rob was right to remind her they were from different worlds.

Her body tingled under his gaze and her heart galloped all the same.

Unable to take more of her escalating desire, she sucked in a deep breath and stepped around him.

"See you later, Rob," she whispered on her way out of the studio.

Rob watched as Jane closed the studio door. He sank into his worn leather chair.

Had she really called her sister? From his eavesdropping, he guessed she had, but he couldn't be sure she hadn't snuck in a call to her old boyfriend.

He reached for the file drawer and tugged. Locked. Just as he'd thought. She'd picked his lock, borrowed his cell phone, made a call and attempted to cover it up.

Damn. Had she leaked information about the show to the press? Any news rag would pay top dollar to find out which bachelor she planned to choose.

He dug his keys out of his pocket, unlocked the drawer the proper way, picked up the phone and pressed the button to pull up recent calls. He stared at the number. Her sister's?

Only one way to find out. He punched send.

"Jilly? I wasn't expecting you to call back this quick," a female voice gushed over the line.

"I must have the wrong number." Jilly? Oh, he remembered reading in her bio information that her friends and family called her Jill. She'd been telling the truth about who she'd called. Why did that make him feel better?

"Wait. My caller ID shows this as the number from where my sister just called me. Who is this?"

"Just a wrong number."

"Is my sister okay?" She sounded a bit panicked at his response. "She hung up a bit abruptly, but I thought that was only because I was . . ." Her voice trailed off. "Who is this?"

Why lie? "Rob Lancaster."

"The host with the most? Oh my gosh. You are such a total babe. Jilly is so lucky. If only I'd . . ." she stopped and Rob wondered what she'd been going to say.

"She's okay?" the woman asked, sounding more subdued.

"She's fine. I must have hit the redial button by mistake after she borrowed my phone and called you. Sorry to bother you." What was her name? He couldn't remember Jane having ever said, although he got the impression her world evolved around taking care of the woman on the phone.

"No bother. Call anytime." Sexual interest was blatant in her voice until he heard a man speak in the background. "Uh, sorry, I've got to go. Tell Jilly I love her and I'm fine. No worries."

Rob stared at the disconnected phone in his hand. He'd swear he heard the man call Jane's sister "Jessie." Must have heard wrong and the guy had been asking about her, to make sure she was okay.

143

Or was he Jane's ex-boyfriend? More likely the guy was her sister's fiancé, the one Jane had mentioned when he'd asked her why she was here.

Rob rocked his chair back and wondered what he should do about catching her breaking into his file cabinet, placing an unofficial, prohibited phone call and making him jealous as hell when he'd heard her on the phone.

At least the call hadn't been to the press. Or her ex.

But he still had an urge to strangle her for putting him in the position of covering for her or revealing to J.P. what she'd done.

He couldn't imagine deceiving his friend.

Surprisingly, he found the idea of ratting on Jane as distasteful as the rest of this sordid reality show.

"The results are in." J.P. burst into the studio where Rob was watching live feed of Jill and the bachelors duking it out in a paintball fight.

"And?"

J.P. waggled his brows. "I'm not going to tell you. You'll find out along with Jane, the bachelors and the rest of the world."

Rob nodded, his attention more on Jill falling to the ground in laughter as the bachelors pummeled her with paint pellets. Her team had won—of course. Did the woman excel at everything physical? His gut clenched, and he reminded himself he'd never know the answer to that question except in his fantasies. All the bachelors, including her teammates, had ganged up and bombarded her, covering her in splatters of multicolored paint.

"Yoo-hoo, anybody home?" J.P. waved his hand in front of the monitor.

Rob frowned at his friend and clicked to turn down the volume on his headset. "What?"

J.P. rolled his eyes. "I just told you I'm not revealing to you which bachelors were eliminated until we tape the show, and you agreed."

"Not hardly." But even as he said it, his gaze went back to the screen. Two bachelors—he couldn't tell which ones in their paintball paraphernalia, but he could guess—had picked her up and were carrying her as she kicked and fought to free herself. The cameramen followed closely. One so much so that paint splattered onto his lens. Where were they taking her?

When they entered the back patio area, he knew. The pool. He grinned as he watched them toss a squirming, shrieking Jane into the water, gear and all. She sank to the bottom.

He held his breath and waited for her to surface, which she did almost immediately. He clicked the mouse to up the volume again so he and J.P. could hear the feed from the microphones.

Bobbing in the bright blue water, she whipped off her helmet and tossed it onto the concrete at the men's feet. She shook her hair out, long wet strands slapping against her beautiful face, and then she grinned a heart-stopping grin at her assailants. "Aren't you boys coming in? The water's perfect."

And just like that, she was no longer alone in the pool.

"Damn, she's good," J.P. said from beside him, reminding Rob he wasn't alone. They watched as the paintball tournament turned into an all-out water fight.

Yeah, Rob thought, she was too good. He couldn't stop thinking about her. He wanted her all to himself. Damn it.

"What were you saying about the results being in?" he asked, dragging his gaze from the monitor.

"I've gotten the official report from the accounting firm handling the viewer voting. We have the names of our three bachelor bootees." J.P. passed Rob the hand-delivered message.

Rob scanned the names of the bachelors and their individual scores.

"As you can see, Jeff Kensington ranked as America's number one choice. Steve Jernigan came in second."

"Great," Rob muttered. They'd run the new footage, boot the bottom three—#3, #7 and #9—and open the polls for next week's show.

"Kensington also won the letter poll and will be awarded an evening alone with Jane in the setting of his choice before the next show airs."

Damn. She'd already been gravitating toward Dr. Dolittle Kensington and G.I. Joe Jernigan. He didn't like it. Hold up. Yes, he did like it. It was what she was supposed to do.

Only Rob hated watching her relationship with the bachelors unfold. He knew she was doing exactly what he needed her to do, what she needed to do, but he didn't have to like it.

Aw, hell, he wasn't making sense to himself anymore.

Something was going to have to give. And soon.

Maybe he really should go into the city and pick up a hot babe.

If only the thought held any appeal.

"I want Jeff Kensington removed from the show."

"Why?" J.P. asked as he lounged in the princess's sitting area. "You're the one who forced the network to include him."

"It was a foolish thing to do. Have him eliminated during the next show." Isabella practically shook as she waited for J.P.'s answer.

"No."

Perhaps he had not understood.

"He must be one of the bootees." She could not bear watching any more footage of him and the lovely imposter. Why had she not thought this through to its natural conclusion? Of course the woman would fall in love with Jeff. How could she not?

"I can't do that."

"Why not?"

"He topped the polls and won the date with Jane. Tonight's the big night."

"No." Isabella's heart wrenched at the thought of what the night might bring. Could she bear another kiss between Jeff and the other woman? "You must stop this at once."

"Why?"

"I do not wish for him to remain in my home." More truthfully, she did not wish for him to have a private date with the other woman. The thought only made the tightening in her chest more painful. "Please see to it that he leaves the castle tonight."

"This is outta my hands, Princess. I can't tamper with the numbers. Unless Kensington is legitimately booted, he stays."

All she had wanted was the opportunity to see Jeff one last time. She should have flown to Central America and volunteered once again as Izzy Strover.

But she had been greedy. She had wanted Jeff to visit her country in the hope of . . . what, exactly? Jeff falling in love with her homeland? Since she had manipulated his journey, perhaps it was only appropriate that, instead of soil, he was falling for a savvy American woman.

A woman who was free to choose him.

"Then there is nothing that can be done?"

"The game has already begun. Now we just have to see how it all plays out." J.P. crooked his head at her. "Do you want a live feed of tonight's date?"

Did the man intend to torment her?

"Yes," she breathed, knowing she would not rest until she had watched Jeff and "Jane's" date. "I would appreciate that very much."

"I can't believe my letter got the most votes." Jeff spread out a blanket, then took the picnic basket Jill held. They'd walked to a small private lake on the palace grounds. The moon shined big and round in the star-studded sky.

"I can. It was very sweet." Almost as if he had written it to a woman he'd waited a long time to meet, a woman he'd thought about a great deal and longed to spend time with.

"Sweet?" He laughed. "That's not exactly what I was going for when I wrote it."

"What were you going for? I almost felt as if I were reading a letter from a long-lost lover. One fate had stolen from me. A man asking for a second chance."

"Whoa." He held his hand up, but she noticed a slight tremble in his voice. "That's a bit deep for me."

"Me, too," a deep baritone interrupted.

Jill's head shot around at Rob's words. She glared at him in the soft light created by the equipment the crew had set up.

Why had he insisted upon tagging along on her date with Jeff? Most of the time he stayed hidden in the studio. Which suited her. It was hard to focus on romancing the bachelors when Rob was so near. Couldn't he just leave her alone? Didn't he realize he was breaking her heart?

Sending him a quick frown, she turned her attention back to Jeff. "Well, I thought your letter was endearing, and apparently a lot of other women did, too."

Jeff cast a confused look toward Rob, then offered his hand to her. "Let me help you sit down."

Jill took his hand and lowered onto the rough, thick blanket. *You'd think the crew could have found a more comfortable blanket.* The material almost felt like wool beneath her palm. Thank goodness she'd worn slacks rather than the skirt Gregory had tried to talk her into. Otherwise she'd have had to cut the picnic short from itching to death.

"I hope you like the meal I asked the chef to prepare. I wasn't sure what you'd prefer."

"I'm sure it'll be great. I'm starved."

A snort sounded from Rob's direction. Jill hid her scowl. Was he going to keep interrupting her date all night?

"What can I do to help?" she asked, resisting a peek in Rob's direction. She refused to acknowledge his presence again, even if her body seemed unable to focus on anything but his proximity.

"Nothing. Just sit there and look beautiful."

Jill felt like an even bigger fraud. *Look beautiful.* Funny how she'd never felt that way until she'd crossed an ocean and had men compete for her affections.

Jeff pulled out containers of assorted cheeses, a bottle of wine and two goblets. Delicious aromas filtered from the basket. "May I?" he asked after uncorking the bottle.

"Please." She lifted one of the goblets and allowed him to pour her glass partway full of the ruby liquid, then waited as he filled his own. "Allow me to make a toast?

"To new friendships that last a lifetime."

Jeff raised his glass.

"And to ratings that soar." Oops. Why had she added that out loud? Grimacing, she met Jeff's blue gaze and was relieved when he merely shrugged and clinked his glass to hers.

"To friendships." The corners of his mouth curved upward as he winked. "And to soaring ratings."

Jill took a slow sip of her wine, enjoying the woodsy flavor. "Wow, very nice."

Jeff grinned. "Wish I could take credit, but I'm told it comes from one of the many vineyards in this beautiful country. Seems this place has all kinds of hidden treasures."

"Really? It's delicious." And it was, although admittedly she wasn't an expert of any kind. "So, tell me, Jeff. Why did you decide to come on a reality television show and let the world in on your every move?"

Jeff passed her a plate of cheese and grapes. "A lot of different reasons."

"Like?"

"The conventional ways a man meets a woman weren't working for me." He shrugged. "Why not a reality show?"

"You tell me." She eyed the contents of the plate, hoping the microphone wouldn't pick up the rumble of her stomach.

"I've devoted most of my adult life to mission work, and there isn't an overabundance of eligible women. I came here hoping to fall in love with a woman who could share my dream."

Jill almost dropped the plate, which would have been a shame. Food should never go to waste. But Jeff's admission had startled her. He'd come on this show hoping to meet the woman of his dreams. He'd probably been sorely disappointed in the show's choice of her. Well, of Jessie. Damn, she'd have loved for her sister to meet and fall in love with a man like Jeff. For that matter, falling for him herself wouldn't have been a bad thing.

"You know, when I agreed to come on this show, I really wasn't expecting to meet someone like you."

Yeah, she'd just figured that out on her own.

"Oh?" she asked, once again eyeing the cheese and wondering how many chunks she could take out without looking like a pig. Three? Four? Should she push it and take five? She took five. They were only small wedges, after all. And who knew what else he had stuffed in that basket?

She mentally scolded herself for obsessing over cheese when Jeff was having a serious conversation with her. If only she could have fallen for him.

Jeff laughed, a soft self-deprecating sound. "You'll think me a tad foolish, but I actually thought I'd met you before."

"Really?" Jill's eyes widened as she put a piece of the cheese in her mouth. Yum, it was the same sharp-tasting cheese she'd made her sandwich with. "We've never met that I recall. Until this trip I'd never traveled outside of California."

"As I said, it was foolish to think I'd ever met a real princess, much less—" He stopped, shrugged and grinned. "Well, I'd met a woman a year ago from this country and her name was similar. My imagination played tricks on me."

"I hope you weren't too disappointed when you saw me."

He took her hand in his and squeezed it reassuringly. "Jane, a man really would be foolish if he were disappointed with meeting you."

With wonder, Jill stared into Jeff's intent blue eyes. Maybe she'd only imagined that his kiss had been brotherly? Maybe she should—

Rob coughed. Loudly. As if he had something in his throat.

Jill turned to look at him; so did Jeff and the three cameramen.

"Sorry about that," Rob apologized, waving his hand at them dismissively. "Ignore me and continue filming this scene."

"Date, not scene," Jill corrected.

"Hard to do when you keep interrupting," one of the cameramen mumbled under his breath, but Jill heard and had to stifle a smile. Had Rob heard him as well?

She met his eyes and heat shot through her body.

No need to keep wondering. Jeff's kiss had been brotherly and would remain brotherly, and she had the feeling only one man's kiss would ever fill her with passion.

And he'd ordered her to kiss another man.

She turned back to Jeff and changed the subject. "J.P. told me you went to the day care today. How did it go?"

Jeff glanced back and forth between her and Rob, but didn't comment or ask the questions she saw in his gaze. "It was a riot. Those little scrappers practically had number eleven tied up before I could rescue him."

"Tell me more. The idea of all you hunky guys teaching a day of preschool sounds very interesting." Why couldn't she forget that Rob's gaze was boring into her? Why didn't he go do something else? This was difficult enough without him scrutinizing her every move.

"Well, I think we probably provided a lot of comic relief." Jeff pulled out the rest of the food, and mouth-watering spicy aromas filled the air. Man, she was hungry. How long had it been since lunch? If you could call that measly meal Bachelor #2 had served her lunch.

"J.P. says you stayed calm and collected. You more so than any of the other bachelors."

"It wasn't my hair that had glue squeezed into it."

Jill covered her mouth with her hand, smothering her laughter. "They didn't?"

"Yep, but that's not all." Jeff launched into more tales of his adventures at the day care. Jill laughed so hard her stomach hurt. Which seemed appropriate as her chest ached from longing to picnic with Rob. To lie on this itchy blanket and spend hours talking with him. Then hours making love with him.

Her breath caught at the image of her and Rob tangled together under the moonlight, sans cameras and crew.

She snuck a glance and caught a deep scowl on his face. There would be no moonlight picnics for her and Rob in the future.

With a heartfelt sadness, she faced Jeff, listening to his tales. She laughed again, although the sound came out a tad high-pitched.

CHAPTER TEN

God had sent Jane to torture him. That had to be the explanation for why she kept sneaking glances at him.

Of course, one might argue that he deserved his current state of torment, since he'd booted J.P. and insisted upon supervising the filming of Jeff and Jane's date.

What had he been thinking?

That the crew would hear him this time if he yelled "cut"?

And for a few seconds there he'd almost expected Jane to lean over and kiss Dr. Dolittle. He'd seen the curiosity in her eyes.

And instead of having the cameraman zoom in, he'd hacked like a hyena with pneumonia.

"Boss, I think we've got it from here if you want to go back to the castle," one of the cameramen offered.

Hell, no. "Uhm, I'm fine. Thanks."

The man shrugged. "Just thought I'd offer since you've got that nasty cough."

Rob rolled his eyes and pointed for the man to record Jane and Kensington. "Pay attention to them. Not me."

Because they'd definitely missed something while the man had Rob's attention. Jane now leaned forward and brushed her napkin against the corner of Kensington's mouth.

"There." Jane patted the sauce from Kensington's lips, then dropped her napkin onto the blanket.

The blanket he'd swapped for the nice plush one originally provided for their picnic.

"Thanks. I'd have had barbecue sauce on my face all evening. That probably wasn't a great choice for a picnic."

Jill smiled and patted her stomach appreciatively. "It was delicious."

"Thanks. I brought strawberries and chocolate fondue for dessert." He pulled out two more containers from the basket. Rob frowned. How had Jeff gotten all that stuff into that basket? Next thing you know, he'd be pulling out a violinist for mood music.

On cue, the sound of crickets chirping filled the air.

Well, hell. Even Mother Nature wanted these two together.

He turned to the cameraman. "I've changed my mind. I'll be in my suite. You guys know what you're doing. You'll be fine without me."

Jane certainly seemed to be doing just fine as she was.

Damn it.

"What do you think about Kensington's date?" J.P. asked the elegant blonde, who reminded him of a bird trapped in a cage. Why she had insisted on staying at the castle, when it meant not leaving the west wing, he'd never understand. Only on a few occasions had she left the grounds, and then only for short periods of time.

Although he thought he was starting to get it.

"I do not think about it one way or the other."

She lied. He'd made a point to show up in Isabella's apartments during the date, just to catch her reaction to Jane and Kensington. That was why he'd let Rob accompany the couple in the first place. Otherwise, he'd never have willingly let Rob go on that outing.

"You're the woman Kensington met in Central America, aren't you?"

Her gaze lifted. "Why would you ask?"

"Because it's the only thing that makes any sense." J.P. shrugged. "You know the network had to donate a hefty sum to his mission work to convince him to agree to come on this show? Then someone let your name slip, and the report is he started packing his bags quicker than you can say 'undercover princess.'"

"He did this?" Her eyes glimmered with interest.

Oh yeah, she'd been playing clandestine princess long before *Jane Millionaire* came on the scene.

"Yes." J.P. twirled his cigar, wishing he could light the Cuban and take a deep puff. Isabella would have a fit if she knew he'd had more than one puff in his suite and again on the rare occasion in the studio. Still, what the princess didn't know wouldn't hurt her. "Why do you think hearing about Princess Isabella Jane Strovanik would put the good doctor into a tailspin?"

"Perhaps he is a man who is excited at the prospect of spending time with royalty." But she gave herself away by clenching her fists.

"Or maybe he thought Izzy Strover, who just happened to be from the same small European country, was really an undercover princess?"

Her distressed gaze lifted to his.

"You truly believe he came expecting to find me?" She shook her head and walked across the room. "Why would he think that? I have not seen or spoken to Jeff in over a year."

Did she realize what she was admitting?

"Too much time has passed since I volunteered incognito at the clinic he operates in Central America."

"Obviously he made an impression on you that withstood, however much time has passed. Why shouldn't you have made just as lasting an impression?"

She visibly considered his suggestion.

"Perhaps if my father had not fallen ill." Her eyes closed and she took a deep breath before continuing. "Perhaps had he not passed on to his creator, things could have been different. However, King George has died, and I have obligations to meet. Whether or not Jeff came here looking for a woman he thought he knew is of no matter. That woman was as much a fraud as the one he currently dines with." She sighed, staring at the couple on the screen. "I should not have summoned him into this deception I have created within my home."

"That's where you're wrong. I think it does matter. A great deal." J.P. stuck the cigar back into his shirt pocket and leaned forward. "Why don't you tell me all about it?"

Four days had passed since Jill's date with Jeff. Four days in which she'd spent almost all her waking time with the bachelors and had barely seen Rob.

Was he hiding from her?

She truly believed he was, which she should have been grateful for. So why was she in the studio hoping to see him for a few short minutes? Torture though it was to be so close and yet so far away.

Since the night of her date with Jeff, Rob had accompanied the remaining bachelors as they worked at a local day care. Meanwhile, Jill spent one-on-one time with whomever remained at the castle. J.P. had told her that they'd arranged for three men to teach twenty three-year-olds for four hours each and were capturing it on film—all in the name of finding out what kind of fathers the bachelors might make. The children had been instructed to create as much havoc as possible for each group—and from all reports they had. No wonder she'd cracked up when Jeff had recounted some of the kids' stunts.

She found herself gravitating more and more toward Jeff. Several of the bachelors were great guys—or seemed to be. But of her options, Jeff interested her the most. Unfortunately, he didn't make her body throb with just a look—that response remained limited to one man.

Rob. He'd stolen her breath during his host gig. He'd been wearing his tuxedo, and no man had ever looked finer. He'd glanced at her and smiled at all the appropriate times, but his eyes had never met hers. She'd meant to say hi, to find some excuse to accidentally touch him, to see if he still sent electrical shocks with each graze of his skin against hers. But the gutless man disappeared off the set faster than she could blink.

Oh yeah, he was avoiding her all right.

She should be grateful and not think him a coward.

But she wasn't, and she did.

She'd not been sorry when bachelors #3, 7 and 9 had gotten booted from the show. Although she admitted their obvious disappointment had made her feel badly. Rejection was never nice. And two more bachelors would be booted during the next show. J.P. had told her she'd be sliding Rolex watches onto the wrists of the remaining seven men. The only Rolexes she'd ever touched had been hot or knockoffs.

If Jeff, or even Bachelor #6, Steve, got booted, she didn't know what she'd do. She'd really come to enjoy their company. They both sort of reminded her of Dan.

She'd been willing to settle for a passionless relationship once; why not now?

She knew the answer.

She glanced around the empty studio one last time. Where was Rob? He wasn't in any of the main areas or the exercise room. She'd hoped to catch at least a glimpse of him today, but so far zilch.

She eyed the computer equipment. Maybe she could find him via the cameras stationed throughout the estate. She'd sat with Rob often enough before the bachelors arrived; she should be able to figure out how to operate the system. The cameras were always on. All she'd have to do was figure out how to flip through them, and she would know where Rob was hiding.

"Looking for someone?" J.P.'s question caused her to jump just as she reached the well-worn chair where Rob often sat.

"Oh. You startled me." Did she look as guilty as she felt?

"Not who you were expecting?" The older man's face told her he knew exactly whom she'd hoped to find in the studio. Was she that obvious about her feelings for Rob?

"I wasn't looking for anyone in particular, but I did have a question." Okay, she was covering and had the feeling J.P. knew it. She glanced at the monitors and thought quickly. "There are cameras everywhere. Including my bedroom. I was wondering, just how much privacy do I have? Gregory told me there were no cameras in any of the bathrooms because of some kind of privacy act. Is that true?"

"Yes." J.P. appeared amused. "Nothing that goes on in any bathroom is recorded in any form. Thank God." He grinned. "That's why Gregory told you to always change in your bathroom rather than your bedroom. No free peep shows for whoever edits the film."

"No sound?"

"Not unless you're wearing a mike at the time."

Oh, she'd have to remember that. Just in case.

"Planning on needing some privacy?" he teased.

"Well, a girl does need some time to herself. Besides, it's nice to know that if I need to escape for a few hours, all I have to do is take a long bubble bath."

Instantly the image of being ensconced between Rob's legs in the large tub popped into her head. He could scrub her back. Then she'd do his. She squeezed her eyes shut, trying to block the images of where all that back washing might lead.

"Thinking about taking a long soak?"

She opened her eyes and met J.P.'s amused gaze. "Something like that."

He laughed, wrapped his arm around her shoulder and led her to one of two sofas in the room. "Tell me, Jane. If you had to choose at this very moment, who would you pick?"

"Is this for the record?" she asked as they sat on one of the two flowery couches that had been set up for the crew to use.

J.P. propped his feet up on the sturdy wooden table angled between the sofas. "Does it make a difference?"

"I guess not," she admitted. "Steve or Jeff."

"Why Steve?"

"Because he can laugh at himself." She pushed a strand of hair back. "He doesn't seem to take life too seriously, which is amazing in and of itself with his background. He's ex-military and now works as a private investigator in Texas. He didn't give in to the urge to try to dominate me during our basketball game, and I think he could have won had that been his objective. He's fun, intelligent, athletic and knows how to take care of himself without being overbearing. In real life, we have a lot in common."

J.P. nodded as if pleased with her answer. "And the good doctor?"

She shrugged again. She'd felt a connection to Jeff from that first dance they'd shared. "Jeff's an amazingly generous man. I like him a great deal."

"Why?"

"He's a wonderful man." Even if his kiss appealed about as much as a desk job. Why couldn't he kiss like Rob? For that matter, why couldn't he just be Rob? Or Rob just be one of the bachelors?

"But?" J.P. asked when she didn't elaborate.

"I can't figure out why he's here. He says he needed a break from his mission work, to meet someone and forgo formalities because he's ready to marry and doesn't have time for a normal courtship."

"And what part of that can't you figure out?"

"Why he's really here. He thought I was someone else, and I think that's the only reason he's here." She pulled her knees up to her and wrapped her arms around them as she continued. "He's gorgeous, smart, witty and fun to be with. My date with him was dreamy and superromantic."

Or would have been, had he been the right man, and had said right man not crashed the party to remind me continuously that I was with the wrong guy.

"Why would he go this route to look for a bride? Why would any man?"

"Adventure? Giving in to an impulse? Fame? Who knows what triggered these guys into signing away a month of their lives?" J.P. pulled a cigar from his shirt pocket and stuck it in his mouth without lighting it. "Why did you?"

She should have seen that one coming.

"I was ready for a change." True, although she hadn't known it when she'd flown from California. She'd thought her life was perfect—except for her breakup with Dan, and Jessie's escapades. But she'd been deceiving herself. She'd been lonely even while surrounded by family and friends. "How long have you known Rob?"

Oops. Where had that question come from? She eyed J.P.'s cigar with disgust, grateful that he hadn't lit it. Such a nasty habit, similar to her way of asking questions she had absolutely no business asking. She squeezed her knees tighter. Nasty habit, indeed.

"Since he was fifteen."

"You knew his wife?" She straightened into an upright position as she stared at J.P.

His mouth fell open and the cigar dangled precariously from his lips. "He told you about Mandy?"

"He mentioned her," she admitted, thinking she really needed to learn to keep her mouth shut. "I'm sure it's on tape around here somewhere."

Sometimes she forgot everything was being recorded. Like right now. Although she'd searched for a camera, she had never figured out if the studio was a camera-safe zone or not. But she'd dealt with enough high-tech surveillance equipment to know that even something that looked like a simple fountain pen could record. It was highly possible that Rob could watch this later. Ugh.

"Mandy was an older woman who dazzled Rob during an impressionable period of his life. He'd just hit stardom in the box offices. She swept in and had him chained to her faster than you could blink an eye."

"She was older than him?"

"By a few years. Rob was barely eighteen when they married. Mandy had a few films to her credit, but wasn't the instant success Rob was in front of the camera. Or behind the camera, for that matter. She was a beauty, I'll give her that. Still is, but if she'd been as smart as many gave her credit for, she'd have hung onto her marriage to Rob."

"What happened?" Yep, her propensity to ask questions that were none of her business was one heck of a bad habit. She could have bitten her tongue, but J.P. didn't look irritated.

He considered her with his unusually light blue eyes before answering her with slow deliberation. "Rob's ex wanted things he wasn't able to provide at the time."

"Funny," Jill mused, letting J.P.'s response soak in. "That's practically what Rob said word for word."

Not-so-shameful guilt plastered itself onto J.P.'s face. Jill's eyes widened and she play-punched him. "You sly dog, you."

The sofa springs groaned beneath J.P.'s laughter. "Well, *someone* has to edit the tapes."

Rob stopped halfway through the studio doorway. Fifteen feet in front of him, Jane and J.P. huddled on one of the overstuffed sofas.

Jealousy slapped him in the face.

What were they doing? Why was Jane smiling

pretty as you please? She hadn't smiled at *him* in over a week.

As much as it pained him to admit it, he missed her. But how could you miss someone who was everywhere you looked? Who was the entire focus of your work?

And how could he be jealous of a man twice his age? One he respected and trusted with his life?

Stupid. J.P. might be a big flirt, but he was harmless where Jane was concerned. J.P.'s career ranked first in his life, always had, always would—just ask any of his ex-wives.

But Rob wasn't so sure about himself. Not anymore. He hadn't questioned his lifestyle until recently, and now that he had, he couldn't say he was satisfied. He had an expensive house filled with expensive toys. A big house. A big *lonely* house.

Was that why it never bothered him to be gone for months at a time on a shoot? Because when it came down to it, he had nothing to go home to except an empty mansion in Beverly Hills?

He didn't like the thought any more than he liked how cozy J.P. and Jane looked. He popped his neck from side to side, hoping to ease some of the tension knotting there.

Both J.P. and Jane turned at the cracking sound, as he'd known they would.

"Rob." She jumped to her feet. She wore casual clothing, jeans and a clingy dark green knit shirt. He couldn't help but notice how her breasts gently bounced with her quick movements.

He forced his gaze to her face and his mind from

thoughts of peeling her clothes from her body. Not that he couldn't still see the image plastered in his mind.

J.P.'s eyes narrowed suspiciously. "There you are. Have a good shoot?"

Had the old man known he was standing in the doorway?

"We finished the last group of bachelors." He never looked away from Jane.

"How did it go?" she asked, gazing intently at him with her big green eyes, although she didn't bestow a smile on him. Not even a tiny one.

Damn, he wanted a smile. Her smile. Just for him. Insane as the desire was, since her interest only complicated matters more.

But he was beyond caring. He'd already decided he'd gone irrational with longing. She'd worn him down, made him insane with her kiss.

He wanted a smile. That wasn't too much to ask for, surely?

"As expected, the kids gave them hell. You'll get to watch the videos later tonight."

"With you?" Her bright eyes took on a hungry appearance. Hungry was good. No. Hungry was not good. That was why he'd avoided her as much as he possibly could—because he was starving, and she was banned from the menu.

"Actually, I'll be taking care of that," J.P. interrupted. "Rob has other plans for tonight."

"I do?" he said, then realized J.P. was giving him an easy out. Just as he'd been doing since that garden kiss. Damn it.

Not that he could satisfy his hunger anyway. He was doomed to starve.

"Oh, yeah. I do."

He did have a hundred things that needed doing, and feasting on Jane's delectable body wasn't one of them.

CHAPTER ELEVEN

Later that night, a supposedly ready-for-bed Jill paced across the elaborately woven rug that covered the marble floor of her suite.

Lost in thought, she picked up a porcelain vase, ran her finger across the hand-painted surface and set it back on the intricately carved wooden table.

She couldn't take much more. It was torture to know Rob was so close and yet so removed from her. Staying far away was the smartest, safest thing she could do, but it was driving her insane.

A little over two weeks remained.

Two weeks and she'd have to choose one of the dwindling dirty dozen. Striding back across the room with nervous energy, she rubbed her arms when she stepped off the rug and her bare feet touched the cold marble floor.

Two weeks until her romantic week in paradise.

Once her pretend honeymoon was finished, she'd never see Rob again.

And that was just if one of the bachelors chose her

over the money. It was highly likely that she only had two weeks left with Rob.

An invisible vise squeezed her heart.

A month from now when she was far away from this castle set in a fairy land of rolling green hills and men clamoring for her attention, what would be her most cherished memory when she looked back on her *Jane Millionaire* adventures? Her biggest regret?

Without a doubt, Rob Lancaster would star in both.

His kiss in the garden ranked as her most treasured moment. Not kissing him again was her biggest regret. Her gaze landed on the solid wood door connecting their rooms.

Rob was less than twenty feet away, but more than a locked door separated them.

What would he do if she knocked on that door and kissed him? Told him she wanted to know what it felt like to make love to him? Would he turn her away? Or would he give in to the passion she'd seen in his eyes?

Darn it. If Jessie were here, she'd put on a naughty nightie and seduce him senseless. Jessie had never had any qualms about going after a man she wanted.

So why couldn't Jill do it?

She was supposed to be Jessie, after all. But her supplied wardrobe didn't include any outrageously sexy lingerie, and even if it had, she doubted she'd wear it. Because even though Rob wanted her, he would more than likely send her back to her room a very disappointed woman.

But what if he didn't? What if she floated back to her room a very *satisfied* woman? She'd never know if she didn't knock.

Of all the things she'd ever been called, a coward wasn't one of them.

She walked over to the antique dresser, ran a pearl-backed brush through her highlighted hair until it shined, and stared in the mirror at her makeup-free face. What would Rob see when he opened the door?

A pretend princess who was really a jock police-woman? A Hollywood starlet looking for her road to fame?

Heck, at this moment, she was none of those things. She was a woman so caught up in one man's spell that she knew if she didn't act on her feelings, she'd wonder "what if" for the rest of her life?

Before all the reasons why she shouldn't go to his room popped into her head, she dropped her brush onto the silver tray. The loud clang reverberated straight through her. Taking a deep breath, she crossed the room, heedless of identity crises and contracts and fraud and every other reason why she should crawl into her own bed and forget about Rob.

Knock. Knock. Knock.

Nothing.

"Rob?" Could he hear her? Was he even in his room? She glanced at her watch. Only a little past eleven. He was there. "Are you awake?"

On the other side of the door, Rob looked up from his computer monitor where he was editing the script for a planned episode of *Gambler*. He cursed.

A quick glance at his watch told him Jane should be asleep. Why wasn't she?

He ran his hand over his face and sighed. He'd done

a great job avoiding her. Much better than he'd expected. Of course, J.P. had run interference, always providing a buffer on the occasions when Rob and Jane had to be in the same room. Recalling his jealousy when he'd spotted J.P. and Jane on the sofa made Rob cringe. Where was J.P. now? He had a feeling he was going to need interference.

"Rob? I know you're in there. Open up," she called, knocking more loudly than before.

Lots and lots of interference. Truckloads of interference.

"Go to sleep, Jane." He rubbed his hand across suddenly tired eyes. Would she listen? He doubted it. One thing he'd learned watching all the footage of her was that she wasn't afraid to face a situation head-on. Normally, he liked that about a woman, but not when the attraction between him and an off-limits woman comprised the situation.

He supposed it was possible her knocking on his door late at night had nothing to do with personal reasons. But somehow he doubted it.

"If you don't open, I'll go to the other door, and I'll keep knocking until you do. Even if I wake every last man in this castle."

Damn. She would, and the camera in her room was recording everything she said. Had she forgotten that or didn't she care?

He saved his work and walked to the door. Too bad he didn't have a safety chain. Safety would be good right about now.

"You rang?" he asked as the door squeaked open.

"We need to talk." She barged into his room with a gust of rose-scented air.

172

"About?" His hand stayed on the knob as he stood at the door. If he left it open, would that give her the hint not to stay long? Or maybe an open door would let the whiff of flowers drift right back where it had come from? He wouldn't be able to sleep a wink if her fragrance lingered in his room.

"Anything. I just need to talk to you."

"Huh?" Maybe he should open the door leading into the main hallway as well. The more un-Jane-contaminated air, the better.

"There aren't any cameras in here, are there?" She looked around suspiciously.

"Hell, no." Why would there be cameras in *his* room?

"Good." She faced him, pinning him with her gaze. "You're avoiding me."

Head-on. No holds barred. That was Jane. Her eyes sparkled with hurt, longing, desire. Her long hair caught the light from his lamp and shined like a halo around her beautiful face. Had she just brushed it? His gaze traveled lower over her emerald silk gown, which closely matched the color of her eyes. Gold buttons ran down the front. Delicate straps held the gown up over her pert breasts and lithe body. Her nipples pebbled against the material, torturing him.

"It's in our best interests for me to keep avoiding you." Had that hoarse croak been him?

She stepped closer. The scent of roses grew stronger. How did she always manage to smell like a rose garden? He backed up, bumping into the ornate wood door that separated their suites, knocking it shut. Not good. Now he was trapped in her intoxicating fragrance.

Where was J.P.? Interference was needed. Quickly.

"Don't you tell me what's in my best interest, Rob Lancaster. You have no idea." Her cheeks flushed and her eyes glowed.

God, she was beautiful.

And dangerous to his resolve.

Not to mention what she was doing to his rising libido.

"You shouldn't be here." Another croak. Worse than before. He sounded like a damn frog. Or a boy just hitting puberty. Pathetic. And his rising libido had just gone literal.

"I know, but I couldn't stay away. I feel like I've waited too long already. I keep thinking about how I'll wonder for years to come what it would have been like. What *we* would have been like." She took another step. "I'm not willing to go through life without knowing. Are you?"

He resisted his urge to inhale deeply. To do so might allow the roses to overpower what little good judgment he still had with her looking like something straight from a sexy lingerie catalog.

"A relationship between us can't happen, and even if it could, I don't do relationships. I'm a one-night stand kind of man." He didn't want to think about the rest of his life. Just managing the next few weeks without knowing how it felt to be inside her was almost more than he could deal with—especially with her tempting him like Eve's apple being wagged in front of a starving Adam day after day. *J.P., where are you?*

"Fine." She shrugged a bare shoulder. "I want one night."

Oh hell! He hadn't seen that one coming.

Or had he?

"Jane," he began, trying to marshal his thoughts. He had to order her out of his room. There were so many reasons she couldn't stay, and yet not a single one left his mouth. All he could think was that maybe one nibble would satisfy his hunger. One little nibble. What could it hurt?

She closed the gap between them. "If one night is all I can have, I want my night. Now. Tonight. With you. No more waiting."

Her arms wrapped around his neck, and he had the sensation of rose petals raining upon him, beating his power to resist down to almost nothing.

Power to resist? What power to resist?

"It'll ruin everything." He stared into her eyes and wanted her more than any man had ever wanted a woman. He *knew* he wanted her that much.

"How?" Her lips inched closer to his.

Just one little nibble . . .

"The show," he muttered halfheartedly. "Us becoming involved could ruin everything we've worked to achieve with *Jane Millionaire*. You know that as well as I do."

"I won't tell if you don't," she whispered against his mouth.

"Tomorrow? When the sun comes up and you're faced with the harsh truth that one night is really all we had? What then?" He held himself rigid, knowing that if he dared move, it would be to possess her, body and soul, and to hell with the rest of the world.

"One night. You and me. Tomorrow we'll go back to

playing our roles, and we'll pretend like tonight never happened."

Hope glimmered, irrational as it was. Irrational as *he* was. If Jane meant her words, maybe they could have tonight. If he got his fill of her ripe body, she wouldn't monopolize his every thought. He wouldn't question his empty house and emptier life. If he could get over his obsession with her, life would be better, *right?*

"You'll choose one of the bachelors and go on the honeymoon?" Her offer seemed like manna from heaven. What was that old saying about offers too good to be true?

"Tonight changes nothing regarding my role in *Jane Millionaire*." She whispered the words he desperately wanted to hear. "I'll fulfill the terms of the contract. Whether or not you make love to me tonight doesn't affect my obligations to the network."

Her fingers twined into his hair just as he'd wanted them to do while he'd watched her with Jeff in the garden. He groaned.

"You're sure? You have to be sure you can go on as if nothing has happened between us."

"Has anyone ever told you that you talk too much?" Her lips touched his.

All desire to ask questions, to verify that he wasn't destroying J.P.'s career, his own career, fled. All he could do was feel. Feel the woman against him. Besides, he told himself, if they made love, they could put this raging fire behind them.

Making love was the best thing they could do for *Jane Millionaire*. He was sure of it.

"I want you, Rob," she breathed. "So much."

He kissed her. He didn't have to tell her what he wanted. The undeniable evidence of his desire pressed against her belly. Her mouth opened, and this time he took what he craved. He plunged into her sweet mouth and tasted mint toothpaste and Jane. A heady combination. But then Jane in any combination added up to a dizzying effect.

He pulled her closer, kissed and conquered her mouth. Or maybe she was doing the conquering, because he was without a doubt captive to her every whim.

Her hands descended, and she tugged his T-shirt loose from his jeans. Was that moan from her or him? He helped pull his T-shirt off. Damn, were they moving too fast? he briefly wondered. Her palms ran over his bare back, lower until she cupped his jean-covered buttocks. Quivers of need shook him. Not fast enough, he answered his own question. Not nearly fast enough.

They kissed, touched, for how long he didn't know. Time no longer mattered. Just Jane. When her fingers moved to the button on his jeans, he grasped them. "Slow down, or I'm going to take you standing right here."

Her eyes widened, and damned if he didn't see excitement glittering back at him. She wanted him hard and fast and wild, and he was about to lose it.

"I want to make this good for you," he somehow managed to grind out, battling his urge to throw every good intention to the wind and possess her with all the intensity coursing through him.

She nodded and didn't pull her hands free when he

loosened his hold. He took a deep breath, counted to ten. Forwards. Backwards. In Spanish. Counting didn't seem to be helping.

Slow, easy. That's what she deserved and that's what he'd give, even if it killed him.

"Tell me what you want." He bent and kissed beneath her earlobe, lower, lower still until he caressed her delectable neck.

"I want *you.*" Her breathing was ragged, but then, so was his.

"How do you like a man to touch you, Jane? Slow and sensuous or hard and demanding?" He ran his fingertips down her neck, lightly grazing her soft skin. She shivered.

"You're doing just fine on your own."

He pressed a kiss into the indention at the base of her neck. Her hair brushed his face as she nodded her agreement. The scent of flowers from her shampoo intoxicated him. Was that why she always smelled like roses? From her shampoo? He breathed deeper, needing a stronger fix.

Barely managing to keep his fingers from trembling, he unbuttoned her gown one golden button at a time. He started at the top and slowly slid each button free, his knuckles grazing over the delicate flesh he revealed. The silk of her gown had nothing over the smoothness of her skin. Soft. Sensuous. Sexy. When he reached the button over her navel, he pushed the material aside and watched as it slid from her shoulders to lie in a silky green puddle around her feet.

Sweet heavens above.

He stepped back to admire the work of art he'd uncovered. A masterpiece. Tan skin turned into milky white globes that he yearned to sample. Starved. What a great description of the ache inside him. His gaze skimmed lower, over her flat abs to her black silk-covered hips. Long, graceful legs stretched on forever to feet covered only by the deep red polish on her toenails.

"You are so damn beautiful."

"I feel beautiful when you look at me like that." Her voice was husky.

Male pride surged. He planned to show her just how beautiful a woman could feel. How good a woman could feel. With his hands, his mouth, his body. His gaze locked with hers. He cupped her breasts, caressed, stroked, teased each nipple until they strained toward him, until she leaned into him. With a groan, he lowered his head and suckled until she whimpered.

She reached for his jeans again, and this time he let her. Let her? He might die if she didn't touch him soon. He needed her hands on him, around him, stroking him. She shoved his jeans and boxers down, and he kicked the clothes from around his feet.

This time she looked.

Feeling like a schoolboy hoping the homecoming queen would find him worthy of her attention, he stood still as she inspected him. The look in her eyes when they met his told him he measured up to her expectations in every way, even surpassed them. He sucked air into his oxygen-deprived body just as his vision started to blur. When had he forgotten to breathe?

He reached for her, needing to experience her body

next to his. Mouth to mouth. Chest to chest. He rubbed his palms over her until he cupped her tight bottom and ground himself against her. Hips to hips.

Hot madness spread through him. A strong and swift need to bury himself in her until she exploded around him, slammed into him weakening his knees, weakening *him*.

"Touch me." His request bordered on a plea.

"Yes." Starting at his shoulders, she massaged and kissed her way over his body. Exploring every sinew, every part of him until he thought he might burst from pent-up longings.

But he only had one night. He didn't want it all to be over in a frenzied rush. Patience. Slow and easy. He had to keep his cool. Maybe he should try counting again. She touched her hot mouth to his nipple and gently nipped. One . . . for the life of him he couldn't remember what came next. No, wait, he did know. Jane. Jane came next. Over and over. Then he'd come.

He pulled back to stare into her passion-filled eyes. "I'm going to have you, Jane. Tonight. If you aren't sure, stop me now."

"Call me Jill," she demanded breathlessly. "I want to hear my name when you're inside me. Not some fictional character from a television show."

" 'Jill'?"

She paused, looking uncertain for the first time since she'd entered his suite. "It's a nickname my friends call me. 'Jane' is off-limits to you. Right now, tonight, I'm not Jane. Make love to me, to Jill."

"Okay." She was right. He wasn't making love to Jane. He wanted Jess—er, Jill Davidson.

"Say it," she whispered, moving sensuously against him, making his blood throb through his body.

"I'm going to make love to you, *Jill*, and I'm going to thrust into you until you scream *my* name over and over in ecstasy."

She smiled. The smile of a woman who knew she was going to be thoroughly satisfied before the sun rose. He scooped her into his arms.

"Oh!" she exclaimed, wrapping her arms around his neck.

He lowered her onto his king-sized bed, gently, reverently, with shaking arms and burning desire. His need to possess her urged him to strip off her panties and sink inside, but he restrained himself. They had all night, right? He wanted to make this last, to feel her orgasm time and time again, not take her like a seventeen-year-old novice only out for his own satisfaction. But hell if he didn't feel like a seventeen-year-old about to experience sex for the first time. He had to get control of his body, and quickly. One . . . Wait, he'd already tried counting, twice, and it hadn't worked either time.

"No one's ever done that before." Her eyes shined as she gazed up at him.

"What? Carried you to bed?" He ran his fingers down her face, wondering if a more beautiful woman had ever lived. Her thick lashes swept across her cheeks. A soft whimper escaped her lips.

Something unrecognized, protective, probably unwanted, moved within him, but now wasn't the time for analyzing the rampant feelings she elicited within him.

"They should have. You deserve to be swept off your feet, Ja-ill."

Her hand grasped his, and she tugged him to her. She rained blistering kisses over his chest. Surely, if he looked, his skin would be scorched, branded by her hot mouth.

"I want you. Inside me. Now."

His abdominal muscles clenched in response to her demand. Oh, yeah. He wanted that, too. So desperately and for so long that the intensity of his desire to possess this one woman almost scared him witless.

"Yes." He stretched out next to her on the hand-sewn quilt, greedily stroking the creamy flesh of her breasts.

"Yes," he repeated, his hands roaming her, touching, seeking. "I want to have you again and again until you can't see straight."

"Prove it," she challenged softly, rotating her hips against his throbbing manhood.

He'd been trying to slow things down, to be patient. To hell with slow. And since when had he ever been patient? Deep and hard. That's what this situation called for. Fast and furious. He wouldn't wait another second.

He hooked her panties with his thumbs and slid them down her long, long toned legs. She didn't move except to lift her hips and watch him gawk like a schoolboy at her amazing body. Could she see the awe he felt? The fire in him to seize her perfection?

He kissed her breasts, her stomach, the trim triangle of chestnut curls, lower. She squirmed, undulating against his mouth, her fists clasping and unclasping the folds of the quilt as he flicked his tongue across her sweet nub.

Roses. Sweet, sweet rose petals. Rose petals that fed a starving man's obsession.

"Rob. Oh, Rob," she cried. Her head tossed back and forth in rhythm with the motions of his mouth as he pushed her closer and closer. Her spine bowed, and he knew she was almost there. "Rob, please, oh, please."

Her frantic pants were nearly driving him crazy with the need to thrust into her slick heat. But he wanted to make her come first. To taste and feel her response to his touch. To know she needed him as he much as needed her. More.

"Rob, I can't stand any more. Please. Please come inside me," she begged, her voice raspy with ardor. "Now."

Almost. She was almost where he wanted. But not yet. Not until she lost control would he fill her with his rock-hard length, complete them as one being.

"Rob." Her voice was becoming more and more urgent. Desperate. Her back arched, her legs tensed, her abdomen contracted. "OhmyGodohmyGod!"

Now. Continuing his gentle sucks and tongue flicks, he slid his finger deep into her hot dampness. She convulsed around him, grabbing his shoulders as though she held on for dear life. Her fingernails dug in as she cried out, her orgasm hitting them both full force.

"Oh my God. I've never. Not like that. Oh, Rob. Oh. My. God." She sounded as though she'd just run the hundred-yard dash—and won.

But she couldn't have, because he'd won whatever race had just taken place. Won the prize of her wild release. Damn, but he felt smug in the knowledge of her words, of her powerful response. Smug and victorious.

Oh hell. He was about to come.

Think cold shower. Think pain. Think taxes.

Think it's time to put a condom on.

Where was his wallet?

There. On the nightstand. Next to an ornamental bowl and pitcher.

Rolling from her, he removed the foil pouch and took care of protection. He positioned himself above her and stared into her dazed eyes. Dazed, but quickly returning from bliss to hungry passion.

She nodded languidly, begging with her eyes for him to make them one.

He thrust inside.

And drowned.

Drowned on the emotions that flooded through him. Like a leaf crossing over Niagara Falls, he plummeted into unknown waters.

Ecstasy. Perfection. Heaven.

Alpha and omega.

Everything. It all started and ended right here in this room with himself and Jane. Where his body connected with hers.

She wrapped her legs around his waist, taking him deeper still. How she managed he didn't know because he was already lost inside her. Lost to everything but the woman rocking the foundations of his definition of sex, of life.

Skin to skin. Body to body. He sank deeper and deeper under her spell.

He was in major trouble.

Sex had never been like this.

"Rob." Her thighs quivered around him, and all rational thought disappeared. Loving her, driving her wild with frenzied desire, took precedence over everything.

"Tell me, Jane," he grated between clenched teeth, barely containing his need to thrust into her violently, uncontrollably, instinctively. "Tell me what you want."

CHAPTER TWELVE

Jane? Somewhere in the recesses of her hazy mind, the wrong name registered.

"Jill. Call me Jill," she reminded him.

"Jill." Guilt flickered briefly across his face, but he didn't pause as he conquered her body. Thank God. She'd probably almost blown it by asking him to call her Jill, but she didn't want to hear another woman's name on his lips while he was inside her, making love to her. Even if she was supposedly the other woman.

If she only had the one night, it would be *her* night.

Sex had never been this good. *Chocolate for breakfast isn't this good.*

Searching to see if he felt the same magic that coursed through her body, she met Rob's gaze. Perspiration dampened his hair, slicked his skin. His wide shoulders bunched into tight muscles. He held his upper body off her as he pumped deeper and deeper. His pulse throbbed erratically in his neck, assuring that he was just as moved by their lovemaking.

She twined her fingers into his dark hair and tugged him to her, smashing her mouth desperately to his. She lifted her hips to meet him, thrust for heavenly thrust.

His entire body hardened, his muscles contracted, his abdomen rigid, his hips poised above hers.

"Jill." It was all he said before his determined control snapped. She caught his strangled cry with her mouth as he hammered into her, hot flesh slapping against hot flesh. Heat, tension built until she imploded into hot lava. A fire that started where her skin touched his and spiraled in liquid, pulsating waves to her very core.

"Rob!" she screamed. Her fingers clasped his hair, twisting, pulling him closer. "Now, Rob. *Now*."

His body pummeled her with his climactic release.

"Jill," he growled before collapsing onto her, his breathing ragged and his heart racing against her chest.

Oh yes. This was what it was all about. All the hoopla about sex. Finally she knew.

She kissed his cheek. Oh God, Rob Lancaster had just stolen a big chunk of her heart and given her the biggest O of her life. The biggest? Heck, the little twinges she'd previously experienced no longer even qualified as orgasms.

Her feelings for Dan had never been like this. And she didn't just mean the out-of-this-world sex. Neither Dan nor her previous lover had managed to propel her to the moon, much less another solar system, but her emotions had more to do with this unique man lying on her, squashing her.

Not that she was willing to give up the glorious pressure of his body on hers. She only got the one night and she planned to touch him every single glorious second of it.

"Wow," she whispered against his damp hair. He smelled wonderful, all musky and manly. Satisfied.

He started to roll off her, and she tightened her grip. "No."

He lifted his head. "I'm too heavy for you."

"No, you're not."

"Yes, I am." Not giving her the opportunity to protest, he rolled, pulling her with him. In one swift movement, he'd reversed their positions.

"Okay, so you were a little heavy. You didn't hear me complaining." She smiled down at him, wiggling her head back and forth to tickle him with her hair.

"No, I can't say I've ever heard you complain." His hand swept up, brushed her hair back. His gaze searched hers. "You're amazing."

Her smile brightened, reaching deep inside to warm her innermost being. "So are you."

"Did I hurt you?"

"Not hardly," she scoffed, loving the warmth emanating from his eyes. She arched a brow in challenge. "I was more afraid I might have hurt you."

He laughed and playfully swatted her bottom. The contact of his palm against her bare bottom stung.

"Ouch," she complained. "Now, that hurt."

She reached around and rubbed her sensitized skin.

"Want me to kiss it and make it better?"

Her gaze shot to his. "So soon?" she asked, awed at his stamina.

"Not yet, but if you keep wiggling like that, it won't be long." He grinned, mischief playing in his eyes. "Well, actually, it will be long. And hard. And . . ."

"You are so bad." She kissed him, deep. "And I like it." Another kiss. "A lot." And another. "A whole lot."

Much later, Jill lay in Rob's arms listening to the thump-thump of his heartbeat. He was awake, but neither of them had spoken for a while. Not since he'd taken her on the wildest ride of her life. She smoothed her hand across his chest, wishing she could reach inside and make his heart her own.

What was he thinking about?

Was it possible he'd tell her to end this ridiculous charade as Princess Isabella Jane Strovanik and spend the next hundred years or so being his love slave? At the moment, she had no doubt she'd agree to be his sex servant and live but to serve her master.

And just what did that say about her?

She'd never before had sex with a man who she wasn't in a committed relationship with. There had only been the two men. The one during her early college days and Dan. Dan. How could she not have realized before coming to Europe that they were all wrong for each other? Thank God he'd ended their romantic relationship. He was like a brother to her. Did loneliness really drive one to ignore logic and believe a good friend was much more?

Obviously so.

And what about Rob?

How did he feel about her? About what they'd just shared together. Phenomenal sex, to say the least.

For her the sex had only been the cherry on top of the sundae. Rob was ice cream topped with chocolate syrup, whipped cream and, oh yeah, a ripe, juicy cherry on top.

She wanted another bite. And another. And another.

But she'd agreed to one night.

How could one go back to ordinary sustenance every day after she'd tasted something so scrumptious?

She eyed Rob's naked body. Scrumptious indeed. How had she once thought he looked like Benjamin Bratt? She bet Ben didn't look this good on his best day. Although after her *Jane Millionaire* experience, she had a totally different perspective on *Law & Order*.

"Why don't you have an accent?" she asked before she could think better of it.

Rob shifted next to her, his muscles tensing. "What do you mean?"

"When I first met you, I expected you to have a Spanish accent. It surprised me when all I heard was pure Californian charm. Was I wrong in thinking you had Latino heritage?"

He inhaled and took his time before answering. "My father was Puerto Rican, but he wasn't part of my life. Left before I was out of diapers and I haven't seen him since. My mom was of mixed European descent, the good old melting pot put into effect. Other than having grown up in East L.A. with a mostly Mexican population, there isn't any reason I'd have an accent."

"So you do speak Spanish?"

He laughed and pitched his thumb and index finger

together. "*Un poquito*. You couldn't get by in the neighborhood I grew up in without knowing a little, but my mother always insisted upon English being spoken. Because of my father, I think."

"You said 'was' when you spoke of her." She hated asking, but she wanted to know more, to understand this man who had come to mean so much to her in such a short amount of time.

His body coiled with tension. "She died right before I turned eighteen."

Which would have been right before he married. "I'm sorry, Rob."

"Me, too. She was a wonderful woman and mother."

Ah, there was something attractive about a man who loved his mama. Jill grieved his loss, the knowledge that she'd never meet the remarkable woman who'd given birth to and raised Rob. "Did she remarry after your father left?"

"No, to my knowledge she never even went on a date after he ran out on us. There wasn't enough time for her to go out." His hold tightened, and Jill winced. She'd stumbled onto a subject she should have left alone.

Why did she always have to push further? To ask one more question?

"I'm sorry. It's the badge. I just have to ask whatever pops into my mind," she said, trying to smooth things over. Under no circumstances did she want to lose this warmth between them.

"It's okay." He rolled onto his side to face her. "Like I said earlier, you're an amazing woman."

191

Oh my. Her cheeks blazed. "Okay, then, finish telling me about you."

He chuckled, but she didn't pick up on any real humor.

"Me?" His expression turned thoughtful, and she wondered if he thought she'd gone too far by asking for personal information. "I guess you could say I'm one of the lucky ones. As I mentioned, I grew up on the poor side of L.A. Mom worked all the time trying to support my brother and me. There were days we barely saw her, but she did her best to make sure we had the things we needed and finished school."

"You have a brother?" she interrupted.

"Yeah, Ben's a year older than me."

Ben? His brother's name was Ben? She stifled a grin. Last name hadn't been changed to Bratt, had it?

"I went to Hollywood. He went to Uncle Sam, supposedly for four years, but he keeps reenlisting. He's one of those true-blue military guys." Rob's gaze grew nostalgic, and Jill got the impression he and his brother had been very close while growing up. Something told her Rob missed that closeness.

"Sounds like a neat guy."

"Oh, he is. Never a dull moment with Ben around." He shook his head, laughing. "As I was saying, I went to Hollywood with big dreams. At fifteen, I lied about my age and worked on one of the construction crews for a film J.P. produced. He needed a stand-in for an actor who failed to show, and picked me. One thing led to another and J.P. took me under his wing and helped me land a few more roles. Money was rolling in. I moved Mom to a big house a year before she died."

He grew quiet for a few moments and Jill bit her tongue, refusing to ask the questions running through her mind.

"One day," he finally continued, "I mentioned to J.P. that I wanted to write, direct and produce my own show. He laughed and told me to tell him all about it. I did, and he made it happen."

"Wow. That's amazing." J.P. had been more of a dad to Rob than his biological father. "So you've known J.P. for most of your life."

"Yes." Rob's face turned sour. "My show didn't hit the ratings it should, thanks to my ex-wife's interference. We were having marital problems at the time. I'd asked her for a divorce shortly into the first season, the only season, and she used the show as a backdrop for her tantrums." He turned thoughtful. "But the show got my name out as a director, and a fairly steady line of work followed. Now here I am in Europe. With you."

"I'm glad," she admitted, snuggling closer and squelching her curiosity about his ex-wife. The woman must have been an idiot to let Rob go. To have wanted any other man when she'd had Rob.

"About?"

"That you're here with me." She touched his face, tracing the strong planes. "So very glad."

"Just for one night, Jill. Tomorrow we both forget tonight ever happened, and we go about our lives separately," he reminded her.

She bit back a gulp. "You're sure that's what you want?"

His eyes closed. "It's what has to happen."

"If you say so." So she sounded like a spoilsport. She didn't care. She didn't want to pretend an interest in one of the remaining bachelors. She already had an interest in the man lying with her.

"I can't believe I told you all that stuff."

She lifted her head to search his face. Did he regret having revealed so much about himself? "Why not?"

"Because I don't usually share personal information with anyone. Too much worry about the press printing every word from my mouth."

"I'd never repeat the things you just told me."

"No, I don't think you would." His chest rose and fell against her. His frustration was a viable entity. "But I've been wrong before."

"You're not this time. When I asked you about your past, I wanted to know for me. No one else. I'm sorry if I gave you reason to think otherwise."

"I bet you're one hell of an interrogator for the police force. No criminal stands a chance. You ask a question and they just start blabbing." He half smiled, although she could tell he was starting to overanalyze the night's events.

She laughed softly, wanting to hang onto their temporary closeness. "If only they'd let me interrogate bad guys. I just get to catch them and haul their butts in for someone else to question."

"Will you go back to the force after you leave Europe?"

"Yes. Why wouldn't I?"

"I assumed you'd relocate to Hollywood."

"You assumed wrong."

"Maybe." His expression shifted, as if he were battling a losing war. "Jill, you need to go back to your room."

"Huh?" Whatever war he'd been waging, she'd apparently come out the loser.

"As much as I'd like you to remain in my bed all night, you can't stay. The cameras in your room recorded you entering mine."

Uh-oh. That one had flown right over her head. She should have tossed a towel over that blasted camera.

"No one will know what we're doing." She didn't want to go to her room. She wanted her night. Her whole night. Not just a stolen snippet. She wanted to wake up in his arms. Was that asking for too much?

"No, but you have to go to your room before it's too late. For the record, we reviewed the video footage of the bachelors' day care shots. Not the most brilliant of plans, but at least it gives a halfway plausible reason for you to have been in my suite this long. If anyone asks, I'll simply say we were going over your options again."

"My options?" How was she supposed to go on with this charade now that she knew what being with Rob was like? She didn't want options—unless they included him.

"Regarding the bachelors—" He paused. With every second that passed, she knew her fate was sealed. "Nothing's changed. We'll stick to our original agreement."

Their original agreement. One night, then they moved on with the show.

"Okay." Even if she'd tried, she couldn't have hidden the hurt in her voice.

"Jil—Jane," he corrected, looking uncomfortable.

When he insisted upon calling her by her show name, she knew he was once again throwing barriers between them. She'd lost him. No, she hadn't ever had him to lose. He'd given her exactly what he'd agreed to, and she had to live with that.

And she would. Honor demanded it.

"Don't say it. I don't need a reminder that you're a one-night stand man. As I told you when I came in here, I'm okay with that. I'll stick to my end of the deal. I'll choose one of the bachelors and continue with this crazy show. But know this." She leaned forward and brushed her lips across his with a light, feathery touch. "That door"—she motioned to the one separating their rooms—"won't be locked on my side. I'm not looking for marriage or long-term commitment from you, but I do want you and freely admit to wanting a repeat of what we just shared. The choice is yours."

With that, she leapt out of his bed while she had the strength to do so, scooped up her clothes, dressed and disappeared through said door as regal as any true royalty.

Rob watched Jill leave his suite, her head held high. Sweltering heat spread through him. Which was utterly ridiculous since he'd just had the most passionate sex of his life. Twice. He should be totally satiated.

Or maybe the sensation running through him was regret. Regret at not being able to call her back. Regret at the knowledge he'd never again experience the emotional and physical high he'd just shared with her.

He'd made a mistake. A big mistake. Huge. Horrendous. *Gigante*. *Enorme*. Okay, he'd made his point. He'd messed up by thinking making love to Jill would ease the tension between them. Because now that he knew how hot she was, how she could bring him to places he'd never been, staying away was going to be almost impossible.

Jill. That was another thing. He needed to think of her as Jane, not Jill. Jill was off limits. Jane wasn't. He had to think of her as Jane.

Jane. Jane. Jane.

It was no use. No matter what he called her, she was still the woman he wanted. The woman he'd had, twice, and it hadn't been nearly enough. A rose by any other name . . . damn.

What a fool he'd been to think sex would diminish the sparks between them. He'd only been fooling himself when he'd bought into that line.

He swung his feet over the bed and sat up. As he ran his fingers through his damp hair, old insecurities filled him. Would he pick up a tabloid and read about the things he'd told her? Or worse, had she had sex with him because he was the producer and she believed he could do wonders for her career?

Why was it that any time he had sex, that question always remained in the back of his mind? That was why he normally avoided flings with women working on his productions. Mandy had taught him not to get involved with actresses.

Several girlfriends since had provided refresher courses. Sleeping with him until a bigger fish came along, or until they landed the role they wanted. Sex to advance one's career seemed to be par for the course in this industry. But not where Rob was concerned.

Truth be told, sleeping with him was probably the worst thing Jill could have done for her career.

When *Jane Millionaire* aired, viewers were going to want her to fall in love with one of the bachelors. Having a hot affair with the producer probably wouldn't ingratiate her in America's hearts. If what they'd done leaked out. Which he'd do his damnedest to prevent.

For everyone involved, he had to pretend he didn't want her with a fervor that scared the hell out of him.

And just how was he supposed to do that when just the thought of that unlocked door sent him up in flames?

The next few weeks couldn't go by quickly enough.

Jill smiled at the remaining six bachelors before taking her seat at the breakfast table. They stared at her curiously. Heat tinged her cheeks. Could they tell what she'd done during the night?

Maybe having glorious sex made a woman look different. Certainly there had been a gleam in her eyes that morning when she'd stared at her reflection in the mirror. She'd looked . . . alive, really alive, for the first time.

"Good morning, gentlemen." She nodded at Jeff and Steve in particular. "I'm sorry you had to wait on me. I overslept."

Which was the truth. Once she'd drifted to sleep, she'd slept surprisingly well considering that she'd been kicked out of Rob's bed.

Too bad she hadn't even showered when Gregory woke her, expecting to do her hair and makeup rather than drag her from bed.

She glanced around the breakfast nook where they generally ate their meals. Floor-to-ceiling windows, a relatively recent addition to the castle, let the bright morning sunshine filter into the room.

"Late night?" Jeff asked as he passed her a butter dish.

"Wouldn't you like to know?" She winked, amazed she felt as chipper as she did. She'd expected to wake teary-eyed at what could have been, but would never come to pass. Apparently memories of making love with Rob outweighed any remorse she experienced over knowing he didn't plan on a repeat performance. She'd count her blessings. "So what's on the schedule this morning?"

"A trip to Paris for shopping and amour."

Jill's gaze shot suspiciously to Bachelor #4. "Really?"

"Don't listen to him. You know we agreed to stay within these stone walls until the filming is finished," Steve reminded Bachelor #4 with a glower.

Jill shot him a scowl of her own. She hoped he got booted on that night's show. His jokes just weren't funny. She might have been able to get past that if he didn't think he was the funniest thing since knock-knock jokes. Surely he'd get the axe soon.

She chatted with the bachelors for a few more minutes, enjoying the delicious eggs, sausage and pastries.

"That's a wrap. You guys enjoy the rest of your

meal." The cameraman lowered the camera from his shoulder. He shot Jill a glance. "You, too."

"Thanks." She always felt more relaxed when the cameramen weren't in her face. Of course there were still the mounted cameras, but it was easy enough to forget they watched her every move.

Too easy as she'd discovered last night.

J.P. entered the room. Was it her imagination, or did he look harried this morning?

"Jane, you and the bachelors are going canoeing today."

"Canoeing?" Now there was something she'd never done. "I don't know how to canoe, but sure." How hard could it be to sit in a skinny boat and paddle?

"Then this will be an enlightening experience for you, won't it?" He sank into one of three empty chairs remaining at the large round table.

"I can teach you," Bachelor #4 spoke up.

Maybe they'd lose him in the lake where she and Jeff had picnicked. She gave a tight smile in his direction before turning to J.P. "Okay, if canoeing is on the agenda, I'm cool with that."

"Smile. It's not like we're talking extreme sports here," J.P. advised. "You'll have a great day."

"Sure." Canoeing would eliminate the possibility of seeing Rob.

She wanted to look in his eyes to see how he felt about last night. Did he have an extra bounce to his step? A satisfied gleam in his eyes? Or would she see regret? Regret for making love to her? Or regret for asking her to leave his bed?

Maybe when they got back from the lake, she'd have the opportunity to search him out.

Luck was on her side. After changing into a pair of shorts and a plain taupe T-shirt, she ran into Rob in the corridor outside their suites.

"Rob," she breathed when she almost collided into his thick chest.

He winced. She might have been hoping to catch a glimpse of him, but Rob clearly hadn't wanted to see her. He must regret their night together and obviously preferred to forget. "Ji-ane."

Hope spiraled down like a fighter jet shot from the sky. So he wanted to avoid her. Fine. That was what she'd promised to do when she'd seduced him.

" 'Morning, Rob." She hoped her smile might blind him with its fake brightness. "Did you sleep well?"

Okay, so maybe she wasn't feeling quite so generous after all.

"Not particularly." He raked a hand through his already tousled hair. He didn't appear to have slept at all.

"Sorry to hear that," she lied.

"I'm sure you are."

"It's a beautiful day. I'm heading to the lake with the bachelors. Will you be joining us for the trip?" Her face hurt from holding her smile in place.

His gaze narrowed and he looked at her, really looked at her, for the first time since she'd almost ran over him. "No. J.P. will be supervising this morning's shoot. I'm working on tonight's show. We'll boot another two bachelors."

"Can I pick which ones?"

His brow lifted. "No. Not until the last show do you get to choose."

"I know." She nudged his arm playfully, pretending not to notice how sparks of awareness dug into her from the contact. "I was just teasing."

One corner of his mouth lifted in a tight smile, and he looked beyond her to the door of his suite. "Have fun on your trip and don't get wet."

She waved and brushed past him. She hoped he'd grab her, pull her into his arms and kiss her senseless, but knew he wouldn't.

And of course, she was right.

She moseyed down the stairs, passed a grim-faced Gregory on the landing and joined the men waiting in the foyer.

"Ready, boys?" she asked when she saw that the bachelors and crew were all present. It seemed she'd been the last one to arrive on two occasions today.

She chatted with Jeff and Steve for a few moments before J.P. joined them.

"You look lovely, Your Highness." J.P. grinned at her, then shook his head with regret. "I apologize for the change in plans, but I'm no longer going to be able to accompany you. Gregory's on his way to inform Rob he'll be supervising today's outing."

At that moment, a red-faced Rob bounded down the stairs.

"We need to talk." He grabbed J.P.'s arm and tugged him across the foyer and into a neighboring room.

Although she couldn't make out Rob's words, it didn't take a genius to figure out he wasn't pleased

202

about the change of events. Undoubtedly, spending the day watching her wasn't on his priority list.

Too bad, because the grin J.P. shot her when he reentered the room assured her that once again he had gotten his way. Rob would be going on the canoe trip.

Jill smiled and hooked her arms with Jeff's and Steve's elbows. "So, which one of you gents am I going to be rowing with first?"

CHAPTER THIRTEEN

Who'd have known canoeing would make her seasick? She'd never been seasick. She couldn't believe something as serene as a paddle across the private lake would make her regret her breakfast. Nothing should make a woman regret delicious food. But with each shift of the elongated metal boat, her stomach pitched.

Things might not have been so bad, but after three trips across the water with various bachelors, she wasn't sure she'd be able to take much more. Especially since her current companion was Bachelor #4.

"Has anyone ever told you the one about the preacher and the four cops?" he asked, ignoring the fact that she hadn't laughed at his last three jokes.

Would he just please shut up? Who wanted to hear lame jokes about body functions or another one downing cops when one's stomach threatened to revolt?

Rob and two crew members trolled beside them in a small gas-powered boat. Knowing Rob was near, if inaccessible, helped. She snuck a quick glance across the twenty feet or so separating them.

He wore a headset, listening in on their conversation courtesy of the mikes they wore. His face looked terse, unyielding. She guessed he didn't find any of the jokes funny either. Despite his grim expression, he provided the only bright spot in her current excursion across the lake.

Turning back to Bachelor #4, she tried to ignore her aching stomach and imagine Rob across from her. Would he smile at her as he rowed them to the middle of the lake? Would he take her hands and kiss her to distract her from her uneasiness?

"Wanna hear something really funny?" Bachelor #4 asked.

Did he know anything really funny? If so, why had he been holding back all these weeks?

"Why not?" Jill smiled politely, although she'd have preferred to keep fantasizing about Rob and pretending she didn't feel nauseated.

He launched into another terrible joke. Jill's stomach pitched, and so did the boat as the man slapped his knee in amusement at his own tale. In his merriment, the oar slipped from his fingers and dropped into the water.

Had Jill not been fighting to keep her breakfast down, she'd have foreseen what the man was going to do. Instead, she was just grateful he'd shut up.

Until the canoe tilted at an awkward angle.

"What are you doing?" she exclaimed when he stretched over the edge of the precariously balanced canoe. The oar remained out of his reach. "Sit down. Now."

"Just a little more and I'll have it." He leaned out farther and managed to capture the oar. Looking quite proud of himself, he stood, waving the oar in the air. "See, I told you I'd get it."

"Please sit down." She covered her mouth with her hand.

His face wrinkled in amusement. "Scared we'll flip?"

"Yes."

"Sit down," Rob and one of the crew members called simultaneously from the neighboring boat.

The bachelor shifted his weight, and Jane fought an urge to knock him into the water with her paddle. He lifted his oar triumphantly over his head, bobbing the canoe back and forth. This crazy man was going to make her toss her cookies on national television. Jill took aim. This was one bachelor she was going to eliminate herself.

Too late. His eyes widened as he lost his balance and the canoe tipped, tossing them into the lake.

Just great, Jill thought as she was dumped into the water. All Gregory's hard work primping her hair, and she'd come up looking like a drowned rat.

But at least she'd be out of the rocking boat.

Although she knew the lake wasn't that cold, the water felt like icy fingers grasping at her as it soaked through her clothes and pulled her into its murky depths. She kicked her feet to resurface, but the edge of the canoe spun, righting itself, and caught her on the head. Hard.

A searing stab of pain shot through her, momentarily blinding her. She gasped. Water filled her lungs, gurgling in her throat. She sputtered, trying to rid herself of the liquid as she ached for air.

206

Blinking her eyes, she forced them to stay open and tried to keep from panicking.

Stay calm. You're a strong swimmer. Just swim to the surface. That's all you've got to do.

But the light letting her know where the surface lay faded into darkness as her face grew cold.

No. She wouldn't black out. Not from a little bump on the head. She struggled to keep conscious, to find her way to where the water met life-giving air, but the darkness took over.

Images of Rob making love to her, whispering her name—Jill, not Jane—beckoned her to close her eyes and dream sweet dreams.

Where was she? Rob searched the glossy water for some sign that Jill had surfaced. He saw nothing but Bachelor #4 waving in their direction.

He'd wanted to pound the man's face in when he'd realized the idiot was going to topple them over. Still might once they'd reached shore.

He made one more visual sweep of the area where Jill had gone into the water. Nothing.

Her mike only registered static, an eerie sound that taunted Rob.

"I'm going in." He tossed his headgear to the two cameramen as he dove into the water.

He swam quickly toward the spot where Jill had disappeared. Where the hell was she?

His lungs began to cry out for a breath. He'd have to surface soon.

That was when he caught sight of her hair floating

loosely about her. Red tinged the water like a luminous cloud above her still form.

Dear God. No.

Ignoring the pain in his chest from the lack of oxygen, he cut through the water and grasped her limp body.

With a few powerful kicks, they surfaced.

He gulped a lungful of air as he lifted her chin. "Jill, wake up. Jill."

Using the arm wrapped around her, he jerked hard against her chest, hoping to clear her lungs. Rubbing her cheek with his free hand, he prayed he'd been in time. Water spilled from her lips and she coughed. Blood trickled down her face, oozing from the gash on her head.

"Jill, open your eyes."

Her lids sprang apart to reveal dazed, dilated pupils. She coughed again and sucked in air. Her body trembled against his as he kept them above the surface.

"Rob."

"Shh, it's going to be okay, babe." Without thought, he kissed her temple. "I've got you."

The boat pulled up to them, and Rob reluctantly let go of Jill to assist the crew in pulling her into the boat. As water dripped from her soaked body, the crew hauled her from the lake.

Rob attempted to lift himself into the boat, but found he couldn't. His muscles had locked down. He grabbed hold of one of the cameraman's hands and allowed the man to help him.

He ignored an offered towel and immediately went to Jill.

She huddled on the boat's bottom, shivering, a towel wrapped around her slumped shoulders. Another towel was pressed to her bleeding head. Coughs racked her body as she fought to clear her lungs.

Hell, she could have died.

He sank to his knees beside her, causing her wide eyes to meet his. Amazingly, her trembling lips curved in a small smile.

"Bet you don't use that on tonight's show."

The show? She thought he was worried about the damn show when he'd almost lost her?

Whoa. He was jumping the gun. He didn't have her to lose. They'd had their one night and had both agreed that was all they'd ever have. The show was what mattered most to him. That's why he'd been so worried about her. Without her, *Jane Millionaire didn't exist.* His concern wasn't personal.

Jill was just a sexy-as-hell woman he'd rescued from a bad accident. He would have done the same for anyone. He would have.

But it had been Jill, he'd saved her, and she was smiling at him.

Damn, he'd missed seeing her smile.

With a weak smirk of his own, he ignored the turmoil inside him and squeezed her hand.

"No, I doubt you plunging to the bottom of the lake would help ratings." His gaze dropped to her clinging shirt. "Although if the network ever decides to air a wet T-shirt competition, you should definitely audition."

Her mouth dropped open as her gaze lowered to her sopping clothes. Rob grinned, then remembered the idiot who'd caused all this to begin with.

He glanced around, knowing the crew would have hauled the man into the boat.

Bachelor #4 sat in a seat with a towel draped over his shoulders, looking stunned by the events that had followed his foolish behavior.

Rob's fists clenched as he rounded on the man. "What the hell were you thinking?"

"How was I supposed to know the canoe would tip?"

Rob stood, determined to knock out a few of the idiot's perfect teeth.

A frightened light shined in the bachelor's eyes.

"Don't do it. He isn't worth it." One of the crew members grasped Rob's shoulder.

Rob gritted his teeth as he fought the need to pummel the man. "You're through," he spat out.

"What?"

"You're finished. Off the show."

"You can't do that."

"I don't have to. You've already been voted off." He turned to the cameraman who'd stopped him from creating a potential lawsuit. "Make sure he sticks around long enough for tonight's taping, and then escort him off the premises to where the other booted bachelors are being detained. I don't want him left alone. Remind him of the contract he signed regarding the consequences should he discuss any of the events he's participated in during his stint on *Jane Millionaire*."

"You can't do this," the man repeated.

With barely contained anger, Rob faced the man once more. "If you ever have the misfortune to cross my path again, run. Because I intend to crack a few knuckles beating your face in."

"How the hell did that happen?" J.P. sank onto the settee in Rob's suite. When the crew had told him about the accident, he'd almost had a heart attack. How would they have finished filming if something had happened to Jane?

"Because casting did a crappy job selecting bachelors. The man is a walking disaster." Rob pulled a dry T-shirt over his just-shampooed head.

J.P. experienced a moment's envy at the ripped abs Rob covered. They were similar to the ones J.P. had once sported himself. Growing old really was the pits. Now his stomach looked more like the proverbial beer gut. Maybe he'd hire a personal trainer when he got back to California. A young, frisky female trainer to whip him into shape.

J.P. blinked, pulling himself back to the conversation. "What happened at the lake was an accident."

"An accident caused by the irresponsibility of one of the bachelors. He risked Ji-ane's life unnecessarily. He's to be removed from the castle as soon as taping is finished. Otherwise, I'm not liable for my actions."

J.P. stared at the angle of Rob's clenched jaw and thought about Rob's slipup on her name. When he'd watched the film of Jane's rescue, he'd heard Rob call her "Jill." And he'd kissed her.

J.P. leaned back, reached for a cigar and frowned

when he came up empty-handed. Damn, he'd have to sneak a smoke after he'd approved the clippings to be aired with tonight's episode.

"You know," he drawled, "it's a shame you aren't one of the bachelors. The crew caught your rescue. It would have made some great footage. Handsome bachelor risks life and limb to save the star of the show."

Rob's chest rose and fell in swift succession. "That footage needs to be destroyed. I don't ever want to see it or think of this afternoon again. This isn't some show about getting your jollies off of fear."

Did the boy realize how transparent he was? He'd never seen Rob so smitten by a woman. And the poor lad had been gaga over Mandy before her shine had started to fade and the real witch beneath her gilded surface came through. Yep, Jane had Rob by the ole royal jewels.

"Quite humorous that our pretend princess gets rescued by Prince Charming, but he isn't one of the bachelors she's allowed to choose from, wouldn't you say?"

"I don't see a thing funny about any of this."

No, J.P. imagined he didn't. "'Cause you're looking at it from the wrong perspective."

"Ji-ane almost died this afternoon. No matter how I look at it, I'm not going to see a humorous side."

So transparent.

"So, we'll film the show, and Bachelor #4 will leave immediately following. That should work well enough." JP nodded, considering how far to push. Much further than he had up to this point. "Kensington is with Jane. He put a couple of stitches in the cut on her head. Says she has a light concussion but will be fine as long as she doesn't overdo it for a few days."

Rob's face pinched at the news that Kensington was with Jane. A tic twitched along his jaw.

J.P. almost laughed. And to think, the boy had once been a successful actor. "Too bad we won't be using any of the footage of her rescue. The two of them cozily playing doctor would have heated up the airwaves."

"Isn't it, though?"

"Fortunately, the gash is easily hidden beneath her hair. Kensington was able to keep from making a gap. Only had to snip a few strands." J.P. stifled his mirth. Barely. "The man is really good with his hands."

Rob stuffed his hands into his jeans pockets and let out an exasperated breath. "Don't you have something you need to be doing? Possibly finishing up whatever was so important that I had to take your place today?"

"Aren't you glad you did? I could never have pulled Jane from the water and we both know it."

Rob's face paled, and J.P. regretted his reminder of Jane's brush with death. Still, she was going to be fine, and the show would go on as scheduled. At least, mostly. There had been a few necessary changes. One had to be flexible about these kind of things. Fortunately, he'd learned to go with the flow a long time ago.

"Actually"—he rose from the settee—"I do have a few things I need to attend to. I'll see you in a couple of hours. Maybe you should take a nap. You look worn out. But come to think of it, you did when I first saw you this morning, too. Must have had a long night. Get some rest. We'll film the show as soon as Jane feels up to it."

Standing with his legs slightly spread, Rob rocked back on his bare feet. His mouth twisted in thought, and he finally shrugged. "Okay. If I'm not down fifteen minutes before it's time to start shooting, send someone up for me."

"Sure thing." J.P. opened the door, pausing to throw one last parting shot. "You know, when I was editing last night's film, I noticed Jane disappeared into your room for several hours. What was that all about?"

Gotcha. J.P. smothered a grin at the guilty-as-sin look plastered on Rob's face.

He rocked back on his feet again, his hands digging deeper into his pockets.

"You weren't sticking your hand in the cookie jar, were you?" J.P. asked, knowing exactly what had transpired. He'd known the moment he'd seen Rob this morning. Something had been different. Not that his constant tension about Jane had eased, but it seemed to have transformed into something more intense, more personal.

"No, sir. No cookies for me last night."

J.P. held his tongue. "Yeah, that's what I thought. You were reviewing the day care scenes with her, right? I'm glad I can always trust you to do the right thing."

He slipped out the door and closed it with a thunk. He leaned back against it and huffed a long breath.

Dear Lord, would Rob ever forgive him for what he was about to set into motion?

"I'm fine." Jill swatted Jeff's hands away. "Really. Quit making a fuss over me."

"You took a blow to the head. One that knocked you unconscious. That's a big deal." Jeff hooked his arm with hers again as he escorted her down the stairs and into the room where each show was taped.

Jill hung her head. "I can't believe I passed out because of this little thing."

She fingered the raised bump on the top of her head.

"Quit touching it. You'll end up with an infection."

"I thought that was the purpose of those stitches you put in."

"Yeah, well, if you don't quit touching them, you'll bust it back open."

"If you say so." She smiled at his concern. He really was a great guy, and a fabulous doctor. "Personally, I don't see the reason for so much fuss. All the other stitches I've had never burst open, and goodness knows I put a lot more pressure on them than just my fingers."

Jeff's blue eyes narrowed. "Just what were you doing where you would have gotten stitches, Princess?"

Oops. Maybe that blow to the head had done more damage than she'd thought. "Just because I'm royalty doesn't mean I've spent my life in a plastic bubble. I did spend four years in southern California, you know." Which is how they'd explained her speech.

"Yes, but being a university student isn't generally a contact sport."

"You might be surprised." Jill hid a smile. She'd played many a game during college that had resulted in cuts deep enough to need stitches. Usually on her head. Jessie had always teased that it was a good thing she was so thick-skulled.

Jill came to an abrupt halt on the stairs.

Jessie.

Not once when she'd been struggling in the water had she thought of who would take care of her sister. All she'd thought of was Rob.

Guilt hit her. How could she have forgotten her sister? Jessie needed her. Had needed her from the time their parents had died while on the way to watch one of Jill's basketball games.

"Jane?" Jeff tugged on her elbow with his. "Are you okay?"

She blinked up at him.

"I—" She winced. "Yes, I'm fine. It's just"—she paused, searching for the right words—"I think I forgot who I really am today."

"Huh?"

She shook her head and ignored the tiny spurt of pain the motion triggered. She'd refused medication when Jeff offered. Good thing, too, as she was slipping out of character enough as it was.

When they entered the room where they would be filming, Jill's gaze immediately met Rob's.

Rob's breath lodged in his throat. Jill on Jeff Kensington's arm wasn't what he wanted to see. Although it should have been.

Her wide green eyes searched his. For what he wasn't sure, but could guess. She had to be wondering if her dip in the lake had changed things between them.

It hadn't.

Although he had slipped and called her by the

216

wrong name. Had gotten caught up in the emotions of the moment and kissed her forehead.

None of the crew had mentioned the incident. Possibly no one had noticed.

More likely they just weren't commenting.

Damn, he could have screwed up everything. He wouldn't ruin this show. Not for any reason.

He looked away without acknowledging Jill's presence, determined not to give any indication that she looked lovely in her elegant blue gown or that he wanted to take Jeff Kensington's place at her side.

J.P. walked up beside him. "Wow, I think she's more stunning every time I see her."

He ignored the comment. Why admit that J.P. was right? "Is everything ready?"

"Of course." J.P. nodded at Rob's tuxedo. "Have to say, you're looking quite spiffy tonight yourself."

Rob rolled his eyes. "Come on, let's get this over with."

When everyone was in place, Rob ran through his spiel as host, smiling and providing a witty introduction to each scene. His commentary would be inserted into the show during editing.

When the filming ended, he turned to find Jill standing next to him.

She reached out to touch him, then stopped, her eyes full of confusion. "I wanted to thank you for what you did earlier."

Rob shrugged. "It was no big deal."

"You saved me."

"Possibly."

"I owe my life to you."

"You don't owe me anything."

"Rob, about last night," she said, but he shook his head.

"No. Don't even say it. Last night never occurred." He met her gaze and squared his shoulders. "You think you owe me something? Fine. Repay me by forgetting that last night ever happened."

Shock registered on her face. "But—"

"No buts about it." He scanned the room to make sure no one had noticed them. Only J.P., a few crew members and a couple of bachelors remained. None paid them any attention. "Last night shouldn't have happened. Regardless of what we said, I should have sent you back to your room. If I could do last night over, that's exactly what I'd do."

But he was lying. He knew it and suspected she did, too. But he wouldn't retract the words. She had to focus on Jane. On the bachelors. On Jeff Kensington.

Her gaze lowered briefly. "Okay. I shouldn't have assumed anything had changed, but you called me Jill and I—" her words broke off as J.P. joined them.

"Excellent job tonight." He slapped Rob on the back.

Jill offered him a smile, but Rob didn't bother. "I'm just glad that bachelor is gone."

"Me too," Jill said.

J.P. nodded. "Yep. Can't believe he lasted as long as he did."

"So what's next?" Jill asked.

"Nothing," Rob answered. "You've been given the night off to rest."

"To rest?" She met his gaze. "I'm fine."

"Yes, that's what I've been told. I was also told that you needed to rest."

"Okay." She nodded at J.P. "I'll be in my room."

Rob watched as she spoke to the bachelors before she left the room. Kensington close at her side.

J.P. slapped Rob's shoulder one last time, then walked off, but not before tossing out words that twisted Rob's gut.

"They do make a lovely couple. Maybe the show will have a real honeymoon yet. Wouldn't that just push us right off the rating scale?"

Knock. Knock. Knock. Rob glanced at the connecting door.

Oh no, he wasn't answering that knock tonight. He already knew what heaven waited on the other side.

"Go away."

"Please, Rob. I need your help."

Was she hurt? Had her wound started bleeding again? Against his better judgment, but unable to risk that she might be ill, he opened the door.

She stood, fully dressed and looking nervous. "I need your help."

"You've already said that."

She glanced into his suite, her gaze stopping on his bed. No, he wouldn't be giving her that kind of help. Although hell if his body wasn't responding to the train of her thoughts.

"I need—" She paused, her gaze returning to his face. "I need you to take me to the lake."

"What?" That sure hadn't been what he'd expected her to say.

219

Her weight shifted back and forth. "I have to go back. Tonight."

"The hell you say."

"You don't understand." Her shoulders visibly lowered. "I'm afraid."

"You almost drowned today. I think you're allowed a little fear, don't you?"

"It's not a little. It's a lot, and I have to go to the lake. If you won't take me, I'll find another way. One of the crew, or a bachelor, or I'll go alone. But I have to go. Tonight. Now."

Rob regarded her, trying to decipher the determined glint to her chin, the desperate look to her eyes. "Why?"

"Because if I don't go back in that water tonight, I may never be able to."

"You plan to go in the lake? Tonight?" Over his dead body.

"I face my fears, Rob. It's the only way I can look at myself in the mirror and have any self-respect." She placed her hand over his. "Please take me to the lake."

Rob called himself every name in the book and then a few more as he drove one of the network's Jeeps out to the lake, Jill at his side.

The last thing he needed was to be alone with her. Or to see her floating in the lake again.

With him or without him, she would visit the lake.

Did he have any choice but to take her? If he refused, he'd only sit in his room, agonizing over knowing she was at the lake, wondering if she was okay.

So here he was, bumping along a dirt road to a lake he could have lived without ever seeing again.

Jill hadn't spoken since they'd climbed into the Jeep. He glanced her way. Although she couldn't have been able to see much in the dim light, she stared out the window with her hands twisted around the towel in her lap.

He had to admire her spunk. Few men he knew would have returned to the lake so quickly after a brush with death. Of course, there wasn't much he didn't admire about Jill. Last night she'd convinced him she was close to perfect.

A new surge of regret filled him. One he had to deal with, as he'd been a fool to give in to her sweet seduction. But only a monk could have resisted.

"You okay?" he asked when he pulled the Jeep to a stop next to the small dock.

"Fine." She turned to him and offered a tight smile. "I just want to get this over with."

He could relate. "Let's go, then."

They walked toward the dock. Moonlight reflected off the inky blue-black surface of the water, belying the hidden dangers.

Crickets chirped around them and a frog croaked in the distance. A breeze rustled the leaves of the surrounding shrubbery. Unease settled in Rob's soul.

He watched Jill stare out at the water with mixed emotions. He understood her need, yet he'd have been lying if he didn't admit he feared for her safety. He didn't want her to go in the water. How would he ever find her in the darkness if she cramped in the water?

Then it hit him. He didn't want to have to go in the water. Period.

Aw, hell.

Without a word, Jill stripped down to the swimsuit she wore beneath her clothes. Her lithe beauty momentarily distracted Rob from his harsh realization. With the moonlight bathing her skin, she walked down the length of the dock and dived in without pausing.

Rob's stomach dropped somewhere beneath his feet as he ran to the end of the dock. He skimmed the water's shadowy surface.

"Jill?" he called. Dear Lord, why had he let her talk him into this?

CHAPTER FOURTEEN

Jill dived into the water and prayed this wasn't the most foolish thing she'd ever done.

She refused to live in fear of water. The only means she had of conquering her fear was to confront the terror that had gripped her every time she'd closed her eyes while in her suite.

She sank beneath the dark water. Shock as the cool water chilled her skin filled her with panic, causing her to go still.

What had she done?

Then her reflexes responded, and she kicked hard, propelling herself through the water and toward the surface. Nice and easy, taking time to assure her mind that all was well.

She broke through the surface and flung her hair back just as a loud splash near the dock caught her attention. Rob?

She searched the shoreline for him, but didn't see him until his dark head rose above the water about ten feet from her.

"I didn't know you were coming in."

"That makes two of us."

They swam toward each other until Rob was close enough to touch. Close enough that the moonlight reflected from his tawny eyes.

"Thank you."

Jill stared at him in surprise. "For what?"

"I hadn't even realized I'd decided the lake was evil until you forced me here." His shoulders lifted from the water. His bare shoulders.

She glanced at the dock. Was that dark bump his clothes? She couldn't be sure in the darkness.

"This afternoon was an accident. The water is neutral. Neither good nor bad." Did she make sense or was she merely babbling? The realization that he'd stripped warmed her insides, made her remember how his strong body had felt tangled with hers. She gulped down the lump forming in her throat.

Water droplets ran down his face and Jill decided she'd been wrong. Water was good. Life-giving good.

"You're okay?" he asked, and she got the impression he was not just asking about her fear of the water. There was a tenderness in his eyes that belied everything he'd said earlier in the day.

"I am now." She bobbed in the water, wondering if he'd kiss her. She wouldn't ask him to, but she hoped.

"Jill."

Her chest swelled at the emotions wrapped into her name. Emotions that told her even if he kissed her, even if he made love to her right at this moment, he'd regret it in the morning. She had to let him make the next move.

And he wasn't ready to make that move. Not tonight. Maybe not ever. And if she were wise, she wouldn't be longing for him to make love to her again.

With more courage than it had taken her to dive into the lake, she flung her arms forward and showered an unsuspecting Rob with water.

Surprise flickered onto his face before he grinned. "You're going to pay for that."

"Really?" she taunted, kicking her legs back in preparation to make a quick escape. "By who? You?"

He dived toward her, sending a spray of water in her direction. Jill took off, swimming away for all she was worth, determined not to let him catch her, but honest enough to admit that if he did she wouldn't be heartbroken.

She surfaced quite a distance from the shore. No sign of Rob. Where was he hiding? She turned and scanned the calm lake surface, thinking that the brilliance of the moonlight reflecting from the water was one of the loveliest sights she'd ever seen.

Maybe it was her company that gave the world such a rosy hue.

She leaned back and rewet her hair to keep it from her face. Something grabbed her foot. Rob. She shrieked and kicked halfheartedly, trying to escape his hold.

He surfaced a foot in front of her.

"You should be ashamed, Rob Lancaster. You scared me."

"You expecting Nessie?" He laughed.

"Comparing yourself to a monster?" She splashed a little water in his direction.

225

"Haven't you learned your lesson yet?" He cast a threatening look in her direction.

"My lesson? You were trying to teach me something? When?" She flicked more water at him.

"That's it. You've had it now."

Jill lurched away, but was too late. He grasped her and ducked her under, not holding her there but for a second. Probably in deference to her experience earlier in the day.

She sputtered, clasped on to his shoulders and pushed downward.

"Still haven't learned your lesson, I see." Laughing, he shook his head at her efforts and doused her again.

When she surfaced she flung her hair to shake the water free. The long strands slapped against Rob's face.

"No fair. Sea serpents aren't allowed."

"Sea serpents? Are you saying I'm an aquatic Medusa?"

"More like a siren than a creature that turns men to stone."

She'd take being called a siren. "Okay, you win."

"What?" His surprise was genuine, but he eyed her suspiciously.

"You heard me. You win."

"You'll forgive me if I don't believe you."

"Why not?" She timed her move just right and thrust her body upward as she clamped on to his shoulders. "Because I might do this?"

With her full weight as leverage, she pushed a grinning Rob under. And wasn't one bit surprised when he refused to go down alone.

* * *

226

"Just how long am I supposed to keep filming, boss?" the cameraman whispered.

"As long as their clothes are on." J.P. chewed on the cigar as he squatted in the bushes with the cameraman he'd dragged with him.

Damn arthritis made this spying business hell.

"And if their clothes come off?"

J.P. dangled the cigar from his mouth. Just how far was he willing to take this?

"If clothes come off, you go home."

Jill tried to keep from giggling as she and Rob snuck up the stairs. Why they snuck she didn't have a clue. It wasn't as if cameras didn't capture their every move.

"Quit laughing. You're going to wake the whole castle," Rob stage whispered, humor lacing his words.

"Or the ghosts."

"Ghosts?"

"You remember, the ones you warned me about on my first night at the castle." Had it only been three weeks since then?

"Oh, those ghosts. Can't say as I've heard them creeping around through the castle."

She rolled her eyes at him. "Guess you scared them off."

"Hmm, I was thinking the same thing. Only that you'd been the one to scare them away."

She slugged his shoulder and earning a smothered chuckle.

"I should make you pay for that."

"Like at the lake?"

"No. This time I wouldn't let you win."

"You just keep thinking that you *let* me. I've heard that delusion is a sign of mental illness. Guess you prove that theory."

"Ya think?"

They stopped outside Jill's suite. Suddenly realizing they were alone in the dimly lit hallway, Jill's breath caught.

"I know."

Jill leaned against the hard wood of her door.

Rob stepped closer, placing his hands to either side of her face. "You're definitely certifiable," he breathed softly.

She stared into his golden eyes, wishing she could read what was in his heart as easily as she could see the battle waging in his gaze. He wanted her, and yet he didn't.

And he couldn't enter her suite from the main hallway. Not while the cameras zoomed in on them. She had a role to play. If he wanted her, really wanted her, he knew which door she'd welcome him through. The one she'd left unlocked last night.

And they both knew what it would mean if he opened that door.

Certifiable, he'd said.

"Definitely," she agreed, ducking under his arms and hightailing it into her room before she changed her mind and dragged him to her bed, regrets or not.

Jill sat on a sofa, surrounded by the remaining four bachelors, among them Jeff and Steve. Tonight was her last night before decisions had to be made.

And they were playing a game of Win, Lose or Draw.

It seemed odd to her, but there had been no scheduled activities for the evening that they hadn't already filmed. When they'd looked for a game to play, this was the only one they'd been able to find other than the deck of cards they'd worn out during the late-night hours over the past two weeks.

One of the remaining four was drawing a picture and gesturing wildly with his hands as his teammate, Steve, tossed out guesses. Several of the crew members were hanging with them, but in the background, as J.P. had insisted upon recording the game in case they decided to use it in one of the last two shows.

She hadn't seen Rob all day and had only caught a brief glimpse of him the day before. She'd hoped without success that he would change his mind. Each night she lay in bed listening for the door to creak open.

It never did, and tomorrow was her last day at the castle.

Hard to believe it had been four weeks since the bachelors had arrived. She had no doubt as to which one she'd choose to spend the "honeymoon" week with. For the past two weeks, she'd spent the majority of her free time with Jeff. She really liked him, but she had no illusions about the differences between friendship and romance. Jeff fell into the wrong category. If only she could have fallen for him instead of Rob. Life would be so much simpler. But as always, she'd royally screwed up when it came to men.

None of it really mattered anyway. Tomorrow, Jeff would choose the hundred grand, and she'd be home a few days later. Everything would return to the way it had been before her *Jane Millionaire* days.

Except now she knew what sex could, and *should*, be like.

Damn it, she wanted more.

More of the way she felt with Rob. More of the fun she'd had with him at the lake. More of the hot, wild loving she'd had with him the night she'd gone to his room.

She fanned her flushed face.

"Your turn." Jeff's sharp tug on her sleeve pulled her from her thoughts.

Jeez, she'd totally phased out of their game. She smiled at the camera as she picked up a card, then stepped up to the dry-erase board they'd set up.

She read the card and laughed out loud. Had they rigged the game? No way could the crew not have staged this.

"Go," the bachelor in charge of the timer ordered.

Jill rolled her eyes and began drawing.

Rob leaned back against his leather chair as he watched the live feed of Jill and the four bachelors playing a game. Jill had grinned when she'd looked at her card. Why?

Curious, he watched as she drew a big heart on the board. Next, she drew a dollar sign. Her teammate, Kensington (of course), began tossing out words.

Love. Jill nodded and wrote the word beneath the heart. Immediately, Kensington called out, "Money."

Jill wrote the word beneath the dollar sign.

"For love or money," Rob said out loud, shaking his head in disbelief. Aw, hell. How had that happened?

"Wanna beer?" J.P. asked as he walked into the studio carrying an extra longneck.

"Did you rig their game?"

"What are you talking about?" J.P. looked innocent for once, and Rob knew the older man told the truth. JP couldn't lie worth a flip.

"Nothing." Rob took the bottle and set it down on the desk.

"Are you glad it's almost over?" J.P. asked, taking a long, noisy guzzle.

Was he? Once they shot the "honeymoon"—if they had to shoot it—he'd never have to see Jill again.

That was good, right?

His gaze drifted back to the screen where she was high-fiving Kensington while the other three grinned and rolled their eyes at Jill's antics. Everyone seemed to be enjoying themselves.

Everyone, but him.

He'd had two weeks of hell.

Hell because he'd walked her to her door after their swim and hadn't so much as stolen a kiss. Not that he hadn't wanted to. But he'd known he wouldn't stop with a single kiss. Still, if she hadn't ducked into her room, he might have risked everything.

Hell because he wondered if she'd open her body and heart to him if he threw logic to the wind and entered her room through the door he stared at night after night? Or had she changed her mind and locked him out long ago? After his behavior following their short dose of heaven, he wouldn't doubt it.

He'd been a total ass the night she'd given her

sweet body to him and again after the taping of Bachelor #4's departure.

Jill had stuck to her words. Not once since their swim had she made any move toward him, not a single gesture or look to show she still wanted him, that they'd come unglued in each other's arms, that their night together had meant something to her.

What had it meant to him?

Besides the best sex he'd ever had.

Man, he wished he knew. She was special, totally unlike anyone he'd ever known. He liked being with her. Liked who he was when he was with her.

"You're quiet," J.P. mused, his chair squeaking as he shifted his weight.

"Just thinking."

"About Jane?"

Rob glanced at his friend. "Why would you ask that?"

"Don't give me that crap. I've known you since you had to shave peach fuzz off that famous face," J.P. reminded him with a grin; then his expression turned serious. "You made the right choice by keeping things simple. Sex would only have complicated matters."

Rob grunted and picked up the longneck, deciding he was thirsty after all. Really thirsty.

"I'm sure Jane intends to choose Kensington," J.P. continued. "Viewers should like that. Polling shows he holds the highest audience appeal."

Since she pretty much only spent time with Jeff or Steve except during planned activities, and Kensington got the preferential treatment, Rob agreed.

A romantic week on a tropical island with Jill.

Jeff Kensington was a lucky man.

Rob took a slow, cool sip, letting the smooth liquid slide down, soothing his dry throat.

"Do you think he'll go for the money?"

"Or for love," Rob snorted as his gaze went back to the monitor. The bachelors and Jill were laughing and carrying on as though they were having a blast. Jealousy slammed him. He was as jealous as jealous got. Damn.

Had he ever been jealous over a woman? Not since Mandy, and never with this intensity. Rob set his beer down, not liking how the cold brew churned in his flaming body. Or maybe it was the green monster agitating his insides. Either way, he didn't like the unsettled sensation.

"Huh?" J.P. stared at him, rocking back in his chair.

"You missed it. Jill's card was 'for love or money.'"

J.P. cackled. "You're kidding?"

"Nope. And, of course, Loverboy picked right up on it." Rob put his hand on the mouse and clicked to zoom in on camera number two.

"Kensington answered?"

Rob nodded. He turned and saw that J.P.'s eyes practically glowed. Was that dollar signs he heard cha-chinking inside his friend's head?

"We'll have to use the footage," J.P. said. "Did you plant the card?"

"I figured you had." Rob returned his attention to the screen. Just in time to see Jill kiss Kensington.

Okay, so it was just a quick smack of her lips, but fierce longings shook him. Or maybe he shook because that green monster was battering his body, trying to break free.

"Nope. What a damn coincidence."

Rob had decided long ago that there were no coincidences. Only actions and reactions. The fact that he wanted to punch Jeff Kensington in the face—now, there was a classic example. Jill had kissed Kensington and was possibly going to go on a "honeymoon" with the guy, and Rob wanted to punch his lights out. Action. Reaction. Simple enough.

See, he was still keeping it simple. J.P. should be proud.

Nonetheless, he squeezed the mouse as if he could somehow diminish his frustrations by doing so.

"A few months after the show airs, when the media hoopla has died down, look her up if you've still got an inkling to have her."

Rob forcibly loosened his hold on the defenseless computer mouse. "You don't think Jill and Kensington will stay together?"

J.P. snickered and shook his head. "She wants you. A blind man could see the lust in her eyes when she looks at you. Frankly, I'm damn jealous of the way women fall at your feet. And Jane's a looker. Three or four months from now, you should go for it if you still want her as another bedpost notch."

He had a feeling he might still want Jill in three of four years, possibly longer. Why did life have to be so complicated? And he cringed at classifying Jill as just another notch on his bedpost. Whether or not he wanted to admit it, his feelings for Jill were not of the one-night stand variety.

"Three months from now, I may be on the other

side of the world," Rob answered noncommittally, staring at the monitors.

"Great. That should put you right smack-dab in California where she just happens to live when she's not fulfilling her duties as a European princess."

"Smart-ass."

"And don't you forget it, boy." J.P. guffawed as he took another sip. "I like her, you know."

"What's not to like?" He wished he knew. He'd focus all his energies on that flaw in hopes of dashing his ever-increasing fascination with her. He'd already tried to focus on the fact that she would likely turn out to be just another casting-couch starlet wanting to use him to advance her career.

Unfortunately, that didn't fit his gut instincts about her.

"Yeah, she's nothing like Mandy, is she?"

"Thank God." J.P. had never liked Rob's ex-wife. If only he'd asked for J.P.'s advice before he'd given the fame-hungry witch his name. Maybe his view of the fairer species wouldn't be quite so jaded had he not married Mandy and had their marriage end so publicly. "One Mandy in the world is more than enough."

But he'd run across many more women with hunger for fame and fortune in their eyes. Mandy had only provided the initial inoculation for him to develop immunity to that greedy breed. Or so he'd thought until meeting Jill.

"Have you seen her lately?"

"A couple of months before we started filming *Jane*. I ran into her at an opening. She was with husband number five and contemplating divorce once again."

Obviously impressed, J.P. widened his eyes. "One more and she'll catch up to me. Guess I'd better start the search for lucky number seven."

Rob rolled his eyes. "I thought you swore you were finished with marriage after number six took you to the cleaners?"

"But the down and dirty sure was fun while the getting was good." J.P. waggled his bushy silver brows, no doubt thinking of the blonde who'd been so much fun, albeit expensive, for the eighteen months she and J.P. had been married. J.P.'s expression sobered. "Man wasn't meant to be alone."

"I like being alone." Rob adjusted the mouse to keep from meeting his friend's eyes. Alone was much better than his marriage to Mandy or the revolving-door bride-and-groom swap most of his Hollywood counterparts, including J.P., participated in.

"If you say so."

"I say so." And it was the truth; being alone had never bothered him. At least not before meeting Jill. But the thought of facing that unlocked door tonight, knowing it was his last chance, made him seriously doubt the conviction he heard in his voice.

Only one more night to be haunted by thoughts of what lay behind an unlocked door, to be haunted by thoughts of an empty house half a world away.

Alone. Yeah, he liked being alone all right.

Long into the night, Rob lay in his king-sized bed, still trying to convince himself he wanted to be alone. Not an easy thing to accomplish while lying in a bed that had seemed much too large for just one person ever since he'd shared it with Jill for those few brief blissful hours.

He blew out a frustrated breath.

The sun wouldn't be up for several hours, but it didn't matter. He couldn't go back to sleep and it was too early for a jog. He'd dozed off and on all night. The few times he had slept, he'd dreamed he was a knight come to rescue a beautiful princess, Jill, from her castle prison. He'd dreamed of knocking down the door between them, of making love to her, of her sweet moans as he thrust inside her, dreamed of her fiery, demanding kisses.

God, it was hot in here. Rob kicked his covers off his bare body and flicked on a lamp that looked like a lantern of some sort, although, like everything else in the castle, it ran on modern-day electricity.

His gaze landed on the connecting door. Just as it had a thousand times during the long hours he'd lain awake fighting his body's need for a certain woman.

Need. He needed Jill. The realization terrified him, yet on some inexplicable level the admission freed him. What would she do if he opened that door and made love to her? Branded her with his kisses? Told her he didn't want her to choose Kensington or any of the bachelors?

Now where the heck had that come from?

He wasn't going to open the door. Nor was he going to make love to her. Branding her was simply out of the question, although he wouldn't mind stamping a big R across her forehead. Of course, she'd take that to mean "rejected" rather than "claimed by Rob."

Not that he was claiming her.

He couldn't. Not for at least three months, probably more, if he didn't want media backlash. The press could kill a career faster than ten bad films in a row.

Or make a career, as he suspected would happen with Jill. Offers would pour in, and she'd move on to bigger and better things just as the other women in his life had.

Rob groaned. The sad truth of this whole reality nightmare was that he might never make love to Jill again if he didn't go to her tonight.

But opening that door, well, he was pretty sure she'd take it to signify more than what he was willing to give. More than what he had to give.

When she'd come to his room, she'd mentioned regrets. What regrets was he going to have tomorrow afternoon when their time together would end with the arrival of the real princess? What regrets would he have two weeks from now? Two months?

Since the night she'd taken the initiative, he could have been with her, spending time with her. Could have opened that connecting door on the night they'd gone to the lake, and she'd have welcomed him. Instead, he'd done the professional thing and stayed away in halfhearted hopes she'd fall for another man.

He'd watched the footage of her and Kensington. She liked him. A lot. She'd even kissed him a couple of times, more than the pert smack she'd given during their drawing game. Damn it all to hell. He'd had to vent his violent emotions after each kiss by punishing his body in the exercise room. He'd barely been able to walk the next morning after his last grueling workout.

He'd ached in more ways than the physical ones.

And those aches were the ones that plagued him. Jill had gotten under his skin. More than Mandy. Which was saying a lot, because at one time he'd have hung the moon for his ex-wife.

What if Kensington chose to go on the trip with Jill and she fell for him during their "honeymoon"? So what if she'd had the hots for Rob first? She might marry Kensington and then where would he be?

Because even before J.P. had suggested it, he'd known he would look Jill up after the show's media attention had settled. He wanted to explore a relationship with her outside of this dreamy setting that was more like a nightmare.

If she fell for Kensington, he'd never have the opportunity to hold her, never be able to kiss her lips or taste her honeyed sweetness again. Could he live with the knowledge that he'd willingly shoved her into another man's arms and allowed that to happen?

And just how was she going to react when the real princess was thrown into the whole twisted equation?

Reality television. He hated it with a passion.

When Isabella made her appearance, who knew what Jill would do? Certainly forgiveness wouldn't come easily.

Tonight could truly be his last opportunity to hold Jill, to breath in her rose-scented fragrance, to feel her heartbeat next to his.

Rob stood, raked his fingers through his already tousled hair, flicked off his lamp and strode soundlessly toward the connecting door.

The cold floor of his suite sent chills down his spine, or maybe it was anticipation of the prize that lay behind door number one that had goose bumps covering his skin.

His heartbeat bounded. *Lub-dub*. *Lub-dub*. Harder. Faster. Until he felt like a star in a thriller movie, and a slasher was going to jump out at any moment.

Was he a fool?

Probably, but he couldn't stay away. The cameras were still in her room, but it would be dark. He'd toss a shirt over the video equipment. If they were quiet, no one would ever know he'd been there.

If she didn't throw him out, which was probably what he deserved. He'd known when she slipped into her room on the night they'd gone to the lake that she'd wanted him to join her. And he'd not gone to her. Because he'd been afraid.

When had he turned into such a coward?

With trembling fingers, he twisted the skeleton key to unlock his side of the door. Heaven waited on just the other side.

CHAPTER FIFTEEN

Lying in her made-for-a-princess bed, Jill reached over and picked up her watch from the antique nightstand. She shifted the jewel-encrusted loaner until the moonlight hit the face.

Four o'clock.

Breakfast with the bachelors was at eight. And she had to make her decision at noon. Today.

When all was said and done, she'd be on a plane back to California. Possibly tonight.

Alone.

She didn't want to be alone.

Oh, she'd have Jessie—if she didn't kill her sister for getting her into this mess.

She sighed. No, she wouldn't threaten her sister. Instead, she'd hug her. Without this trip, she wouldn't have realized what a rut she was in. She had needed to quit hanging on to the idea of her and Dan getting back together. She hadn't even realized that was what she'd been doing. No wonder Dan's girlfriend hadn't trusted her.

She should have gotten out, dated, and looked for Mr. Right.

Rob's image plastered itself in her mind.

No, he wasn't her Mr. Right. He was a famous Hollywood producer, and she was a cop. Had they met under different circumstances, he wouldn't have given her the time of day—unless she'd pulled him over for speeding. Then, he probably would have flashed his toothpaste-ad-perfect smile and tried to schmooze his way out of his ticket.

And darned if she probably would have let him.

She grinned and pulled the covers tighter around her as she realized she most definitely wouldn't have let him sweet-talk his way out of a ticket. She'd have slapped handcuffs on his wrists and hauled his sexy Hollywood butt into the station.

Oh, yeah. She'd have made a lasting impression on him, one way or the other.

She rolled over to stare across the moonlit room at the shadowed corner where the connecting door loomed. She'd offered her body to him and he'd refused, had continued to refuse each and every night that door remained shut. She had too much pride to go to his room again and throw herself at him.

She wasn't a fool. She meant nothing to him except a quick tumble in the sack to pass time. Not really. She'd never had any great expectations of them having a happily-ever-after together. Rob wasn't the type. He was pure Hollywood, with all its glamour and glitz.

She suspected that, for her part, their time together had meant much more, and if he'd been receptive, she would have offered him her heart along with her body.

Tugging the goosedown covers closer around her, she closed her eyes and prayed sleep would come.

Squeak.

Her eyes sprung open.

Had she imagined the noise? Her gaze focused on the dark corner. Nothing. No shafts of light indicating the door had opened. Nothing at all.

Go to sleep, Jill. You're imagining things.

Or maybe she'd gone to sleep and was going to have one heck of a dream starring Rob Lancaster in the buff. Maybe of him carrying her from the lake, peeling her swimsuit off with his teeth and making love to her on the dock. A girl could hope.

Squeak.

Still no light, but she had heard a noise, and it had come from the direction of the door.

The connecting door.

The moon had apparently gone behind a cloud, because she could no longer make out much of anything, but she wasn't dreaming. That much she was sure of. The door had opened.

Instinctively, she sensed that someone was in her room, and even though she couldn't see him, she knew that someone was Rob. Excitement shimmied through her. He'd come to her. What did it mean?

"Who's there?" she asked anyway, barely daring to breathe.

"Shhh," came a low masculine voice from close to her bed, causing her to jump. She hadn't realized he'd crossed the room. Had she been away from the force so long that her police instincts had dulled completely?

"You scared me." She sat up in her bed, finally able to make out his outline.

"Shhh, don't talk. I covered the camera, but our conversation will still be picked up if we don't keep our voices down." Rob whispered. He reached out and touched her braid, stroking his fingers over the long rope she'd plaited her hair into prior to crawling into bed. His touch bordered on reverence. And uncertainty. "Am I welcome here?"

He was asking . . . Her heart skipped a beat. Not that she hadn't known immediately why he'd opened the door, because she had. There could only be one reason.

She should say no. She should tell him to get lost after the way he'd completely ignored her since the night at the lake, but to do so would be punishing herself.

This was their last night. Forever. Because once they left this idyllic setting, they'd each go back to their lives and he'd forget about her. He'd even told her as much.

But she couldn't deny him. Didn't want to. She'd love him with all she had and make memories to cherish during the lonely nights ahead.

"Yes," she whispered, clasping his hand and pulling it to her lips. She pressed a kiss against the surface of his palm. "I left the door unlocked, didn't I?"

"Shhh, no talking. Just feel." He climbed into her bed, and she welcomed his warmth by wrapping her arms around him.

"Okay." Talking wasn't what she wanted anyway.

She wanted his touch, his caresses, his body.

He gave her all those things and more.

Occasional moonbeams illuminated his naked form above her, casting a dreamlike glow to his skin.

A god. He looked like some Greek god come to Earth for a night of human passion. She whimpered as he kissed, suckled, touched, stroked, tasted every pore on her skin. When she knew she was going to cry out if he didn't fill her body with his hard shaft, his mouth took hers, capturing any sound she might have made.

Now, she silently begged. *Oh, please now.*

As if he could read her thoughts, his hardness nudged her slick, wet folds, separating her mound of hot flesh. He clasped her fingers with his and pushed their locked hands down on each side of her head as he rose above her and thrust inside.

Deep. Hard. A shiver passed over her skin, and she wondered what he was feeling as he held his passion under tight rein. Did he feel the completeness, the oneness of their connected bodies?

His hips moved slowly at first as he drove his thick length into her time and again, filling her with him. Then his rhythm picked up speed and intensity. Her body and heartbeat matched his pace as his pelvis's pistoning movement swept her sanity far, far away to a fantasyland where she was a real princess being eternally claimed by Prince Charming.

As much as it scared her, Rob was her Prince Charming—the only man for her.

Her breath caught as swirls of heat began to ignite in her boiling center. Tiny bursts of electricity exploded, each one gaining momentum until Jill felt she was going to explode like a Fourth of July fireworks display.

Then she did.

Her back arched high off the bed, her hands clamped tightly to Rob's, her heart hammered. She gasped for breath that seemed impossible to catch as wave upon wave of sweet spasms rocked her.

Just as her inner thighs clenched with the peak of her orgasm, Rob covered her mouth with his. He came with her. Hard.

Ohmygod. Oh. Yes. Yes. Yes.

Heady dizziness overtook her. She held her breath until her chest threatened to burst.

Then, in a soft, swift gush she released the air in her lungs and sizzling quivers sent her over the edge again, falling right into one amazing climax after another.

Rob's gentle, searching kiss told her he also sought reassurance in the emotional aftermath of their joining. It stood out as the most phenomenal experience of her life.

How was she supposed to choose a bachelor when her heart had made its choice and no other man would ever do?

"I cannot do this," Isabella informed J.P. moments after he entered her suite.

"Why not?"

Funny, he did not seem as upset as she had thought he would.

"Because this is wrong, and I cannot see the purpose of my interrupting your show. What difference could it possibly make for me to show my face? Your show has been a success in your country. My appearance would only cause pain to your Jane Millionaire."

And possibly to Jeff. Had he fallen in love with the beautiful "Jane"?

J.P. shrugged. "Okay, if you don't want your moment in the spotlight, that's fine with me."

"Really?" Not in her wildest dreams had she envisioned her conversation with J.P. going this well. She had expected to have to plead with him.

"Sure, but I have to admit, you surprise me."

There the man went with his disgusting cigar. Did he think she did not know he snuck in a smoke when he was in his rooms? Did he think her staff not loyal to her, their princess?

"Why?"

J.P. laughed, walking over to look at an antique gold-inlayed snuffbox that had been her father's. "Well, you're missing your chance with Kensington, for one thing."

"My chance with Jeff? What do you mean?"

"Cut the crap, Your Highness. We both know you brought him here because you're in love with him. Nice fellow, too."

In another century she could have had him beheaded for speaking to her in such a manner. At times, Isabella longed for the past ways.

"I do not see your point. What do my feelings for Jeff have to do with today?"

He picked up the snuffbox and Isabella had to squelch the urge to ask him to set it down. "If you don't make your appearance at the taping of the show today, you'll never know how he really feels, will you? You'll basically be giving your blessing for him to woo another woman. Come to think of it, that's what you've already done by bringing him here under false pretenses."

"I—" She wanted to deny his words, but could not. She had arranged for Jeff's inclusion. Just so she could see him once more.

And the truth was, she loved him. She had known when she had been at his mission site and had volunteered to stay longer. She had only left when news of her father's illness had been delivered. Left without telling Jeff goodbye. How could she explain that her father was king and might be dying? That although she had fallen in love with him, she did not know if she would ever see him again?

But she had had to. Her heart had demanded to know if the emotions in her chest were real or the figments of her vivid imagination.

"I will be married before the end of summer. Jeff need never know I was here."

J.P. shrugged. "That's your choice, Princess. Your choice."

She nodded. Her choice. If only.

"But it's a shame, as we both know he came here for you. Don't you think he deserves to know the truth?"

The truth. Isabella closed her eyes. Tell Jeff that after a year apart she still loved him. But even if he loved her, they could not be together because he was not royalty.

"Just think about it. You've still got about an hour before the show starts. Why not let Jeff know you're here? What's the worst that can happen?"

Did he mean other than the possibility that she might selfishly renounce the throne by choosing to be

248

with Jeff, if he would still have her? That she might let her honorable but chauvinistic cousin become king and halt women's rights and equality?

Then the truth occurred to her.

The worst thing she could imagine would be Jeff seeing her and not caring one way or the other that she had stepped back into his life after a year's absence.

Was that the real reason she had decided against her arranged role in the grand finale of *Jane Millionaire*?

What was the worst that could happen, indeed?

Breakfast was a tense affair.

All the bachelors were on edge. Jill wiped her sweaty palms with a perfectly pressed white linen napkin. Heck, she was edgy, too.

A fire roared in the six-foot-wide fireplace along one stone wall. The blaze had to be for ambience, because the weather was gorgeous and this room felt hotter than Hades.

She shifted in her seat of honor at the elaborately set twenty-foot dining table. Fine china, antique silverware, crystal goblets, gorgeous fresh floral arrangements. She halfway expected Jeeves to come ask if she'd like some Grey Poupon with her eggs Benedict. Would she miss being waited on hand and foot when she went back to California?

Somehow she doubted that's what she'd be missing.

Two bachelors were sitting by her side, Jeff on her right and Steve on her left. All four of the remaining candidates stared at her as they picked at their breakfast.

She certainly was the center of attention this morning.

She averted her gaze to the intricate imperial pattern on the edge of the china and caught a faint whiff of the vivid blossoms' fragrance over the aroma of their food.

Their last meal together.

She hadn't said much this morning, and even Jeff had quit trying to elicit conversation after several failed attempts. She simply didn't know what to say. Not to Jeff or Steve. Certainly not to the other two bachelors.

She didn't want to spend a week on a tropical island on a pretend honeymoon.

At least not with any of them.

And she was tired of pretending. She just wanted to be herself and to hell with anyone who didn't like it. And before long, she'd go back to being plain Jill Davidson instead of Princess Isabella Jane Strovanik.

She should suck it up and quit sulking. It was unlikely she'd have to go on the "honeymoon" anyway.

She'd pick Jeff, he'd choose the money, and that would be the end of her royal stint.

The end of her time with Rob.

But, oh, what an ending it had been.

Her stomach flip-flopped at the memory of what they'd shared earlier that morning.

Hot, sweaty, glorious lovemaking.

And Rob had made love to her.

She dropped her fork onto the lacy white tablecloth. Its tines clanged against a saucer, the noise reverberating around the silent room.

"Excuse me," she murmured in her princess voice and picked up the utensil to take another bite of perfectly prepared sex—er, eggs.

Oh, man. She had to get her mind off Rob before she made a complete fool of herself in front of the ever-present cameramen.

But the more she tried, the more memories flooded her.

Rob had been wild and wonderful, and she'd felt the desperation in his lovemaking. Feral. Hungry. Out of control. Yet tender, giving, almost worshipful in his touches, his kisses.

In the two hours he'd been in her bed, he'd loved her thoroughly. Over and over.

Had he been memorizing every touch, every scent, every taste, as she had?

They'd both known they were saying good-bye.

Even if she hadn't been able to tell him how he affected her, at least she'd had the opportunity to show him. No words had passed between them. Only the guttural sounds of shared ecstasy.

Words hadn't been needed.

He'd taken her, and she'd been his willing captive.

Of course, in round two—or had it been three?—she'd devoured him right back. A smile played on her lips. If his powerful climax had been anything to judge by, he'd been a happy camper as well.

In some ways she was glad he'd insisted upon no words—and not just because of the camera.

What could be said at this point?

They were two very different people stealing a few passion-filled moments in time, a fantasy affair in a fantasy castle, nothing more. For sanity's sake, she'd leave it at that and not ponder that, had they talked this morning, she might have whispered words of love.

Which would have been totally dimwitted.

Thank goodness they hadn't been talking, because she did *not* love Rob Lancaster.

She swallowed the tasteless lump of egg in her mouth.

She didn't love Rob. She couldn't.

What she needed was to finish this day, go home, and be thankful no one had figured out she wasn't the woman who'd signed up to play this part.

Which amounted to fraud.

Fraud.

She, Miss Upstanding Citizen and Dedicated Police Officer, had committed fraud. If she got discovered, she would most likely lose her job, not to mention the possibility of going to jail for thirty days. Not a pleasant prospect for a cop to be incarcerated alongside criminals she'd helped put away. Life would be hell.

Might be anyway.

Jeff leaned close and whispered, "Are you okay?"

She stared at him, but didn't speak. Maybe she still wasn't talking? Maybe she'd never talk again. Then she wouldn't have to choose to go on a fake honeymoon with the wrong man.

Not that Rob was the right man. He was a big-shot producer. A man with money and prestige.

"Everything's going to be all right." He patted her hand, offering assurance. "Just wait and see."

He was wrong, of course, but then for Jeff everything would be all right: before the day ended, he'd have a hundred thousand dollars to go along with his new tie, Rolex, flat-screen television and media center—to watch reality TV on, no doubt—and, since he'd made it to the final round, a new luxury car. All generously provided by the show's sponsors.

Her stomach roiled.

She took another bite, hoping the tasteless food would settle her stomach.

As the morning passed, Jill jumped through all the hoops J.P. put forth. She smiled, spent time with each bachelor and discussed her choices as the cameras recorded every move she made. She posed for more publicity shots. Hadn't they done enough in all the hours prior to the bachelors' arrival and the ones they'd done of her with them since? Apparently not. Rob stayed conspicuously hidden, even though he'd supervised all her previous photo shoots.

Despite the deep hurt in her chest, she smiled some more.

Her face ached from smiling so much.

She was so ready to have this over and be on her way to California, back to her own familiar, safe world. But even as she thought it, she knew she'd never view her world the same way again.

Rob had changed how she looked at life.

At the dreaded noon hour, she and the four bachelors sat in an awe-inspiring hall of the castle. With its marble floors, tall wooden pillars and vaulted ceiling it resembled a small cathedral. It was a room where kings had once made decisions much grander than the one she'd make today.

The bachelors were seated on wooden pews, like subjects at her court. The walls were stone, but beautiful paintings of victorious battle scenes covered each one.

Shivers ran down her spine.

Surely, kings had knighted brave men in this very room once upon a time. It seemed a travesty that she, with a jewel-encrusted tiara upon her head, was sitting on the throne. Under less stressful circumstances, she'd have laughed her butt off at the pure hilariousness of it.

Jill Davidson on a throne.

The only throne she rated was of the porcelain variety.

God, she felt like such a phony.

Most of the crew members had gathered in the back of the hall to watch as she made her choice. Rob, in his fancy duds and host-with-the-most smile, stood a few yards away. But he'd yet to meet her gaze. She fought the urge to make him look at her, to make him admit that this was what he really wanted.

It had to be, since he was going along with the whole scenario.

If he cared about her, he'd stop this foolishness.

Bright lights focused on where they stood, almost blinding her with their intensity and making her uncomfortably hot. She might just melt.

Hmm, would melting save her from an even worse public humiliation?

Regardless, the cameras were rolling and sweating wasn't allowed today, as J.P. had reminded her after breakfast. You'd have thought fanning herself was a major crime with the way he'd carried on. But then again, this gown was too gorgeous to sweat in anyway.

A white material as luminous as pearls accented the

curves of her upper body, and the skirt flared out at her hips, falling in delicate folds. Hints of gold laced the material. Tiffany's had once again provided jewelry that probably outshone many a real princess's jewels. Teardrop-shaped diamonds and pearls ornamented the platinum chain that draped her neck. A matching tiara graced her head.

At least she looked like royalty, even if she didn't feel it.

She glanced at each bachelor, following J.P.'s instructions to the T. She listened to Rob make his speech, then began her own rehearsed spiel.

"I have to make a hard decision today. I've enjoyed the past month. Getting to know each of you has been a pleasure, and all of you have become dear to me." She paused, wishing her heart was behind this. "But I can only choose one."

She looked at each bachelor in turn. Why was her heart beating so fast? She fought the need to glance at Rob, all decked out in his tuxedo and looking snazzier than any man should be allowed.

And lost her battle.

He looked so good in his spiffy clothes. So very good out of his clothes.

She shuddered as an onslaught of memories hit her. Only hours before, they'd been wrapped in each other's arms. She remembered the way the moonlight had illuminated his toned flesh as he'd loved her.

Another glance revealed that his dark hair was stylishly tousled, much like it must have looked when he'd crawled into her bed. Had he been running his fingers through it? Was he as frustrated about this setup as she was? What would he do if she chose him instead of one of the bachelors?

When her gaze collided with his, she knew. Knew that the man staring back at her with hot whiskey eyes owned her heart.

She could deny it all she wanted, but the truth couldn't be suppressed. Jill Davidson loved Rob Lancaster. Forever and always. With all her heart and soul and most definitely her body.

She swallowed and looked away, accidentally catching Jeff's gaze. His eyes were warm and friendly, and he smiled genuinely at her. Not an "I'm in love with you" smile, but a kind expression that showed he cared about her as a person.

Why? Why couldn't she have fallen for him?

She felt totally ridiculous. The cameras were rolling. Everyone was waiting on her to make her great revelation. Time was ticking away. She had to say Jeff's name. For her sake. For Jessie's sake. For Rob's. J.P.'s. For everyone's.

Just say the words. Say Jeff's name and be done with it, she told herself. *It's not like you'll have to go on the trip anyway. He'll take the money. You want him to take the money.*

Still unable to speak, she tilted her head to stare at Rob once more.

His eyes were unreadable. Though she had a feeling the message for her was to forget her feelings for him and do what needed to be done.

"I choose—"

"Stop." Every head in the room turned to stare as a

willowy blond woman gracefully walked up the aisle toward the throne. "This woman is not who she says she is. She's an imposter."

Jill's mouth fell open.

Uh-oh. Somehow this regal woman—about the same age as herself, only much prettier and more feminine—had discovered the truth about her and Jessie.

Fear and relief simultaneously flooded her.

"I—" she began, but the woman interrupted.

"You're not Princess Isabella Jane Strovanik."

Not what she was expecting her to say, but nonetheless true. Jill watched apprehensively as the woman stepped between her and Rob. Jill went on the offensive. "Who are you?"

The blonde smiled gracefully, but cast a nervous glance toward the bachelors. "I'm Princess Isabella Jane Strovanik. The real Princess Isabella Jane Strovanik."

Oh heck. Now what was she supposed to do?

Jill searched the crew for direction. J.P. had stepped closer to the front of the room, but he offered no guidance. She glanced at Rob. His face was blank, but his eyes had turned to tumultuous molten gold. Neither of the producers seemed surprised.

They'd known about this woman? That she would be here today? Why hadn't they told her? What was going on?

"Gentlemen, it seems we have a dilemma." Rob stepped up, seeming to have shaken whatever had caused the earlier turmoil in his eyes. With finesse and an ease that belied the possibility that the interruption hadn't been planned, he spoke to the cameras

257

and the bachelors. "Which one of these lovely ladies is the real princess? The gorgeous Jane whom you've spent the last month getting to know, or this majestic vision who claims she's of true royal lineage?"

The bachelors murmured among themselves. All but one. Jill stared at the openmouthed Jeff. He looked as if he were seeing a ghost.

"Izzy?" Jeff squawked, rising from his seat.

Izzy? What was he talking about?

The woman's cheeks blushed a bright pink as she glanced at Jeff; then she quickly averted her gaze.

Jill frowned. Had *Jane Millionaire* turned into an episode of *The Twilight Zone* or what? She expected to hear creepy music start up any moment. Maybe Rod Serling's voice announcing some strange occurrence. Remembering the cameras, she forced the frown from her face and glanced around the room, looking for a clue as to what was really going on.

"It's time," Rob said, this time to Jill. "Make your choice of who you want to spend the next week with on your Caribbean 'honeymoon.'" Was this for her benefit or for the cameras? She glared at him, wishing she could demand to know how he could do this to her. Why demand something she knew the answer to? He'd used her, and she couldn't even blame him. Hadn't she practically asked for him to?

Honeymoon, he'd said. God, just hearing the word made her stomach pitch. How would she manage another week of pretending? And why should she, when they'd deceived her?

Her gaze flicked back to Rob. He'd stepped closer, and she studied every lovely angle of his face. Her heart thudded and her tongue stuck to the roof of her dry mouth.

She knew what her responsibilities were.

For Rob, she had to do this. This was his career. Her career. Her life. Jessie's life. So many people could be hurt if she didn't do the right thing. She knew all these things, so why was she still hesitating?

She gulped. "I choose Je—"

"Wait a moment," Rob interrupted. Was this planned? Or had he been unable to hear her say Jeff's name?

"The bachelors don't know the new rules. Once Jane makes her choice, the chosen bachelor may take the romantic getaway with Jane—or he can choose a cash prize of one hundred thousand dollars, and walk away."

The men's eyes widened. Except for Jeff, who had gotten over his initial shock at the appearance of the blonde and now looked torn between disbelief and anger. Was he upset on her behalf? Why did he keep glancing at the woman who professed to be the real princess? The newcomer stared at him with her heart on her sleeve.

What was going on?

"Or he can opt to stay at the castle for another week with this woman who claims to be the real Princess Isabella Jane Strovanik."

Jill's eyes widened too. This new woman, who might really be a princess for all she knew, had been thrown into the prize pool? And Jeff knew her? From the looks passing between the two of them, they knew each other quite well.

This had to be a nightmare. She'd wake up and be at home in California, and the past month would only be one long bad dream—except for the Rob parts. The scenes with Rob were sheer fantasy. Too good to be true.

Maybe this really was *The Twilight Zone* disguised as reality TV.

CHAPTER SIXTEEN

Rob's heart lurched, and lodged in his throat.

Jill was going to choose Jeff Kensington, and the two of them would spend a fun-filled, romantic week together on a tropical paradise. One thing might lead to another. . . .

Jealousy pricked the armor around his heart. Jill was his. He'd claimed her this morning. The other night. He'd branded her as his woman. His urgent need to stop this disaster from unfolding stomped all over his better judgment.

She was unlike any woman he'd ever met, and he was going to lose her for a television show?

A damn reality show, at that. Why had he let J.P. talk him into this drivel?

After loving her this morning, while the first streaks of dawn filtered into her suite, he refused to risk her falling for Kensington. Not when he was confident she had fallen for *him*. He'd felt it in her touch, in her kiss. He'd be a fool to send her on a romantic interlude with another man.

Rob Lancaster wasn't a man known for foolishness. Jill's eyes were locked with his. She was more beautiful and royal than the regal woman standing between them, the real princess. Jill looked confused, unsure of how she should proceed. She also appeared more than a little ticked off. He should have told her about the real princess. He should have told her that she made him want things he'd never dreamed of wanting.

"I choose—" She started over. Despite the anger she targeted at him, her expression also begged him to rescue her. He could see the plea in her wide green eyes.

She wanted him. And damn it, he wanted her. In the worst kind of way.

Jeff Kensington couldn't have a honeymoon, fake or otherwise, with *his* woman.

Turmoil raged, churning reason with emotion until he couldn't tell the two apart. He had to stop her. He couldn't stop her. Or could he?

He opened his mouth, willing words that would prevent her from choosing Kensington, but not a sound came forth. He was the producer, the host of this show. He'd given his word to J.P. His dreams for *Gambler* rode on *Jane Millionaire*'s success. He wouldn't blow his career over a woman.

"—no one," she finished.

The entire room fell silent.

"No one?" Rob's mouth closed. He stared at the beautiful woman whom, he'd mere hours ago buried himself in until he'd been too exhausted to do more than collapse upon her.

Shame and relief washed over him. Shame that

he'd not been able to publicly acknowledge his feelings for her. But, then, he'd never been one for public displays of emotion. He valued his privacy. How could he openly stop Jill when he wasn't even sure what the emotions rushing through him meant? He did recognize the relief he felt, though—relief that she wouldn't be honeymooning with Jeff Kensington.

Jill's gaze touched each bachelor in turn, but didn't flicker to Rob. He'd disappointed her by allowing her to voice her decision. What had she expected him to do? Declare he couldn't live without her in front of the cameras for all of America to watch? Not hardly. His personal life was just that: his.

When they discussed whatever was happening between them, it would be in private, and it would be kept there.

"The rules state I have to choose whichever one of the bachelors I want to go on a honeymoon with, and very simply put, I don't want to go on a honeymoon with any of you." She sighed, confidence, regret, and hurt evident on her face and in her stance. "As I said earlier, I've enjoyed meeting and getting to know each of you." She smiled, and Rob's heart performed an acrobatic stunt worthy of a gold medal. "I've learned more about myself in the last few weeks than I imagined possible. And one thing I'm sure of is that I'm not willing to settle for anything less than real love with a man who's not afraid to admit he cares for me." She shrugged.

Rob held his breath, knowing her remarks referred to his silence when she'd debated her decision.

"The past month has been a fantasy come true in so

many ways. But I didn't fall in love with any of you, and it doesn't seem right to spend a week pretending otherwise."

She took the tiara off her head, walked to the closest pew and handed the glittering crown to Jeff Kensington. Oh God, had she changed her mind?

Rob took a step in their direction.

She smiled at Kensington. Her eyes glittered more brightly than the diamond-and-pearl necklace around her neck, but her head remained high and her bare shoulders never sagged. Damn, she was something else.

"I hope we can continue to be friends. You've come to mean a lot to me over the past month, and I don't want to lose your friendship," she said. "A part of me wishes we could have fallen in love, but we both know it will never happen. As far as I'm concerned, you're free to choose one of the other two prizes. I'm just removing myself from the list."

Kensington took the bejeweled offering, stared at it a moment before kneeling to kiss Jill's hand. They looked like something straight from a fairy tale.

"In my heart, you are a true princess, and I wish things could have worked out differently between us."

"Me too." Tears shimmered in her eyes as Kensington took her in his arms. In a hug between friends.

Rob stood mesmerized by the scene.

Hell, all of America would be pissed these two hadn't gotten together, and it was his damn fault. Could a man cry and shout for joy at the same time?

"What's she doing?" J.P. hissed from beside him, ob-

264

viously not caring if the cameras recorded him. No matter, since any good cameraman had his sights trained on the embracing couple. Rob didn't turn to look at his friend, just watched Jill and Kensington whisper back and forth to each other. What were they saying?

"She can't do this," J.P. continued. "Her contract. We'll sue."

Rob started to answer his coproducer when a stunning beauty with hair a shade lighter than Jill's stepped into the room. A woman wearing a sleek black pantsuit—a woman who could easily be mistaken for the woman he'd spent the past six weeks lusting after. The woman from the interview tape and photos.

What had Jill done?

"Another interruption?" one of the ignored bachelors grumbled as Rob stepped toward Jill. The need to protect her from saying something incriminating, not to mention his desire to strangle her, coursed through his veins as the enormity of what she'd done rammed home.

"Jessie!" Jill exclaimed, obviously too shocked at the woman's appearance to censor her response.

Damn. He'd been right on the money. This was her sister. The one he'd spoken to on the phone. What was she doing here? Rob started toward them, but J.P. tugged on his sleeve to hold him back.

"Think about what you're doing. Just let this play out. It should make for one hell of a show."

"Thirty seconds ago you were planning to sue," Rob reminded him, knowing J.P. was right. He had no business interfering. Actually, his business was *not* to interfere when something this juicy happened. Damn.

"Yeah, well, this just got better than anything we could have cooked up."

If J.P. realized Jill was a fraud, he might cook her up. No, J.P. wouldn't have to cook her up. Rob was going to do the job for him.

She deserves to be cooked up.

She'd lied to him. To them all.

What had she been thinking? And why the hell was her sister here? Didn't she realize how obvious it was, with the two of them together, what had taken place? Anyone who'd seen the footage of the audition interviews would immediately make the connection.

Nothing good could come out of this.

"I came to rescue you," the woman who looked remarkably like Jill answered. Jill's sister. Jessie Davidson.

"Rescue me?" Jill's forehead furrowed as she stared in apparent amazement at her sister. "Since when do *you* rescue *me?*"

"Since I got you into this mess." Jessie walked onto the platform as if she owned the castle. She smiled beatifically at all the men, dazzling most if not all, Rob was sure. "You heard her. My sister is not available for your honeymooning pleasure. She'll be accompanying me home tonight. That's all, folks."

And she winked outrageously at the camera, grabbed Jill's hand and tugged her from the platform and toward the door.

Rob blinked.

J.P. scratched his head, an odd look on his face. Those looks usually meant he was guilty of something.

But for the life of him, Rob couldn't think what J.P. could be guilty of in this situation.

"They aren't really leaving, are they?" J.P. asked.

Hell if he knew.

Leaving. Jill was leaving.

Heedless of J.P.'s continuing commentary and the stare down between Jeff Kensington and Princess Isabella, Rob raced after Jill.

"I suppose you are surprised to see me." Isabella wondered how she was expected to run a country when she could not manage to form a coherent thought. Jeff had always affected her in such a manner. She had wondered if time would dull her response to him. Now she knew it had not.

"Surprised?" Jeff's eyes closed as he shook his head with disbelief. "Why should I be surprised?"

"I'm sorry."

"For what, exactly? For disappearing during my shift at the hospital without so much as a good-bye? Or maybe for that crappy little note you left thanking me for a good time?"

"That is not what my note said," she denied fervently. "I thanked you for making my trip special."

Jeff continued as if she had not spoken. "Or maybe you're sorry for the fact that I came on this Godforsaken show thinking I would find you. I mean, what are the odds of me being contacted out of the blue by a major network to appear on a reality television show? One with a princess named Isabella Strovanik? Oh, and she's from the same country as Izzy Strover? I'd say the chances are zero to none."

"I never meant to hurt you."

"Did I say you'd hurt me?" His gaze pierced straight to her heart.

Isabella winced. "No, but if you would let me explain."

"Explain what? How you disappeared from my life for a year?"

"Yes." This was much harder than she had imagined it would be. "I do want to explain that to you. And much more."

"Have you considered that maybe I no longer want to hear it?"

Yes, she had considered that possibility many times. Why had she listened to J.P.? He had only wanted her here for his show. She sighed. No, he had been right to push her. She had to start facing her fears. As the soon-to-be ruler of this country, she would not be able to cower when unfortunate circumstances arose.

"I hope that is not true."

Jeff looked around the room. What was running through his mind? He looked harassed. And she had done this to him. All because she had selfishly wanted to see him.

"Can we please go somewhere away from the cameras to discuss this in private? I have much to tell you."

His blue eyes jerked to her. "In case you haven't noticed, the cameras are everywhere except the johns. You wanna talk in there?" His biting words did not suit him, but she understood his anger.

Isabella stood her ground, drawing upon all her courage to see her through. "Come to my apartments.

There are no cameras in the west wing. I would not allow them in my family's private quarters."

His chest heaved. "This is your castle? You're really a princess?"

"Yes. That is why I had to leave you. My father became ill. A stroke. He passed away a few months ago, and I am left to fulfill his duties."

Jeff laughed, a humorless sound that echoed around the room. Isabella glanced around, meeting the gazes of the curious onlookers. All the cameras were pointed in their direction. She and Jeff were the center of attention now that the two other women had exited the room.

"Please, may we go to my quarters? You have traveled so far thinking you would see me. I am here now. Would you refuse to listen to what I have to say?"

He threw his hands up. "I can't believe any of this is happening. Jane isn't Jane. You're Jane. Some crazy woman who looks like Jane drags Jane out of here. Or who I thought was Jane out of here." He touched his forehead. "I think I need an aspirin."

Never had she seen him so upset. So very distraught.

"I will have one of my servants attend to you. Follow me, Jeff. Please."

He stared at her, then nodded. "Sure, Your Highness. Whatever you say. After all, I'm in your country, and you could probably have me thrown in jail if I disobeyed."

"Yes." She would agree to whatever he suggested if it would get them out of the spotlight. She did not want to bare her heart with cameras capturing every word. "Come now, or I will have my chief of security lock you in the dungeon."

It was an empty threat, as the castle's dungeon had not been in working order for several centuries.

Mouth clamped shut, Jeff followed her. When J.P. and two cameramen went to join them, Isabella shook her head. She would not have her private quarters invaded by the film crew. Her gaze caught J.P.'s, and she braced herself for an argument.

Instead, he smiled and gave her a thumbs-up motion.

Americans were so confusing.

Or maybe it was just men that she did not understand.

Breathless with disbelief, Jill yanked free of Jessie's grasp.

Where was the freaky music? This was one hundred percent *Twilight Zone*. Or maybe one of those "Jill Davidson, you're on *Candid Camera*" moments. Jessie couldn't possibly be here, in Europe, at the taping of *Jane Millionaire's* grand finale.

Thank God it hadn't been live.

Impossible or not, her sister stood two feet away, looking as if she'd just stepped off the cover of *Cosmo*.

Jessie was here.

Jill noisily sucked air into her lungs. If Jessie was here, it meant something terrible had happened.

"Are you okay?"

"I'm fine."

"Dan?"

"He's fine, too. We all are. Except I've been worried to death about you." Jessie gazed at the elaborate hallway, the portraits of royalty, the handmade rugs and the marble sculptures. She whistled. Loudly.

"Doesn't look like you've been roughing it. And

those men are absolutely scrumptious. Much more so than they appeared on television." She waggled her brows. "Lucky you."

"Why are you here?" Jill tapped her foot on the hardwood floor. The sound seemed to echo up and down the long hallway.

Jessie's glossy lower lip pouted. "I've already told you, I came to rescue you. Come on, let's go."

Her sister grabbed her arm, but Jill resisted. "No."

"No?" Jessie's eyes widened. "What do you mean, no?"

"I'm not leaving like this. Not without saying good-bye."

A perfectly drawn eyebrow arched. "Well, duh, that's what we just did."

"I have to stay." Jill paused. Maybe Jessie was right. Maybe it would be better to just disappear. Technically, she had fulfilled the terms of the contract.

The contract. Now everyone knew she was a *fake* fake. Oh God. *Rob.*

"You idiot," she blasted her sister. "You've ruined everything by coming here."

Jessie grimaced. "What are you talking about? I thought you'd be glad to see me."

Jill took a deep breath and glanced around. They were alone in the long corridor. "I am glad to see you, but don't you think someone on the crew might figure out you're the person who auditioned for *Jane?*"

"So what? I spoke with some guy on the crew before I flew here. How do you think I found you?" Jessie waved her French-manicured hand as if to wave off Jill's concerns. "Besides, you got what you wanted. What you needed. A month of men lollying after

271

you." She grinned, a wicked expression on her face. "Did you have a good time?"

Jill wanted to scream. Instead, she took another deep breath. Not that it made a difference. She didn't think breathing all the oxygen in Europe would help.

Jessie's mouth dropped, and her eyes danced with bedevilment. "Oh my God." She did a little bounce that only Jessie could pull off without looking ridiculously childish. "Tell all."

The last thing Jill wanted was to tell Jessie about Rob. "Jess, you seem to be ignoring the fact that we've committed fraud by my coming instead of you."

Jessie shrugged. "What do they care if you came instead of me? Obviously, you gave them what they wanted. The show's been wildly successful, and there are only the three final episodes left—the one that airs tonight, the honeymoon trip next week and then the finale. America loves Jane. Your picture is everywhere."

"My picture?" Jill gulped. Was she going home to a media circus?

"You're on the cover of half the magazines on the newsstands." Jessie pointed a finger at her. "You, my dear sister, are famous."

"Famous?" Why hadn't she thought about what would happen when she returned to San Padres? Her life would never be the same.

"There's even a letter from *Playmate* magazine at the house," Jessie crowed. "They want you to pose nude for them."

"*What?*" Jill steadied herself against a mahogany table.

"Oh yeah, but for what they were offering to pay, I

don't think you should do it." Once again her sister waved a hand dismissively. "At least, not unless you get them to triple the amount."

Had Jessie lost her mind? She wouldn't take off her clothes for a magazine no matter how much they were offering. She could just see the guys on the force having a field day if they ever caught wind of it. She met her sister's curious look. "And you know this how?"

"Because I read the letter." Jessie gave her a duh look. "Now tell me about the guy." She lifted a brow and added mischievously, "Or is it guys?"

"Does my privacy or committing a felony mean anything to you?"

Jessie waved her hand again. "Well, technically, it would have been my mail if I'd been Jane."

"But you aren't. I am—was." Jill touched her throbbing temple. This was too confusing, too surreal. She had to be caught up in another dimension. One where her loony sister had just made null and void everything Jill had put her own life on hold to protect. One where a man could bring her to unbelievable heights, yet want her to go on a romantic interlude with another man. One where Jill Davidson had fallen in love only to have her heart broken.

"Yes, and," Jessie continued, "I want to hear all about those gorgeous hunks of men I just glimpsed. Especially about number ten, Steve. Oh, and the yummy host."

No way was she going to talk about a certain yummy host.

Jill crossed her arms and shook her head. They were standing in the middle of an open hallway less than twenty feet from the entrance to the room where said gorgeous hunks were. She was *not* going to discuss men with her sister, period.

"Oh, come on." Jessie pouted. "At least tell me if you got laid? Surely with this many single men, you quit moping over Dan long enough to help some guy get totally lucky?"

"I can not believe you just said that." Jill eyed her sister in disapproval. Jessie's audacity amazed her, although it shouldn't have. She'd lived with her all her life. "Let me get this straight. No one's hurt or dying. Yet here you are making a grand entrance—during filming—to rescue me after I've been here five weeks to keep you from being sued for breach of contract?"

Jessie shifted her weight in her high-heeled black boots. "Uhm, well, you sounded so pitiful on the phone. What did you expect me to do? I came to help you out of a miserable situation."

"It's the very last day. I would have been on the plane home in a matter of hours. Don't you think your rescue comes a little late in the game?"

"I was only trying to help."

And the worst part was that she probably had been. Jessie just never thought things through, and when faced with the consequences of her rash actions, she always relied on Jill to bail her out.

"You've risked everything by showing your face here. Possibly made my reason for being here a vain effort." Let Rob in on the fact that she'd lied to him. "Oh Jessie, how could you?"

"I thought you'd be glad to see me." Jessie's lower lip quivered slightly as her brilliant green eyes watered.

"How was I supposed to know you were coming home today?"

Okay, she had a point. Jessie couldn't have known she hadn't intended to go on the honeymoon.

Jill sucked in another gulp of air. Reality dawned. "We could go to jail."

"No way." Jessie's look bordered on total disbelief.

"Yes way."

"Damn, can't you sleep with the producer or something?"

No matter how much Jill tried to prevent it, heat flushed her face.

Jessie's glossy mouth plopped open. "You didn't."

Jill didn't answer, and avoided her sister's curious gaze.

"Oh my God. You did." Jessie did her bounce again, sounding impressed. *She would be.*

Jill looked at her beaming sister in wry amusement. Jessie's eyes shined with excitement and love. Instantly, Jill reconnected with her sister in a manner that went a long way in dousing her frustrations at her last-minute rescue attempt.

"Why, you little casting couch crawler, you," Jessie teased. "Trying to land yourself another acting gig?"

Jill rolled her eyes at Jessie's outrageous suggestion. Knowing there was nothing that would tempt her to repeat this fiasco and nothing she could do to change what had already been done, she grinned and answered in kind. "Well, you know how I've always dreamed of making it in Hollywood."

"Yeah, I know. You plan to sleep your way right to the top." Jessie giggled and threw her arms around Jill. "God, I've missed you!"

"I've missed you, too." Jill couldn't help herself. She returned her sister's hug. No matter what their differences, Jessie loved her. That she'd never questioned. Her sister's ability to reason, yes. Her love, no.

They hugged a moment longer before Jessie pulled back.

"You know, I really don't think we'll be in trouble over this. I mean, some guy from here called me and, like, invited me. He even sent a private plane and arranged a hotel for me." Jessie's lip puffed out. "I slept for like sixteen hours after arriving, and I'd meant to check out the local studs. But without his help, I could never have gotten into the country."

"Someone helped you get here? Who?"

"James somebody." Her gaze landed behind Jill. Her eyes lit up as though she'd just spotted a winning lottery ticket. Had to be a man.

Jill turned to see which male her sister was seductively smiling at. Her heart fell.

Rob.

A pissed-off Rob.

A very pissed-off Rob if his narrowed eyes and rigid posture were anything to judge by.

Fine. She was more than a little ticked at him, too. He'd been willing to let her go with Jeff. And he'd known about Princess Izzypoo or whoever she was. He'd made a fool out of Jill in more ways than one since crawling out of her bed that morning.

"Hel-lo." Jessie's voice dropped to an almost purr. In direct contrast to Rob, her stance welcomed. Sickeningly so.

276

Wait a minute. Wasn't Jessie supposed to be in love? Engaged? Jill's gaze dropped to where, a month ago, her sister's diamond ring had flashed. It was gone. Uh-oh. Looked as if Jill's European hiatus had been in vain in more ways than one.

Frustration, ripe and raw, seized her. She looked at Rob, half expecting him to be gaga over Jessie. Most men were. But instead his gaze bore into Jill. His intense, accusing, betrayed gaze didn't waver. He hadn't even reacted to Jessie.

As elation that he seemed immune to Jessie's charms filled Jill, so did the realization that it didn't matter. Not one bit.

Rob's eyes told her much more than she wanted to know.

He'd cared about her. She'd known it in her heart. But he didn't bother hiding it from her now. Or maybe he couldn't.

Still, he hadn't cared enough to try to stop her from spending a romantic week with Jeff. If Rob had loved her, he would have stopped the show, or at least let her know he didn't want her on a tropical paradise with any man but him.

She'd hoped. Hoped she'd meant more to him than scratching a sexual itch. The tenderness of his touch that morning had solidified that hope. He'd made love to her during their early morning tryst. There had been more between them than just sexual attraction, and not just on her side. He may not have said the words, but he'd shown her in his touch, just as she'd attempted to show him.

Whatever she'd meant, she could see the cold, harsh reality in his eyes. She'd hurt him, and his frosty resolve announced he wouldn't forgive her lies.

She'd lost Rob forever. Not that she'd ever really had him.

"Let me explain," she began, despite the anger and hurt coursing through her. He'd lied to her, too. She took a step toward him and caught her slipper's heel on her skirt hem. She stumbled, grabbed hold of the mahogany table again and managed to knock a vase onto the floor. The probably-priceless urn shattered. To Jill it seemed to symbolize the cracking of her heart at the thought that Rob had cared and she'd destroyed those precious feelings by not being honest with him. If she'd trusted him enough to tell him the whole story, would he have risked his heart?

Her gaze flickered from the broken porcelain to the tense man eyeing her with disgust and disbelief. "I'm sorry."

He didn't speak, just watched as she stooped to clean up the mess she'd made. One of the messes she'd made. She doubted the urn could be repaired, and she knew all the king's horses and all the king's men couldn't put her heart back together again.

Jessie bent down and covered her hand. "He's who you slept with?"

Jill nodded, not meeting her sister's gaze. Her hand shook beneath Jessie's steady one.

"Go. I'll take care of this."

Shocked, Jill glanced at Jess. She'd seen the lust in her sister's eyes when she'd looked at Rob. It wasn't like her to back down. "You're sure?"

Jessie looked taken aback. "Of course I'm sure. He's yours. I should have realized when he called me that you were involved with him."

"Rob called you?" He'd brought Jessie over? He'd known? That didn't make sense.

"Right after you did." Jessie got her "duh" look again. "I'll tell you everything later. He just spun on his heels and vanished down that hallway to the left. If he's the one you want, Jilly, go get him."

Jill looked at the suddenly empty spot where Rob had been standing. Her stomach knotted. "I'd like to wring his neck right now, but"—she dropped the pieces of porcelain she'd gathered—"I love him, Jess."

"Like, I kinda figured that. *Go get him.*"

"Yeah." Jill kissed her sister's cheek, stood, and ran in the direction Rob had disappeared.

Chapter Seventeen

Rob took the steps of a narrow back passageway two at a time. He wasn't sure where he was headed, but the air in the hallway had become too thin. He hadn't been able to breathe. Jill's beautiful face and harsh words had made his chest constrict. To save himself, to be able to think clearly, he'd had to leave.

Jill had admitted to being like Mandy, a starlet willing to sleep her way to the top. Was Jill really no different from Mandy? Mandy had been so cold, so calculating, so careless with Rob's feelings. She'd had an affair with the star of Rob's first production, leading to the show's demise when the man walked off the set and refused to finish shooting. Was Jill also capable of such treachery?

He paused on the stairs and clasped his fingers around the wooden railing as blinding pain burned across his chest. How could he have been so wrong about Jill?

He'd known better than to care about a woman.

But she'd snuck around his defenses. Or more likely she'd plowed right over them.

And he'd let her. Because he'd believed she was different from every other woman he'd ever known. That she cared about *him*, not what she thought he could do for her career.

He'd been wrong. So wrong.

"Damn!"

"Rob?" the source of his pain whispered from a few steps behind him. He hadn't heard her. Admittedly, in his current state, she could have stomped down the stairs and it was unlikely he would have noticed.

He didn't look at her. He'd seen the guilt, the shame, the regret in her eyes when she'd turned and seen him in the hallway. She hadn't known he was listening when she'd blurted out the truth. The truth that she'd been faking a whole lot more than just her identity.

She should do just fine in the acting world. She'd certainly fooled him.

"Rob," she whispered again, placing her hand on his shoulder. He flinched, but didn't jerk free from her scalding touch. "I know none of this looks good, but you have to let me explain."

"No, I don't have to do anything." Except find better-quality air. The stairwell seemed to have been overcome with roses.

Death by roses. Would he ever be able to smell the flowery fragrance without thinking of her? Somehow he doubted it.

"Please." Her fingers tightened on his shoulder, and

this time he pulled away, but only to turn toward her. She stood on the step above his, which put her mouth at his eye level. Memories of that mouth against his reminded him of what he'd thought they'd shared this morning.

"Please what?" he asked as a wave of exasperated anger shook him. "Please forget you're not who you claimed to be? Or please forget you made a mockery of my production? Or, even, please forget I heard you admit that you slept with me in hopes of my helping you land another role? Not that you'll need any help with your acting talent. You certainly had me fooled." He took a breath. "Please what, *Jilly?*"

She met his gaze head-on and, except for the slight quiver of her lower lip, she showed no outward signs of being affected by his outburst. "I never meant for anyone to find out."

Yeah, announcing she'd only slept with him to advance her career probably hadn't been on her agenda. Of course, he knew producers who wouldn't care. Heck, most didn't care.

Rob cared. Too damn much.

"Lesson learned. Next time keep your mouth shut."

"Huh?" He had to give her credit. She looked genuinely confused. He watched as understanding dawned on her face. "Oh, you mean that last bit about my sleeping with you."

She reached out and cupped his jaw, her soft palms pressed on either side of his face. "Having been right there, how can you possibly think I made love with you for any reason other than the fact I'm crazy about you?"

His heart slammed into overdrive at her words. He

wanted to believe, but Jill was a skilled actress, and he'd taken the crash course in Lying 101 from his ex-wife. He wouldn't be taken for a fool again.

"That was just sex."

She looked taken aback. "I made love to you, Rob. Couldn't you tell? Feel it in my touch? My kiss? The way I couldn't get enough of you?"

She was good. He could almost believe her. Almost.

But he knew she was a liar and a fraud, not above breaking rules and laws to get what she wanted. He wrapped his fingers around her delicate wrists, her deceptive wrists—she was much tougher than she looked. He removed her hands from his face.

"You should leave. Tonight. Consider your early-morning services repayment for my not prosecuting you and your sister for fraud and the countless other felonies you've committed by being here."

"Rob, don't do this," she pleaded.

"Do what?"

"You didn't stop me from choosing one of the bachelors when you could have, when you should have. I'm willing to put that behind us, but don't make the same mistake twice. Don't throw away what we have together," she said softly.

He chuckled without humor. "That's just it, honey. We don't have anything together. I told you from the beginning you'd never be more than an itch I wanted to scratch. Did you think a tumble in your sheets would change my mind? Not hardly."

Her eyes filled with tears. If he'd thought she was sincere, he'd have dropped to his knees and begged her forgiveness, but for her this was all just another rung on the ladder of her acting career. Hell, she was good enough that he might be tempted to cast her in another role—just so long as he wasn't physically working on the set.

No, he'd never willingly have anything to do with this woman again. Her talonlike clutch on his chest had already created gaping wounds. Another go-around would likely kill him.

Her lashes lowered, her chest rose with a deep breath and she visibly trembled. He had to leave before he wrapped his arms around her and begged her to go right on pretending, because he didn't want reality.

Reality. What a joke. The biggest joke of all was on him.

Her eyes opened. Her gaze full of pain, regret and one last glimmer of hope, she stared at him. "Regardless of what you believe about this morning's activities and the events that followed, I made love to you, Rob."

She reached for him, but he flinched away, unable to bear her touch.

"Because I love you," she finished in a breathy rush, as if her heart were really on the line.

His gut knotted. She really knew how to hit below the belt. Somebody should give her an Oscar.

"Pity for you if that's true. You mean nothing to me." He wished to hell he was telling the truth. Maybe they both should be nominated for best performances.

She gasped, and all the stairwell's already too thin and rose-tainted air vanished right along with that flicker of counterfeit hope in her eyes.

Before he spat out any more lies—or worse, started

believing hers—he turned from her sinfully expressive eyes that so falsely mirrored his own hollow ache.

"Who'd have seen all this happening?" Bachelor #6, Steve, asked as J.P. sank down beside him in the throne room.

"Any good producer, I imagine." J.P. dropped his head back against the pew, staring at the ornate ceiling.

"This was all staged from the beginning?"

J.P. snickered. "No. Not from the beginning. Just from the time several of the show's key players got bitten by the love bug."

"Several?" Steve's brow rose. "Who? Kensington and Jane are cozy, but both admitted to just being friends. And what about this new chick? Who's she? The real princess?"

"Yep. The genuine article."

"So Jane's an imposter?"

"Yep. She's a wannabe actress who stepped in to fill Isabella's shoes when the princess got cold feet and decided she wouldn't do the role herself."

"And the princess and Kensington had a thing before the show?"

J.P. straightened. "Sounded that way, didn't it? I guess we'll find out for sure when all this settles."

Jane's sister came back into the room carrying broken pieces of porcelain. That was going to cost the network's insurance company a pretty penny.

Jane's sister glanced around and spotted him and Steve. Flashing a smile that would make a blind man see, she walked toward them. He and Steve both sighed in appreciation of the way her hips swayed with each step.

"I had a little accident in the hallway." Her shoulders lifted as she made an "oops" expression. "What should I do with this?"

J.P. pointed to a spot on the pew. "Just set it down here. I'll have one of the crew take care of it later."

"Hey, I recognize that voice. You called me and invited me here, didn't you?" Her face screwed into a mock scowl. "Did you set me up?"

J.P. laughed. "Set you up?"

"Jill seems to think we're going to be in trouble for our little switcheroo, but you wouldn't have sent for me if you were, like, upset, right?"

Her lower lip pouted and her eyes flashed with flirtation. J.P. almost laughed. Had Jessie Davidson fulfilled her contract, *Jane Millionaire* would have been an entirely different show. Hell, she'd have had the men in such a heated rut, they'd have been at each other's throats. And the glint in her feline eyes assured him that she'd have enjoyed every second of it.

"She's with Rob?"

Jessie shrugged. "The crazy man took off after Jilly broke this vase. Was it worth that much?"

J.P. suspected the vase hadn't had a thing to do with whatever put a fire under Rob's shoes. More likely the boy had been stunned to discover Jane was an imposter. It wasn't often something slipped past Rob. But then the boy hadn't thought straight since he'd become twitterpated five weeks before, when Jane had made her practice descent down the stairs.

"Well, aren't you going to introduce me?" Jessie's

eyelashes batted back and forth as she sized up, Steve. She held out her hand. "I'm Jessie Davidson, and I know who you are. You've been coming into my living room on a weekly basis. I think there's still steam on my windows from your last visit."

A bedazzled Steve took Jessie's hand—to shake it, J.P. imagined—but the sexy wench laced her fingers with Steve's and tugged him closer.

"You have really big"—a smile played on her painted lips—"hands."

"Thank you." Steve gulped. J.P. bet Steve had never been this hot under the collar even during his combat stints.

As if Jessie had read his mind, she grinned. "Like, I've always been fascinated by Navy SEALs. I bet by the time Uncle Sam is finished with you guys, your endurance is something to be marveled at."

"Something like that."

"I've got some time to kill while I wait on Jilly. Wanna show me around the castle and tell me why SEALs do it better?"

J.P. shook his head as the two walked off, deep in conversation. Oh yeah, had Jessie been Jane, the show might have turned X-rated.

Had Jill and Rob gotten together yet?

The boy was going to owe him big-time for setting this up. But just seeing the lad happy would be enough.

And Isabella and Kensington. Jessie and Steve had looked pretty cozy, too. Hell, he was pretty good at this matchmaking stuff. Maybe he could pitch another reality show to the network. One where he played Cupid.

* * *

"Let me get this straight."

Isabella sat with her hands folded in her lap as she watched Jeff pace across her room.

"You brought me here so you could see me again. Yet you don't want to continue our relationship." He shot her an exasperated glare. "Not that I'd necessarily be willing, mind you. But why bring me here if all you wanted was to see me? Why not just return to Central America?"

How could she explain that her heart belonged to him, even if her obligations belonged to her people?

"I am sorry. What I did was wrong. Forgive me."

"Forgive you? This isn't a joke, Izzy. You're talking about my giving up five weeks of my work because I thought I'd see you when I got here."

"Which you did," she reminded him.

"For what purpose? To be told you're a princess?"

"Jeff, there is something I have to tell you." How would he take her news? "I must marry."

"What?" He stopped walking and turned to her. "Are you proposing, Izzy?"

She closed her eyes and swallowed the bitter taste duty left in her mouth. "No, I cannot marry you. I must marry royalty and take my place as queen of this country."

"Queen?" He sank next to her on the settee. "You're going to be queen?"

She nodded. "It is my destiny."

"Why were you at my hospital? What was your trip to Central America all about? And why under an alias?"

288

"I believe in helping others. My country funded many charitable works before my father's death. I wanted to do something that was not simply monetary. My father agreed under duress, as long as I traveled with bodyguards." She shrugged. "It was not as if I had not had them my entire life. Even while at university in the U.S., two bodyguards disguised as students accompanied me to every class."

"Why as Izzy Strover?"

She shrugged, knowing he could never understand the burden of constant surveillance and expectations. "I did not want to be treated differently from any other volunteer when I visited mission sites. Being a princess can bring undue attention. I wanted a chance to just be a woman."

His jaw tightened. "Is that what I was all about? Making you feel like a woman?"

"I will always treasure the time we spent together." She placed her hand over his. Her heart sped up at the contact of his skin against hers. Goose bumps covered her skin. It had been so long since she had felt the heat of his touch.

Jeff's gaze dropped to their hands. "I don't understand why I'm here."

"I had to know how I felt about you."

His blue eyes searched hers. "And do you?"

Heaven help her, she did. "My heart has belonged to you from the first time you kissed me."

"At the hospital."

"Yes." Memories flooded Isabella.

Jeff twined his fingers with hers. "You took my breath away, Izzy."

"As you did mine." His musky scent tantalized her senses. She inhaled deeply, embracing the powerful way her body reacted to him.

"You are engaged?"

"Soon." She leaned closer, her gaze focused on his lips. She wanted him to kiss her. She wanted much more than that. Which was wrong. They had no future. She would not use him to satisfy the ache within her chest.

"Don't look at me like that."

"Like what?" But she knew.

"Like nothing has changed between us."

"Has it?"

"You know it has."

"No. Everything is as it was. Only now you see more clearly who I am. Who I must be."

"A queen?"

"Yes."

"What about the woman, Izzy? What is it she wants?"

Isabella's gaze lifted to his eyes. She had never seen a color so blue. Not even the sea could compete with the hue of his eyes. "She wants you," she admitted honestly.

She heard his sharp intake of breath seconds before all thought disintegrated at the touch of his lips.

"Izzy." His breath was warm against her mouth as he stared at her, a slightly dazed look in his eyes.

This was why she had ensured she would see Jeff one last time. Because she had needed more memories of his touch to hold her through a lifetime of royal service.

"Would you think me improper if I asked you to kiss me again?"

"No more so than my kissing a woman who just told me she intended to marry another man."

She nodded, understanding the implications of his words.

"Jeff, I want much more than a kiss. Knowing we have no future together beyond the present, I want you to choose to go on *Jane Millionaire*'s week in paradise. With me."

"Where's Jessie?" Jill asked J.P. She'd expected to find Jessie waiting for her in the hallway. She should have known better. Jessie had never been one to wait around.

Some of the crew members were milling around in the throne room. Jill's gaze had immediately landed on where J.P. sat in one of the pews. He looked alone, and she had the urge to wrap her arms around him. Not that the older man would appreciate her gesture.

"Your sister wasted no time in snagging a bachelor of her own." J.P. patted the pew. "Have a seat."

Not one bit surprised, Jill collapsed onto the bench. "Steve?"

"Yep. Last I heard they were discussing his endurance and she'd asked him to explain why SEALs did it better."

"She didn't." Jill covered her face.

"I'm afraid she did. But she looks like she can handle herself. Now, tell me why you're not with my boy."

Jill peeked at him from between her fingers.

"Don't act like you have no idea what I'm talking about. Do you think I couldn't see what was happening right in front of my eyes? I may be old, but I ain't dead."

"He hates me."

"Somehow I doubt that."

"You didn't see how he looked at me."

"I imagine he was a little upset about Jessie showing up. Personally, I thought it made a nice twist."

Something in his tone triggered suspicion.

"You brought her here."

"Yep."

"Then you knew I was a fake."

"Not at first."

"When did you figure it out?"

"Your personality is quite different from your sister's. On her interview tapes, she was a total flirt. That's one of the reasons I chose her. I wanted sparks to fly on *Jane Millionaire*. The more sensational, the better. Everything about Jessie screams sensational."

"You can say that again."

"At first I thought you were just shy. Rob commented that comparing you to the woman on the tapes was like looking at a different woman. I had to agree, and found myself watching Jessie's interview once again. The resemblance between the two of you is remarkable, almost as if you were twins. There are differences, though. She lacks your grace and strength, but has a verve for life that is enchanting."

"Why didn't you say something?"

"Because Rob refused to see the truth when it was right before his eyes. All he could see was you. Since

Mandy, he's never let a woman close. With you, he was so busy focusing on all the other reasons why you two shouldn't be together, he forgot to protect his heart."

"You're wrong."

"Am I?"

"Yes. He asked me to leave the castle. Just as soon as it can be arranged."

"Then he's a fool."

"No, I deceived him. I admit I was wrong, but he deceived me, too."

"You mean Isabella?"

She nodded, fighting to keep tears from falling.

"He couldn't tell you. To do so would have been betraying me. He may be as thickheaded as a Neanderthal, but the boy is loyal. I'd trust him with my life."

"Yes, he cares a great deal for you."

"As he does you."

"I thought he did, but I was wrong. When it comes down to it, Rob isn't willing to risk getting hurt again. He'd rather I went on that stupid honeymoon with Jeff than have to admit he cares about me. I deserve better."

"Agreed. Give the boy some time. He'll come around. Apparently you had a conversation with his foolish pride."

"No." She shook her head, knowing she spoke the truth. She and Rob were finished. Even if he hadn't meant those harsh words, too many things stood between them. Things like their backgrounds and financial status. His past and her desire for a real relationship rather than a clandestine one hidden from prying eyes. "Please help me to leave tonight. I don't want to see him again."

"Now whose pride is talking?"

"Not pride. Reality. My reality is that I'm a police officer who for a short while got to live out a fantasy. Rob's a famous producer who got sucked into that fantasy. What we had would never last under the strains of the real world."

J.P. sighed. "You're sure about this? Because once he's had time to calm down and think about this, he's going to realize that your having taken Jessie's place isn't the real issue."

"He already knows. And yes, I'm sure. Please help me go home."

"I'll arrange for you to leave tonight. But we have to record your final interview. If you're sure this is what you want, I'll set everything up."

She nodded. "I'm sure. I want to go home."

CHAPTER EIGHTEEN

"Do you have any idea how fast you were driving?" Jill asked the grinning man in the gleaming red Porsche she'd just pulled over on the San Padres highway.

"Why don't you tell me, sugar?" The man's gaze raked over her uniformed bosom before he met her eyes again.

What a jerk. "I'll need to see your license, registration and proof of insurance, please."

"Baby, you can see anything you'd like." He reached into his glove box, withdrew papers and handed them along with his license to her.

She glanced over his information and started to walk back to the patrol car where Dan was running the guy's tags.

"Hey, while you're writing my ticket, do you mind autographing this?" He handed her a copy of a magazine with her smiling face on the cover.

Not another one.

She forced a smile, tight though it was, took the magazine and resisted the urge to fling it into the ditch. She opened the door and slid into the front seat of the patrol car.

"Ugh," she grunted in frustration.

"What? Did he offer you a part in a porn flick like the last guy we pulled over?" Dan grinned at her from his seat, enjoying this way too much.

"No. This one just wants my autograph." She rolled her eyes and handed Dan the guy's information. "Here, you finish this. I think I'm going to be sick."

He took the papers, but didn't start filling out the ticket. His expression grew serious. "You really should have taken Chief's offer of a desk job until all this blows over."

Jill shot him a dirty look. "Not you, too."

"Hey, I'm on your side, but, honestly, knowing we're being constantly followed by the press is getting a bit old. Did you read this week's issue of *Tattler*? It has a spread on us that claimed our love affair was why you didn't choose that doctor dude." Dan rolled his eyes. "My phone is ringing off the wall, and Kathy is threatening to dump me if something doesn't give. She would have if you two weren't getting along so well since you've come back. I think she actually feels sorry for you."

Dan's girlfriend felt sorry for her. What a great testament to the state of her life. Jill sighed. Yeah, her life had been topsy-turvy the entire two weeks she'd been back in California.

Poor Dan. He didn't deserve any of this three-ring circus. Neither did she, for that matter. But try explaining that to the nuts breaking the law to flash a camera in her face, attempting to get an interview with her or to offer her the lead role in *Jane Does Porn*.

She'd never expected her every move to continue to be scrutinized after she left the castle. The castle. She and Jessie had left a couple of hours following her last conversation with J.P.

She'd fulfilled her duties by filming her comments on her role as Jane, although she couldn't recall a word of what she'd said. The show had given Jeff the cash in addition to the week with Princess Jane—or Izzy, as he'd known the woman when she'd volunteered incognito at his medical mission. It seemed Izzy had been responsible for Jeff's personal invitation to appear on the show.

Jeff had seemed happy when Jill had said her goodbyes and exchanged addresses with him. She hoped things worked out for him. He really was a great guy.

The show had presented Jill with a matching check. She'd tried to refuse it, but J.P. hadn't budged. She'd earned the check, he said. She'd tried not to flinch at his words. Rob might have had a different perspective on what she'd earned and how she'd done no.

Rob. Her heart squeezed. She missed him so much. Although J.P had begged her to reconsider, she hadn't seen Rob since she'd left him in the stairwell.

Well, that wasn't completely true.

Foolish as it was, she'd watched over and over the episodes Jessie had taped of *Jane Millionaire*, just so she could see him. Last week, along with the rest of America, she'd watched the episode where she'd made her choice. She'd cried when the camera had flashed to Rob prior to her making her choice and again immediately after. He'd been tense, then relieved. Why had that footage been included?

Not that it mattered. He'd proven how little he cared. He'd been willing to let her go with Jeff. Would he have encouraged her to sleep with him to improve ratings as well?

And he'd had the gall to accuse her of sleeping with him to help her career. He was the one who put his precious Hollywood career above everything else, though in her heart she knew he had cared for her, despite what he'd said. In the long run, it hadn't mattered. His career meant more to him than she ever could.

"You want me to do this?" Dan asked when he'd finished filling in the speeding ticket. Jill blinked. She'd totally spaced out. Again.

She shook her head, hating that she couldn't seem to keep her mind on her job and off Rob.

"I'll do it." She grabbed the clipboard and the man's ID, scribbled her name on the magazine and climbed out of the car.

Surely with time, this craze would pass?

"Ratings were over the rooftops," J.P. bragged as he leaned back in his seat.

In the seat next to him, Rob shifted his gaze from his laptop, where he was working on polishing *Gambler* for his meeting next week with a Wolf executive, to J.P.'s smug expression.

"Yeah, I saw the e-mail with the numbers this morning. Looks like we'll both be working for Wolf next season."

"It'll be a nice change of pace after *Jane*."

Jane.

"Yep."

"Are you going to look her up after we land?"

Rob's forehead pulled into a tight V above the bridge of his nose. "Why would I do that?"

"Because you should have taken her in your arms and told her to choose you rather than one of the bachelors. If you had, you'd have just spent a week in paradise lying on the beach with her rather than filming Kensington and Isabella."

"You aren't serious?" Rob gawked at his friend. "I stayed away from Jill so she could choose one of the bachelors. I worked hard to ensure that the show would be a success."

"America wanted her to fall in love and be swept off her feet."

"She didn't want Kensington."

"No," J.P. agreed. "She wanted you."

Rob swallowed.

"And you were a fool to let her go. You should have been the one down on your knees, not Kensington. A smart man would have proposed to a woman like Jane right then and there."

Rob snorted. "This coming from a man who's had six wives."

"Soon to be seven." J.P. grinned. "I just have to meet the right woman. It'll happen any day now."

Rob rolled his eyes. "I've learned my lesson on that score."

"No, you didn't."

Rob's brow lifted as he met J.P.'s intense gaze.

"Mandy burned you, and you shut down. You

haven't let another woman close since as far as I know. Not until Jane."

"I didn't—" Rob glanced at his laptop screen, but saw nothing but blurred lines.

"Don't try to lie to me. I know everything. Even if the cameras hadn't caught her conversation with her sister in the hallway, I already had a pretty clear picture of what was going on between the two of you. You think I don't know you went to her room the night before her decision?"

"That was just sex."

"Sure it was." J.P. laughed.

Rob scowled.

"It was. She means nothing to me." Not meeting J.P.'s gaze, he saved his work and slammed down his computer top.

"That's why you've been in a piss-poor mood from the moment I told you she'd taken your advice and left."

With stilted movements, Rob pulled out his attaché case and slid the laptop inside. "There was no reason for her to stay, since she didn't choose one of the bachelors."

This time J.P. rolled his eyes. "Not if you don't include the fact that she loves you. Although why she does I've yet to figure out."

"She only pretended to care about me," Rob insisted. Her words in the stairwell had haunted him day and night. Only the knowledge that she'd faked everything from the moment they met had kept him sane.

"Really? Why would she do that?" J.P. asked the question Rob had asked himself a thousand times.

Rob pushed the case under the seat in front of him and straightened. "So I would help her career."

J.P. appeared to consider his answer. "Possibly, but I doubt it. You know, she gave the money to the police fund for the wives and children of officers killed in the line of duty."

"I heard that. Great publicity stunt." Rob settled back into the first-class seat, hoping J.P. would take the hint and drop the subject. He did not want to talk about Jill. Nor did he want to think about her, but his mind had yet to take note. How long would it take before she quit monopolizing his thoughts?

"She's refused to be interviewed, although I know for a fact she's had offers from everyone from Oprah to Leno."

"So?" Rob shrugged as if J.P.'s words were falling on indifferent ears. Unfortunately, they weren't.

"Seems a bit odd that someone seeking fame and fortune would turn down all opportunities to ride the media wave and return straight to her job as a cop."

J.P. voiced what had been nagging at Rob's mind for the past week. Leno's people had called trying to arrange an interview with Jill, and he'd learned she'd already refused their offer. If she had really slept with him to further her career, why would she refuse free publicity now? He'd heard through the rumor mill that several of his colleagues had actually offered her big-screen roles that she'd declined point-blank, stating she was a police officer at heart, not an actress.

But he'd refused to delve into the meanings of Jill's actions. He'd thrown himself into finishing the show.

Not an easy thing to do when the two people being filmed were sickeningly in love.

Had he been wrong? And if he had, the thought of what he could have had, what they could have had together, threatened to destroy his ability to breathe.

She'd claimed to love him. Had she?

J.P. seemed to think so. And he trusted J.P.

The memory of hearing Jill tell her sister that she'd slept with him to further her career rang in his ears. With the clarity of hindsight, he knew she'd been joking.

Why hadn't he realized it then? Why hadn't he been willing to risk his heart, to risk everything he was, to have interfered when she'd sat on her throne facing the four remaining bachelors? He should have resigned from the show and asked her to choose him. Begged her to choose him.

His pulse picked up speed as he remembered the pain on her face as she'd asked him not to throw away what they'd had, that she could forgive him for allowing her to choose another man. And he'd told her to leave.

Could she forgive him a second time?

He had to find her, prove to her that he regretted his foolishness. It would take more than mere words of love for him to win back Jill's heart. But how could he convince her he wanted her in his life? That without her, he had nothing but an empty house and a lonely existence?

He didn't want to be alone. He wanted Jill. Was it too late? Would she forgive him for being scared to risk his heart?

She had to.

* * *

302

A very frustrated Jill sank onto her sofa to curl up with a bowl of popcorn and a soda to watch the final episode of *Jane Millionaire*. She'd considered skipping the show completely, but couldn't bring herself to.

Not that Jessie would have let her anyway.

Her sister insisted she had to watch to see how it all ended. Reluctantly, Jill had given in to her sister's wishes; she was too tired to argue against Jessie's insistence that she couldn't miss this show.

Today hadn't gone well. Chief had pulled her into his office and informed her that he had assigned her to a desk for the next month. A month. She wanted to be out in the field where the action was, not stuck inside four walls where the only action she'd see was that of a computer screen.

But he'd argued that the force didn't have the manpower to leave her out in the field with all the intentional "crimes" committed in the hope that Jill would be the arresting officer. Since she hadn't willingly provided any additional media fodder, the gossip rags were having a field day with the crime wave that had hit San Padres during the past two weeks.

Her choice had been to sit at a desk or go on leave.

She swiped a handful of popcorn and sighed in frustration before taking a bite.

"Things will calm down in a few weeks, and you'll be able to go back to work," Jessie, with a bowl of her own, reassured Jill as she plopped onto the other end of the sofa.

"My life will never be the same again."

"If you really believe that, why don't you start accepting some of the offers you're receiving? My gracious, Jilly, you're the envy of every woman in America right now."

Jill rolled her eyes. "I think you're mistaken. I didn't end up with a man. The real princess did."

"Maybe you should have stuck around and fought for Rob."

"And maybe you're forgetting that I went after him and he told me to leave."

"And you believe that's what he really wanted?"

Jill sighed. "Yeah, I know that's what he wanted. Courtesy of his ex-wife, Rob has a wall around his heart that he's not going to let me or any other woman through. Besides, he hates lots of press attention, and I'm a media magnet. He'd rather walk across hot coals than take this hellish ride with me."

And she'd wondered a few times if knowledge of what awaited back home had played a role in his pushing her away. He truly shied away from publicity except in regards to his productions. A relationship between them would cause a media feeding frenzy.

And she'd meant what she said. She didn't want a man who was ashamed of her, who wasn't willing to let the world know she was his. Nor did she want a man who could willingly send her away with another man. Rob Lancaster hadn't been the man for her.

But as soon as the press quit following her, she planned to start a search for her Mr. Right. So what if she had a feeling they'd all fall short in comparison to Rob? She'd find a way to make room in her heart for a new Mr. Right. Maybe her feelings for Rob would fade with time.

"Oh, it's coming on," Jessie cooed as the theme music Jill had come to hate filled the room. Something along the lines of "Love Is in the Air." Which had to be better than the old episodes of *Law & Order* she could now quote from memory. She couldn't bring herself to actually watch the old films from Rob's acting days, but watching Benjamin Bratt as a character who existed in her law enforcement world provided comfort to her aching heart, made her believe she'd find a man worthy of her love.

Nausea churned the popcorn in her stomach. Uh-oh. Maybe she'd better lay off eating.

For that matter, had she eaten anything today? A bagel early that morning, but nothing since. She probably wouldn't have indulged in the popcorn if Jessie hadn't had a bowl and soda waiting on the coffee table when Jill had finished changing out of her uniform and into a pair of sweat pants and a T-shirt.

A "Got Milk?" T-shirt. Just like Rob's.

She'd seen it in a shop and had to stop the patrol car to go buy one in her size. Completely and utterly stupid, and Dan had laughed his butt off at her, but somehow wearing it made her feel closer to Rob. Like the old *Law & Order* episodes did.

Where was he tonight? Was he with some Hollywood socialite working off his abundant testosterone? Or was he alone, watching the opening to the show they'd helped create?

She probably didn't want to know the answer: the thought of him with another woman might drive her to insanity. She chose to ignore that he would move on, would have other women in his life, in his bed. Probably already had.

She choked on a piece of popcorn she hadn't realized she'd tossed into her mouth.

"You okay?" Jessie set down her fizzing soda.

"Fine," Jill muttered before taking a long sip of her drink to wash down any remaining food in her throat. "Just fine."

And she would be. Eventually.

Just as soon as she forgot Rob.

Does one's heart ever forget?

Jill watched as her face filled the screen. It was a clip of her right before she'd left the castle.

"You can tell I've been crying," she complained. "I look awful. Why didn't they fix my makeup?"

"Maybe that's the look J.P. was going for when he dragged you in front of the camera," Jessie mused.

Jill glanced at her sister. "J.P. wanted me to look bedraggled and upset?"

Jessie shrugged. "You told me he and Rob were good friends in addition to being coproducers of the show. Maybe J.P. wanted his pal to see how heartbroken you were."

"J.P. was one of the reasons Rob pushed me away."

Jessie shrugged again. "Whatever."

Jill's gaze went back to the screen. A segment on Jeff and the real princess's "honeymoon" played, ending with Jeff on his knees proposing to the woman he confessed to having fallen in love with when he'd met her in Central America. Isabella accepted, muttering words of love and what was the point of being royalty if she couldn't make changes to some of her country's more backward laws. In a segment filmed later, Isabella discussed launching a women's rights initiative; while Jeff planned to head up a health program to ensure all the children in her country received proper immunizations and well-child care. The princess never looked happier. Neither had the beaming man next to her. Love and pride shined in Jeff's eyes while he watched Isabella charm the camera.

They sure hadn't dragged out the suspense of how the honeymoon week had gone. Confused, Jill looked at her watch. There were still forty-five minutes left of airtime. How were they going to fill it?

A commercial came on. Maybe she'd just go on to bed and forget watching the rest. What was the point in torturing herself with more memories of Rob?

"Want another soda?" she asked as she stood, stretching her tight, achy muscles.

"Sure." Jessie handed her the almost-empty glass. "I'll have diet."

Jill rolled her eyes. "Like you need diet."

"I'm auditioning for a big part next week. I want to look good."

"You couldn't look otherwise," Jill said, earning a smile from Jessie. Amazing how she saw her sister in a different light now. When had she failed to notice that Jessie had grown up? Funny how it had taken five weeks on another continent for Jill to realize her sister really could manage her own life—albeit in a way that made Jill cringe.

She walked to the kitchen and poured more soda, silently musing over the portion of the show that had aired so far.

"Jilly, get in here. *Now!*" Jessie yelled.

Jill grabbed the sodas and rushed to the living room. Jessie sat on the edge of the sofa, her gaze glued to the television. "Look."

"What's the rush?" Jill's breath caught when she noticed what was on the television screen. She and Rob were chatting in the studio. It was right after she'd read the bachelors' letters. One of the glasses in her hand almost slipped from her trembling fingers.

This wasn't part of the show. Why were they airing this?

Jessie took the sodas from her and sat them on the coffee table, which was probably a good thing because, when the next clips came on, Jill knew she would have dropped them both.

Footage she hadn't known existed of her and Rob together, before the bachelors had arrived. She and Rob laughing, smiling. She'd loved him even then. The evidence was there in the way she gazed at him, as though he were the sweetest thing since chocolate.

Next, a clip of Rob's face when she'd appeared at the top of the stairs on the night she'd first met the bachelors. Had he really looked at her like that? As if she'd totally taken his breath away? Their dance aired next, close-ups of Rob whispering in her ear. Memories ran through her: how his words had sent tingles along her spine, how his scent had intoxicated her senses.

Her eyes watered when she saw the longing—but also resignation—on both their faces as the dance ended. Footage of them in the exercise room quickly followed, and then her challenge in the foyer.

Jill sucked air into her shaking body as the screen cut to a car commercial.

"What's going on?" Jessie asked. "Did you know they were going to show this stuff?"

Jill shook her head and opened her mouth to speak, but nothing came out. What *was* going on? J.P. had to be behind this. Rob would be livid.

"Here, take a drink." Jessie shoved her soda at Jill.

The cool liquid did little to calm her nerves. Had she bumped her head at work today and just didn't remember?

"Oh, it's coming back on," Jessie exclaimed when the commercials gave way to Jill and Rob battling it out on the basketball court: her teasing him about playing for his kiss, his insistence that she kiss one of the bachelors following his win.

"But as this next scene shows, I did kiss Jane. The very next morning." Rob's gorgeous face came onto the screen.

"Oh my gosh. He's in on this. Do you know what that means?" Jessie gushed. "Jilly, do you know what this means?"

"Shush." Jill threw a cushion at her sister as her early-morning run-in with Rob played. She relived his first kiss, recalling how his mouth had felt against hers, recalling how every nerve cell in her body had been singed by his touch. A deep ache settled in her stomach that had nothing to do with popcorn and everything to do with the man who'd stolen her heart.

More clips followed. Clips she'd forgotten. Clips of him gazing at the computer monitors, watching her with the bachelors. Clips of her watching him. Clips

309

of him rescuing her from the lake, him kissing her temple. Clips of their late-night return to the lake. Who had taped those? And thank God she hadn't dragged him onto that dock and had her way with him.

Another commercial break. Jill ordered her lungs to inhale—she wasn't sure she had since the last commercial.

"Jilly, Rob is narrating this. That has to mean he loves you," Jessie supplied helpfully.

Was it possible? Then the truth of what was going on hit her.

"No, he's doing this for the ratings. I didn't fall for one of the bachelors. He's making sure the show is a success. That's all this is about."

But even as she said the words, she admitted to herself that she wasn't sure. Rob liked his privacy. This was the last episode. Surely he'd already far exceeded his rating requirements? From everything she'd seen, *Jane Millionaire* had been a smashing success. Based upon the media's reaction, she'd have thought they'd far exceeded expectations.

"Ratings?" Jessie looked appalled. "I don't think so. Did you see how he gaped at you when he saw you in your princess gown? Oh my gosh. If Larry had ever looked at me like that, I'd still be wearing his ring instead of dating Steve. And that kiss." Jessie fanned her face. "You two were totally blazing!"

"Maybe." The show came back on, saving Jill from more of Jessie's assumptions.

Scenes aired from the day she'd left the castle. Clips of Rob's expression as she faced the bachelors prior to stating her choice. Her comment that she chose no one as she hadn't fallen in love with any of the bachelors. Rob's look of relief.

How had she missed the emotions he'd revealed?

Because he had kept them hidden from her. He hadn't been willing to share his feelings, and she was sure he hadn't meant for them ever to be known by anyone. J.P. must have twisted his arm. Or the network had offered him a deal he hadn't been able to refuse. Or maybe the ratings really hadn't been as good as the media attention had led her to believe.

Tension filled her as she watched herself knock the vase over in the hallway, chase after Rob, and damned if they hadn't even caught them on film in the stairwell, although only a brief segment of their conversation was shown. Thank goodness.

She also realized that no clips of her going to Rob's room had been aired. Nor any of the sound effects of the night he'd come to her room. Had that been intentional, or had Rob destroyed that footage?

Panicky energy shot through Jill. She stood and paced across the room during the next commercial break. What did all this mean? What did she want it to mean?

As if she didn't know. She laughed at herself. She wanted Rob. But how could she ever know that he was sincere in his feelings for her? That he hadn't done this for ratings?

But would he go this far for mere numbers on a show? Her heart quickened, as did her pace.

"Sit down. You're making me nervous," Jessie ordered.

Jill glared at her and continued to pace. She had to figure out what Rob narrating this show meant. When his handsome face came onto the screen, her long strides paused.

"God, he's too good-looking to be real," Jessie sighed, earning another glare.

More clips of her interview, then Rob sitting in the same chair as she had during her final taping, but the background looked different. When had they filmed that? At the castle? Somehow she didn't think so.

"How did I feel when I first met Jane?" He laughed. "Like a two-by-four had smacked me over the head. Here was the sexiest woman I'd ever met, and she was totally off-limits to me."

Jill's eyes widened. He'd thought that?

"I remember taking a cold shower that night. One of many I took after meeting her." He grinned at the camera, and Jill's heart rate sped up. "I didn't know men really took cold showers until I met Jane and I practically took up residence in one."

He'd been taking cold showers when she'd been burning up with need for him? *What a waste.*

"The night she met the bachelors, I watched her float down the stairs and I knew I was in trouble. I tried to stay in the background and watch while she danced, but couldn't. I pushed reason aside and held her in my arms for those fleeting minutes. From there my obsession with Jane only got worse. She monopolized my every thought. The more time I spent with her, the more I wanted her." He paused, as if mentally chiding himself for his omission.

"I won't go into all the reasons outside the obvious why I felt I needed to resist my attraction to Jane. Let it suffice to say I'd been burned a time or two and hadn't trusted women in a long time. Not until Jane. And even with her, I didn't let myself have total faith. Not like I should have. Not like she deserved."

He paused again, looking a bit uncomfortable for a man so proud, so strong.

"Jane." He stopped, took a deep breath. "*Jill*, if you're watching this, I made a really big mistake when I asked you to go." He swallowed. "And an even bigger one when I let you leave without telling you how I really felt."

Commercial.

Jill blinked, wanting to go shake the television set for cutting to a commercial at such an inopportune time.

He'd said "Jill" instead of "Jane."

"He's got it bad," Jessie piped up. "Maybe even as bad as you do."

"Be quiet," Jill ordered, crossing the room to dig in her purse for her wallet. Right before she'd left, J.P. had slipped her a business card with Rob's cell phone number scribbled on the back. He'd told her to give it some time and to call Rob, because he was sure his friend would regret his hasty reactions.

Jill had kept the card, but hadn't believed she'd ever use it. At this moment, she needed to hear Rob's voice. To ask him what this show meant, what he'd been thinking when he'd recorded it and, more importantly, how he felt. Did he love her? Was there even the remotest possibility he could learn to love her?

Okay, so she was upset he'd rejected her in the worst kind of way. If he loved her, she'd forgive him. She might make him eat dirt first, but she'd welcome him with open arms when all was said and done.

Then reality set in. This wasn't just some average joe she loved. Nor was he Benjamin Bratt. He was Rob Lancaster, the famous Hollywood producer. They came from totally different worlds. How could she ever compete with the jet-set life he lived?

She couldn't. He'd tire of her, and then she'd have to go through the rejection again. It wasn't worth it.

She clutched the card in her palm and stared at the cordless phone on the coffee table, but didn't pick it up. What would be the point? She and Rob had no future together.

She inhaled, then forced herself to sit down to finish watching the show. She might have been tempted to turn off the tube if she didn't think Jessie would choke her, but curiosity would have driven her crazy to see how the show ended.

The commercials finished, and Rob came back on-screen. The scene picked up where he'd been at the commercial break. And Jill's breath caught as he repeated his comment and continued.

"My world is empty without you. I'm miserable. Had you chosen one of the bachelors, I'd have gone insane. Or found a way to stop you. I should have offered you another choice." He stared into the camera as if he were looking through her television set and straight into her eyes. "A choice to choose me. I didn't throw myself into your list of options during that last day at the castle, but I'm offering now. Jill, will you spend a week with me in paradise?"

CHAPTER NINETEEN

Jill stared at the screen and wondered if she'd heard right. He was asking her to spend a week with him?

A week to have an affair, and then they'd go their separate ways? Even if they couldn't have a happily-ever-after, there was no reason to insult her in front of millions of people and cheapen what they'd shared.

She grabbed the phone off the cherry surface of the coffee table and punched in the numbers from the back of the card she held with shaking fingers.

The absolute nerve of him to go on national television and ask her to have a weeklong affair with him.

Where was the 1-800 number so all America could call in and vote on her decision for her?

She seethed. This stunt had to be for ratings.

How dare he take advantage in such a callous manner of the way she felt about him? How could he just ignore how much his question would hurt her? The man didn't know the first thing about love.

Right before she pressed the last number, Rob's nervous glance at the camera made her pause.

"Jill, I know this is an odd way to go about this, but I also know I hurt you, and it was going to take something drastic to convince you that I love you." He laughed a self-derisive chuckle. "Yes, you heard me right. I love you. With all my heart. I need you in my life. Forgive me."

Jill dropped the phone.

"I knew this was what he had planned when he told me to make sure you were watching!" Jessie squealed, bouncing around the living room.

Jill stared openmouthed at her sister, at the television, while she tried to make sense of what was happening. Jessie had talked to Rob and hadn't told her? She was dead meat.

Her gaze locked on to the television screen. Rob continued talking to her. "These past two weeks have been hell. I've missed you like crazy. I even went so far as to buy roses to keep in my room so that when I slept, I could feel close to you.

"Pretty corny, huh?" He grinned, and Jill fell in love with him all over again, just as she imagined every woman in America must have. "This is for you, Jill."

He snapped his fingers and disappeared. For about three seconds of heart-stopping silence, only the empty chair filled the screen.

Jill shrieked as Rob reappeared. The camera was so close to him that she couldn't tell where he was. He spoke, but she couldn't understand him over the roar in her head. All she knew was that she had to talk to him now. She jerked the phone up and punched in the last number.

Ring.

Jill frowned as Rob stopped talking on the screen.

Ring.

He grinned as he dug in his coat pocket. The camera pulled back, and Jill's stomach knotted more tightly than if a Boy Scout had used her insides to earn his merit badge.

Rob stood in front of her house.

This was live feed.

Ring.

"Just a minute, folks." He smiled into the camera as he found his phone. "I have to answer this just in case it's Jill telling me to get lost."

Ring.

"Hello?" Rob answered, and she thought she might black out.

For sure, clamminess covered her skin and darkness danced in front of her eyes for a few seconds before Jessie's sharp poke pulled her back to the present.

"Answer him," Jessie encouraged.

Jill opened her mouth, but nothing came out.

Rob shrugged at the camera and began walking toward her front door again, but didn't hang up the phone. "Jill, is that you? Honey, say something."

He climbed her steps, crossed her porch and stood on the other side of her front door.

"Jill?" he asked again.

Still clutching the phone, Jill hurried across the living room and flung the front door open to stare at the man she loved more than life itself.

* * *

"Jill," Rob breathed, his eyes fixed on her face, as he clicked his phone shut and slid it into his jacket pocket. What was she thinking? Did she still feel the same, or had he destroyed her feelings for him?

Was he about to be made the laughingstock of America on live TV?

Talk about your reality show.

He sucked in a deep breath and waited for her to say something. She seemed frozen to the spot. One hand clutched the phone to her ear and the other held the doorjamb as if she were afraid she might slide to the floor if she let go.

"Darling, please say something," he whispered when more time had passed than should have. Was she going to slam the door in his face? Throw the phone at him? Of course he deserved all those things and more, but he'd hoped she'd throw herself at him and slam her mouth to his in a crushing kiss.

He searched her vivid green eyes to try to read her emotions. Overwhelmed. Unsure. Upset.

He'd made another mistake in doing this. He'd wanted to make a grand gesture. To prove his love to her by announcing his feelings to the world. He'd known she'd pick up on the significance of his actions. But she wasn't receptive to his proposal.

His proposal. He really hadn't gotten to that part yet, had he? The diamond in his pocket suddenly weighed a ton, dragging him to one knee.

Her eyes widened. With fear?

Before he put her in a compromising position with more than twenty million people watching, Rob stood, unwilling to place such a burden on her. Not like this. They'd talk in private, and if he could convince her to forgive him, then he'd give her the ring he'd bought for her.

He turned to the camera. "Sorry, folks. Looks like I've miscalculated."

Her fingers closed around his upper arm, pulling him to face her.

"Tell me," she whispered, her eyes large and full of the same emotion he'd witnessed when she'd stood before her throne and begged him to stop her from choosing one of the bachelors.

"I love you, Jill," he said, the words filling his heart.

Her eyes closed. He swallowed the lump in his throat as he wondered if he'd misread her. Had he somehow failed her again?

Her eyes opened, and hope flickered to life deep inside him. She still loved him. He could see it in her gaze, in the tears streaking down her cheeks.

"Don't cry. Not over me. I'm not worth it." He grazed his knuckles over her soft skin, wiping the moisture away.

"Did you mean what you said?" she asked, her tears not slowing.

"About loving you?"

She nodded.

"More than anything. Do you think I'd go through all this if I didn't?"

Her lids fluttered. "Maybe for ratings."

"The only rating I care about is your heart's."

She blinked, went to wipe her tears away and realized the phone was still in her hands. She stared at it a moment before absently tossing it to someone behind her. Her sister, he imagined.

Aw, what the hell? He dropped back to one knee and took her hand in his. "I love you, Jill, with all my heart. And I have to believe you still love me. You told me you loved me in the stairwell. I was too blind to see the truth, to realize I loved you, needed you."

A sob shook her body and he longed to stand and take her in his arms, but if he didn't finish, he might not get the nerve back up.

"Jill, I once said I preferred to be alone, but that's not been true from the moment I met you. I just didn't know what loneliness was until I faced life without you." He squeezed her hand gently. "Please do me the honor of sharing my life."

Her hand trembled in his.

"The honor of being my wife."

Love shined in her eyes.

"Say it," he asked as he stood.

She stared up at him. "But I thought you wanted me to go on a week's vacation with you?"

"A honeymoon, Jill. A real one."

"What about the differences in our backgrounds?"

"You're not willing to tie yourself to a poor hombre from East L.A.?"

"I'm a cop. You're you. How would we ever fit our lives together?"

"One day at a time, Jill. One day at a time." He pulled her hand to his lips and kissed her palm. "I'm willing to do whatever it takes to have you by my side. Are you willing to do the same? To love me even when I'm stubborn and foolish and full of pride?"

His heart lurched as his strong, capable Jill nodded through her tears. "Yes, I'll marry you."

Clapping sounded all around them, but Rob didn't pay any attention to the film crew or to the fact that millions of people had watched him put his heart on the line. He only had eyes for Jill as he stood and pulled her into his arms.

If America wanted to tune in, well, he'd let the networks worry about what drivel they aired next.

He was busy living a reality all his own.

A Connecticut Fashionista in King Arthur's Court

MARIANNE MANCUSI

Once upon a time, there lived a fashion editor named Kat, who certainly was not the typical damsel in distress. But when a gypsy curse sent her back in time to the days of King Arthur, she found she'd need every ounce of her 21st-century wits to navigate the legend. After all, just surviving without changing history or scuffing your Manolos takes some doing!

Luckily, she's got her very own knight in shining armor, Lancelot du Lac, on her side…even though she's not quite sure she wants him there. After all, shouldn't he be off romancing Queen Guenevere or something? Will Kat manage to stay out of trouble long enough to get back to her world? And what will Lancelot's forbidden love mean for the kingdom of Camelot?

COMPLETELY YOURS

SHERIDON SMYTHE

"Your Escort Will Be a Perfect Gentleman"

That was her sister's promise when Callie Spencer agreed to let one of the men from Mr. Complete squire her around town during her Atlanta business trip. But one look at her stud-for-hire makes Callie wish he'd break all the rules. And at first it seems the all-too-appropriately named Dillon Love will oblige. His burning gaze says he takes a very personal interest in their relationship. But his on-again, off-again seduction makes gun-shy Callie want to shoot herself in the foot. Her heart has already been broken once, by her ex-husband the underwear model, no less. Can she trust another breathtakingly handsome man, even when he promises to be completely hers?

Kate Moore

SEXY LEXY

In fleeing to Drake's Point, California, and buying an inn, Lexy Clark stretches the truth. Her bestseller—*Workout Sex, A Girl's Guide to Home Fitness*—was written for active women with busy lives. Its publicity campaign has led to Lexy's days being filled with men who want her to spend her fifteen minutes of fame in compromising positions. Changing her name and moving to a remote little town seemed the best escape.

Until she meets Sam Worth. Lexy can't imagine a better partner for "home fitness"—and maybe more. But Sam is too smart to buy Lexy's innkeeper disguise for long. She is willing to let him uncover everything about her—except the truth. For when fame catches up with her, will Sam still want Sexy Lexy?

TO KISS A FROG

ELLE JAMES

Craig Thibodeaux is cursed. Frog by day and man by night, he has until the next full moon to free himself—by finding someone to love him. Elaine Smith seems perfect. She is beautiful and smart, and even passionate about frogs. But while she came to Bayou Miste at just the right time, the sexy scientist needs a bodyguard—not a boyfriend. And truth be told, he was a bit more frog than Prince Charming even before he tangled with that Voodoo Queen. Elaine deserves more. She deserves to be the queen of someone's pad: a wife. But with a single kiss, Craig might start to believe in fairytale endings.

PHI BETA BIMBO

TRISH JENSEN

Who fares better in the workplace: the brassy bimbo or the plain Jane? For her doctoral dissertation, sociologist—and lifelong nerd—Leah Smith intends to find out. Trading in her mousy brown hair and flat chest for bleached locks and gravity-defying cleavage, she plans a little experiment. And nothing, not even one sexy—and suspicious—company man is going to trip her up.

Security specialist Mark Colson was hired to ferret out corporate spies, and the newest employee at Just Peachy Cosmetics is Suspect #1—posing as two different women, she is a total fake. Ditz or scholar, he will expose her. But Mark realizes to catch the brainy bombshell he'll have to reveal a few secrets of his own.

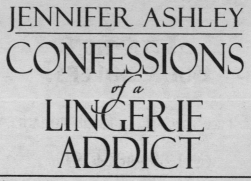

JENNIFER ASHLEY
CONFESSIONS of a LINGERIE ADDICT

The fixation began on New Year's Day: Silky, expensive slips from New York and Italy. Camisoles and thongs from Beverly Hills. Before, Brenda Scott would have blushed to be caught dead in them. Now, she's ditched the shy and mousy persona that got her dumped by her rich and perfect fiancé, and she is sexy. Underneath her sensible clothes, Brenda is the woman she wants to be.

After all, why can't she be wild and crazy? Nick, the sexy stranger she met on New Year's, already seems to think she is. Of course, he didn't know the old Brenda. How long before Nick strips it all away and finds the truth beneath? And would that be a bad thing?
